The SLOPE RULES

Books by Melanie Hooyenga

The Campfire Series
CHASING THE SUN
CHASING THE STARS
CHASING THE MOON

The Rules Series
THE SLOPE RULES
THE FRIEND RULES (short story)
THE TRAIL RULES
THE EDGE RULES

The Flicker Effect Trilogy
FLICKER
FRACTURE
FADED

Anthologies
LOVE ON MAIN
THE ART OF TAKING CHANCES

Praise for THE SLOPE RULES

Gold Winner (YA Fiction General) 2017 — *Moonbeam Children's Book Awards*

Silver Winner (High School Romance) 2017 — *Children's Literary Classics*

Bronze Winner (YA Romance) 2017 — *Readers' Favorite*

"There aren't enough books like The Slope Rules out there in the world of romance. This is a can't miss for anyone who wants more sweet than spicy and needs their hearts thawed on cold winter nights. No one will regret spending time on this book." —*YA Books Central*

"A fun, romantic story with a likeable protagonist and a familiar, yet enjoyable dramatic storyline that will appeal to teen readers." —*IndieRea*der

"Author Melanie Hooyenga tells it like it is in this remarkably honest coming of age story. The Slope Rules offers drama, action and age-appropriate romance all wrapped up in an inspiring, page-turning read." —*Children's Literary Classics*

"Both sporting fans and readers who love emotionally charged novels will adore The Slope Rules,... a great romance for young adult readers... that explores love, coming of age, and personal growth." —*Reader's Favorite*

"The prose is tight and enjoyable from the first paragraph until the very end. The author's descriptions are vivid and beautiful. Cally has a strong, self-confident voice and is a fully developed character." —*The BookLife Prize*

The SLOPE RULES

Melanie Hooyenga

Left-Handed Mitten
Publications

THE SLOPE RULES

Published by Left-Handed Mitten Publications
ISBN-13 978-1542620307
ISBN-10 1542620309

UPC

Book design, cover design, and ebook formatting by Left-Handed Mitten Publications. Author photo by Jenn Marie Photography.

Author website: melaniehoo.com
Email: melaniehooyenga@gmail.com
Facebook: facebook.com/MelanieHooyenga
Twitter: @melaniehoo
Instagram: @melaniehoo
Newsletter: melaniehoo.com/hoos-letter

Melanie Hooyenga
PO Box 554
Grand Haven, MI 49417

For my husband Jeremy,
who's always up for a race

One

My favorite memory of my mom is when she took a massive jump at Killington and the guys around me at the bottom were oohing and ahhing because a chick nailed the jump they couldn't make. And not just any chick—a chick old enough to be their mother. She stayed up in the air so long it's like she was held against the sky with a thumbtack, her orange and white jacket popping against the bright blue, and it was so breathtaking I almost had to look away.

That's the feeling that pushes me now. My skis hover over the lip of the hill, but I catch myself before they plunge forward and reach down to adjust my bindings once more. I bounce my knees, counting off the seconds until the guy ahead of me clears the second jump, then I take a deep breath and launch my body over the ledge.

I'm barely into my tuck when the first voice calls out.

"Girls can't jump!"

I tuck my arms tighter to my body, forcing the comment out of my mind. Some dickweed I don't know isn't screwing me up now. I've taken this jump at least a dozen times today, but this is the first time I'm flipping my iron cross upside-down. Dad would kill me if he knew I was trying this without Coach Brown around, but he's the one who dragged me halfway across the country on vacation to the land with powder so perfect you could—

Whoosh! The tips of my skis slice the edge of the jump and I'm soaring ten feet above the ground. I reach back and lightly touch my glove to my boot—just enough to get the feel for the move I've done hundreds of times—gearing myself up for the second jump. I hold my breath as both skis hit the ground at the same time, then take a deep breath.

The second jump is almost here.

I crouch low to the ground to build speed. I'm sure the boys are shouting after that last air, but I can't hear them. The only voice I hear is my mom, her soft words whispering how she feels closer to god when she's flying through the air. I feel the familiar drop in my stomach and throw my body forward, legs tucked in as close as they can get with two five-foot skis strapped to my feet, my right hand gripping the binding as I somersault through the air.

"She did it!"

"No shit!"

A smile breaks across my face as the ground rights itself beneath me. I unfold my legs, keeping my body loose for the impact of the landing, and I do something stupid.

I glance at the boys on the side of the hill.

Next thing I know I'm tumbling over the packed snow. I keep my bindings tight so they don't fall off every time I land, but that means they refuse to let go as I flop ass over head down the slope. Snow smashes into my face, into my mouth, and my skis finally pop off when my right knee slams against a patch of ice. I come to a stop on my back near the third jump. Heat rips through my knee but I ignore it and roll to my side to watch for the next jumper.

Slope Rule #1: Get out of the way of the next guy.

A snowboarder crests the first jump, his board flipped back so he's parallel with the ground, then he drops out of sight.

I scoot on my butt to get out of the way, pushing with my hands and good leg. My skis are too far down the hill for me to reach so I have to hope he either saw me fall or is good enough not to land on them. He launches off the second jump faster than

I expect, and a burst of air that I will never admit to sounding like a scream escapes my mouth. I give a final push with my boot and watch with a combination of horror and awe as he sails through the air, directly above me, the sun shining behind him like he's a goddamn action hero.

He lands beyond my skis and twists to a stop, then hops to the side so he's clear of the next jumper. He nods at me from behind his goggles. "You okay?"

I look from my skis to my knee, which I'm pretty sure is sprained, and shrug. "I've been worse."

His gaze flicks from me to the second jump. "You're still too close."

Inside I'm grateful that he's giving me enough credit that I know the rules and didn't mansplain that I need to move out of the way. "I'm trying, but I think I jacked up my knee."

He hobbles closer and I notice his lips. Full lips. The bottom one's a little red from where he keeps chewing on it. "Do you need help?"

I scoot farther from the jump and pain slices through my leg. I hate—HATE—asking for help, but either I ask this pretty-lipped boy or I get crushed by the next snowboarder. "Yeah, maybe."

In one swift movement he unhooks his boots and tosses his board to the side before climbing up to me. "This might hurt." He slides his hands under my armpits and drags me away from the jump, sending heat searing through my knee.

I bite back a whimper as I clutch my knee. Dad worries that fifteen is too young to already have knee problems, but whenever I've hurt it in practice Coach Brown sends me to the ice bath and by the next day, I'm fine. But something about the way this is pulsing tells me this is more serious. "I don't know if I can ski."

He lets go of my arms and lowers himself to the ground next to me. "Walk of shame?"

I bury my face in my gloves and shake my head. Riding down on the snowmobile stretcher is complete humiliation.

I feel pressure on my arm and look up. He's pushed his goggles on top of his helmet and I'm staring into the bluest eyes I've ever seen. A different kind of heat warms my belly, distracting me from my knee.

"Don't be a hero."

I wave a hand at the boys who yelled at me when I first took off. "I'm sure they'd love to see me carted off."

"They're not all bad."

"You know them?"

He shrugs. "Yes and no. I was showing them tricks earlier. Now they're following me around."

"Fan club, eh?"

"Something like that." He nods at my knee. "So what are you doing?"

I lock eyes with him. "Would you ride down on the sled?"

A hint of a smile lifts his lips, revealing a dimple in his cheek.

"That's what I thought."

"What if I promise to have hot chocolate waiting for you in the lodge?"

My heartbeat accelerates before I can tell it not to. I don't chase guys. I *am* one of the guys. But here, in a different state, maybe the rules can be different. I smile up at him. "Only if you tell me your name."

His smile broadens and he holds out a gloved hand. "Blake."

I jam my gloved hand against his. "Cally."

Vacation just got a lot more interesting.

two

Riding in the sled was worse than I thought. It took twenty minutes for ski patrol to show up, then they insisted on strapping me to the sled while everyone—including Blake's obnoxious groupies—watched. They drove so slowly that kids snowplowing down the bunny hill could have passed us, and by the time we reached the medical center I was ready to pretend my knee was fine so they'd let me go.

I texted Dad after Blake convinced me to call ski patrol, and now he's pacing behind me inside the med center while a guy in an official red ski jacket appraises my knee. My snow pants are shoved as high up my leg as I can get them, but they keep sliding down. Red Jacket touches his chin before making eye contact with Dad. "Snow pants have to go."

A fresh wave of humiliation sweeps over me. Of all the days to wear long underwear with frolicking bunnies. I unsnap my snow pants and shimmy them to my ankles, then slide the bunnies over a knee that is considerably larger than it was when I got dressed this morning.

"Christ, Cally." Dad forces out a deep breath and rests a hand on my shoulder. "What were you trying to do?"

If I admit I was upside-down without an adult within fifty feet he might not let me out of his sight the rest of the vacation. "Nothing crazy. Just my usual three-sixty. I caught an edge when I landed."

Red Jacket pokes my knee and I suck in a breath.

Please don't let it be serious.

"Looks like a mild sprain. There's a med center in town that can tell you for sure, but I suggest you stay off it for a few days."

I whip around and face Dad. "A few days? That's our entire trip!"

He squeezes my shoulders. "You don't want to risk a serious injury, do you?" That's Dad for you. Always logical, thinking long-term instead of immediate gratification. "Don't think of it as ruining your vacation. Think of it as an opportunity to..." he trails off.

I sigh as Red Jacket unrolls an Ace bandage. "Even Mr. Positive can't come up with a way to spin to this."

Red Jacket finishes wrapping my knee, then slides the bunnies back down, covering my leg. "Could be worse. It could be broken." He glances toward a closet in the corner of the room. "We've got some old crutches you can use."

I grasp the waistband of my snow pants and yank them back on, ignoring the flash of heat that grips my knee. "No, thanks." Dad slides an arm under my shoulder and helps me to my feet.

Red Jacket gives a half wave. "Suit yourself. Take it easy out there."

I roll my eyes. *Didn't he just tell me not to ski anymore?* I'm still looking at the ceiling when Dad stops so suddenly that I nearly lose my balance. "What the—"

"Excuse me," Dad says.

Blake is leaning against the doorjamb just outside the entrance, hands shoved in his pockets, goggles still flipped on top of his helmet. He pushes himself upright when he sees us, his gaze bouncing between me and Dad. "Cally, hey. How's your knee?"

Dad quirks an eyebrow at me.

"Dad, this is Blake. He rescued me from near death."

His eyebrow rises even higher. It's not like me to admit I need rescuing, especially from a guy.

"Okay, not near death. But certain crushing from a boarder."

Dad's face relaxes and he gives Blake a once-over. "Blake, thank you for saving my heart's delight from certain board crushing."

Blake flushes. Dad and I have been like two peas in a pod since Mom died seven years ago, and not everyone knows how to handle our schtick. "Yes, sir. I mean, you're welcome. I'm glad I was there."

Dad releases my arm and watches as I put pressure on my bum leg. Blake seems abnormally interested in my ability to balance, and while I try to play it off, Dad notices. He looks me in the eye, silently asking what I want.

"Can I stay here? In the lodge?"

"You need to ice your knee."

"I'll get ice in the lodge."

"And an ice bath later."

I nod.

"Do you promise to stay there? At least for today?"

I criss-cross my finger over my chest. "I promise."

"Text every half hour."

This time I salute.

Dad points his finger at me the way he has since the first time I rode my bike to a friend's house when I was eight. To anyone else it looks like he's scolding me, but really he's projecting all the worry he's carried with him since Mom died. He smiles at Blake before walking away, and calls over his shoulder. "Behave." He's said it a million times, but this is the first time I've blushed.

That one little word implies so much when you're standing next to a hottie.

"What are you doing—"

"Do you want to—"

Blake and I speak at the same time and I swear my cheeks are so hot I won't need a coat the rest of the day. I smile. "You first."

Blake steps closer to my side and starts to touch my arm, then hesitates. He lowers his lashes and his dimple winks at me. "I owe you a hot chocolate."

How did I forget that? Sophia is right. I *am* an idiot when it comes to boys. Guys-guys—the ones I play sports with and who first taught me to jump—I can handle. It's this flirty-blushy-sweaty thing I'm not used to.

I link my arm through his. "This better be some damn good hot chocolate. That ride was beyond shameful." He laughs, pulling my arm tighter against his body, and my heart pitter-patters.

It actually pitter-patters.

What the hell is wrong with me?

"Are you sure you can walk?"

I shrug. "We're about to find out." But when I put pressure on it I have to bite the inside of my cheek to keep from yelping.

Slope Rule #2: Never let them see that you're hurt.

My heroics don't go unnoticed. He disentangles his arm from mine, steps in front of me, and squats.

"What are you—"

"Let me carry you."

I take a step back. Well, really, I waddle backwards, but the result is the same.

"Cally, I won't stop pestering you until I know you're safe inside the lodge."

The smile falls from my face. I don't move.

He looks up at me and his face grows serious. "What's wrong?"

I shake my head, trying to ignore the sinking feeling sliding around my heart. Of course he's just being nice. If I saw someone biff it after landing on their head, I'd probably stick around to make sure they don't need to go to the hospital, too. But that doesn't mean he's interested in me. Guys don't see me that way.

"Did you change your mind about the hot chocolate?" His eyebrows furrow, making his blue eyes seem darker.

"No, I just... I'm sure you need to get back to your friends."

He turns toward the mountain and shields his face with his hand. "They seem fine."

A laugh escapes me. "You can't even see them."

He raises a shoulder. "Don't need to. So, hot chocolate?"

Fourteen different replies get jammed up in my throat. I choose one that I hope is flirty enough to get Sophia's approval. "How can I resist a guy willing to throw out his back for me?"

Blake locks eyes with me, lips parted, then he smiles so big it's like the sun's bouncing off his teeth—one of which is perfectly non-perfect, chipped just enough to give him character—and I have to blink to stop myself from staring. "Come on." He resumes his squat and I hesitate before wrapping an arm around his neck. He puts one arm behind my back and slides the other beneath my knees, and in one motion I'm in the air, not quite sure how I ended up in the arms of this gorgeous guy who I've known for barely half an hour.

One thing's for sure: I'm texting Sophia as soon as I get inside.

three

I double check that Blake is still in line for hot chocolate, then whip out my phone and fire off a text to Sophia. *Found a hottie. Made contact.*

My good knee bounces in time to my heart, which hasn't settled since Blake deposited me in a chair near the fireplace and pulled off his helmet, revealing shaggy brown hair that falls just above his crazy-blue eyes. The image in my head of us sipping hot chocolate next to the fire is beyond corny, but who am I to argue when they were the only open chairs.

My phone vibrates. *Spill.*

Major wipeout. He came to my rescue. Carried me into the lodge.

I check his progress in line and shake my head. What universe have I landed in where the hottest guy here—and the nicest, and not to mention a kickass boarder—is trying to impress me? It's not like I'm not interested in boys, but I've always been so focused on skiing that by middle school I wedged myself in as one of the guys and now it's too late to change it. The few dates I've been on were with boys outside my circle and they always get scared off once they meet my pack of friends and see how protective they are of me.

And you're having his babies when?

I snort just as Blake sits in the chair next to me. "Was it something I said?"

"Sorry! It's my friend. She's a little... never mind." I tuck my phone into my coat pocket and take a Styrofoam cup from him. Our fingers graze and a little zing of electricity rockets up my arm and straight into my belly. I clear my throat, hoping he doesn't notice that I can't seem to speak.

He sets a bag of ice on the table, slides another chair close to me so I can prop up my leg, and sits in the chair next to me. I grab the bag and roll the ice around to break up any chunks, then plop it on my knee. I should really pull up my snowpants for the ice to help, but the bunny long underwear is staying in hibernation.

Once he's sure I'm situated, he leans forward so his elbows are on the table and points one finger like he's counting. "So here's what I know. You're one of the best trick skiers I've ever seen." He points a second finger. "You're here with your dad and...?" His head tilts as he waits for me to reply.

"Just my dad."

He points the third finger. "And you're gorgeous. Now this would be enough for your average snowboarding fool, but I want to know more."

Who talks like that? I look around, expecting people to be staring, but no one's paying attention to us. "Am I being punked?"

He furrows his brows. "What?"

"I've never once had anyone say something like that to me. I figure it must be a joke."

A blush creeps up his cheeks and he pushes his hair off his forehead. "No joke. I had a lot of time to think when you were with the ski patrol dude. But I mean it. The girls at my school are too worried about their hair to put on a helmet and pull the flip you did."

I shrug. "I guess I don't worry about those things."

He smiles and my belly does another somersault. "And that's why I want to know more about you. Where are you from?"

I take a deep breath and force myself to relax. While I don't want to fall into the friend zone with Blake, I know how to talk to guys.

Pretend he's Hunter or Sam. "I'm from Vermont. South Burlington. I'm on the ski team and wasn't supposed to try that last trick without my coach, but the powder here is so different from back home I couldn't resist." I glance out the window in the direction of the scene of my crash and smile. "He'll be happy you forced me onto the sled."

His dimple deepens. "Right place, right time. So this is your first time in Colorado?"

I nod. "What about you?"

His smile hardens for a millisecond, but it's back so fast I wonder if I imagined it. "I'm from Lake Tahoe. The California side."

"Ooh, a Cali boy?"

He rolls his eyes. "We're not all bad."

"No, I'm intrigued. Us east coast girls don't have too many run-ins with surfer boys."

He bites his lower lip. "I don't surf. I live in the mountains."

"Oh, I figured you're such a good snow boarder that you must surf in the summer." He's quiet, and I scramble for a new topic. I don't know what made him clam up, but I can't blow this in the first five minutes. "How long are you here for?"

The tension in his shoulders relaxes and he leans back in his chair. "'Til Sunday."

"Me too." I can't stop the goofy smile that plasters itself to my face. I met this boy less than an hour ago and I'm acting like we're already in love. Which makes my cheeks flame even hotter.

"When did you start skiing?"

This I can handle. I launch into the story of how my mom was one of the first women in Vermont to do a backflip in competition, and how she taught me to ski by wedging me between her legs when I was barely three—no snowplow on the bunny hill for me. "She died seven years ago in a car accident, and now I feel closest to her when I'm skiing. Especially when I'm in the air." Tears burn my eyes and I drag the back of my hand across them. "Sorry. Didn't mean to drop that on you. We don't talk about her at home as much as we used to, and it's been a while since I've met anyone who didn't know. Back home there's no point bringing it up."

He leans toward me, eyes shining, and rests his hand on my bad knee. "That's cool that you still have a connection with her."

I haven't told many people about my connection with my mom and it touches me more than I can explain that Blake, who barely knows me, gets it. I take a sip of hot chocolate. "So what's your story?"

He gives me his full-wattage smile and I almost lose myself in his gaze. "It's not nearly as dramatic as yours. Where I'm from you either ski or board. I've just always boarded."

"And you've just always been able to get air so massive you practically flew over me?"

"What can I say? I got skills." He pauses, and I feel like he's holding something back, but I don't press him. He moves his hand to the side of my knee, careful not to knock over the ice while lightly rubbing the tendons and turning me into a puddle of mush. "It's too bad you're benched. I'd love to see what else you can do up there."

If he keeps this up I won't be able to sit upright, let alone try to ski. "I'm sure I can go out at least once more. But probably no tricks. Coach Brown will be pissed enough that it's sprained. I could miss the entire season if I blow it out."

"Maybe we could do something that doesn't require us to stand up?"

I pull back, feeling like he smacked me. "What?!"

"What?" Realization of what he implied dawns across his face and he sits up straight. "No! No! Tubing!" He runs a hand over his face, which quickly turns an adorable shade of crimson. "There's a place not far from here and I thought..." he trails off, his hand still covering his face. "I'm such an ass. I'm sorry."

A giggle works its way up my throat as relief sweeps through me. Five seconds ago I thought he'd trashed whatever we had going here. "You know, I hang out with a lot of guys so I'm used to innuendo, but holy inappropes."

He's still not looking at me so he doesn't see my smile. "Cally. That's not what I meant, I swear. I—" he drops his hand and I poke him in the chest, smiling. He exhales and slumps against the back of his chair.

"I'd love to go tubing, but do you think I need protection?" I pause as his jaw drops, unable to stop my shit-eating grin. "For my knee?"

He shakes his head and tilts it back so he's looking at the ceiling. "What did I get myself into?" An alarm goes off on his phone before I can answer. "Oh shit, I gotta go."

Disappointment chases my smile away. What if he set that alarm while he was getting the hot chocolate so he'd have an escape?

He turns off the alarm and leans forward so our knees are touching. "Family stuff. So Cally, will you please do me the honor of flinging yourself down a hill on a piece of inflatable plastic with me?"

A bubble of excitement pushes away my self-doubt. "I wouldn't miss it for the world."

"Please tell me that wasn't sarcasm."

I wink, and my heart's beating so loud I'm sure he can hear it. This is so not me. "Not a chance."

"Is nine too early?"

"I'm on east coast time so that's sleeping in for me."

"You staying here?"

I nod.

"Perfect. I'll pick you up in front of the lodge." He slowly lifts my hand to his lips. My breath catches as he presses a kiss to the back of my hand. "See you tomorrow."

"B-bye." I stammer, as he drops my hand.

I watch as he strides to the door. Several girls turn to stare, then whip back toward me with jealousy in their eyes. I'm used to girls wondering what makes me so special that I'm hanging out with the hot guys, but for once I'm as puzzled as they are.

I pull out my phone. Sophia's text *And you're having his babies when?* is still marked as unread so I fire off an answer. *Soon...*

Slope Rule #3: When the perfect opportunity lands in your lap, you hang on.

four

"You're riding in a car with him? Alone? Do you even know his last name?" Dad paces the small living room of our rented condo.

I scroll through my phone to find him. "McMillan."

"And he's from California?"

"You say that like it's a bad thing. Dad, he helped me yesterday, then waited around to make sure I was okay when he could have been back on the slopes. If that doesn't tell you that he's a good guy..." I stop. There's a fine line with Dad. Push too far and he thinks you're hiding something, but don't give a convincing enough argument and he'll never approve. I'm slowly figuring out the balance but I'm worried he won't give in this time.

"Text me as soon as you get on the road. Then the moment you arrive at the tubing park. And be sure to tell me the name of the place." He throws out rules as they come to him, pointing at me as he strides across the room. "And I want you back by dinner time."

I smile. I've got him beat here. "Blake has to be with his family by three so I'll be back before then."

"Oh. Well, okay then."

I hobble to my feet and he scowls at my knee. "Thanks, Dad. I promise I'll be careful. And if he tries anything inappropriate I'll kick him with my good leg." I kiss Dad on the cheek, then take care to walk as normally as possible, but once I'm outside I pause to regroup. The lodge is on the opposite end of the parking lot but it feels like it's miles away.

The door clicks behind me. "Need a ride to your ride?"

I turn and face Dad. "Thank you."

"I figured you wouldn't tell me how much your knee hurts. And I'd like to meet this boy again."

I fall in step next to him. "Understandable."

"I'm letting you go because I trust you, but I want you to know how hard it is for me to let you drive off with some boy you just met."

"He's not—" I stop. Blake's the definition of 'some boy'. And this will be the first time I've ever ridden in a car with a boy that isn't just a friend. "He seems like a good guy. He was even helping some younger kids with their tricks."

Dad pauses in front of the car. "And you like him?"

"For once I'm not just one of the guys. He seems to really like me."

He opens the passenger door for me but stops me before I can get in. "He'd be an idiot not to."

"Gee, thanks." I roll my eyes, trying to play it cool, but my reddening cheeks betray me. I stare at the parked cars as we roll toward the lodge. "Are you trying to get me flustered before I even see him?"

"Nope, just building your confidence. You have nothing to worry about." He pulls to a stop behind a silver sedan.

Blake is leaning against the passenger door and turns when he hears us. I'm not sure how it's possible, but he's even better looking than I remember. His hair is still messy, but it's a purposeful messy, like he spent some time getting it just right, and his blue eyes are as bright as ever.

Dad nods in his direction. "He's punctual. That's a plus."

My mouth goes dry. "Uh-huh."

He snorts. "I'll help you out." He moves to open the door but Blake beats him to it.

My heart nearly stops when he smiles down at me. "Good morning," we say at the same time.

Dad gets out of the car and moves to Blake's side. He holds

out a hand, brows furrowed, his mouth turned into the closest thing to a scowl I've ever seen on his face. "I'm Cally's father."

"Yes, sir. I'm Blake. I believe we met yesterday?" They grip hands and do that guy thing where they stare at each other for a second before separating and breaking into smiles.

"Take care of her. She says she's okay but it takes a lot for her to admit she needs help."

Blake leans toward me and puts a hand under my elbow to support me as I get out of the car. "Yeah, I picked up on that. I promise I'll throw myself in front of any out-of-control tubers." He winks at me and my stomach does a backflip.

Dad points at me and raises an eyebrow.

I sigh, and press a kiss to his cheek. "Bye, Dad."

Blake slips his hand into mine and tugs me toward his car. "Ready?"

Butterflies carry me the rest of the way.

Once we're settled in the car, he points at two paper cups in the center console. "I wasn't sure if you drink coffee, but I know you like chocolate so I got you a mocha."

I lift the cup to my nose and inhale deeply. My eyes drift closed as the aroma fills my nostrils. I already had my requisite two cups with breakfast—despite Dad's constant protests that it'll stunt my growth—but there's always room for more chocolate.

"I take it that's a yes?"

I open my eyes and reach across the console to squeeze his hand. "Double yes."

He grins as he pulls onto the road.

I toss my bag in the backseat and am surprised that the floor mats are dirty and there are a couple umbrellas jammed in the seat pocket. Our rental car is spotless, but this looks lived in. "Whose car is this?"

My question seems to catch him off guard. "Oh, we, uh, have friends who live here and they let me borrow it. We only have one rental car and my dad needed it today."

Something about his voice sounds off, but how do I know what's normal for him? I haven't even known him for twenty-four hours.

He turns the radio to the satellite alternative station I listen to and I bounce in my seat. "I love them! I saw Twenty One Pilots when they came to Burlington last summer!"

Blake surprises me by singing the words, his voice smoother than I expect, and I can't help but sing along. By the time we arrive at the tubing place my throat is scratchy and my stomach hurts from laughing so hard. Sophia always teases that my true test for a boyfriend will be someone who can tolerate my tone-deaf singing, and either Blake is very gentlemanly, or he actually sees me as more than just one of the guys.

five

If you're ever presented with the opportunity to go tubing with a guy so hot he makes your knees weak, by all means, do it. There are two options at the rental counter: single or double. Take double. Sure the tube is bigger, but there is zero—I repeat, zero—way to ride that thing without some part of your bodies touching. And as we all know, practice makes perfect, so by the sixth or seventh run I'd figured out the optimal way to both protect my knee and make sure the highest percentage possible of Blake's body was pressed against mine.

When we go inside for lunch, Blake loops his arm through mine as we hobble our way through the line, then pays and carries our tray to the lounge area. No private table today—we're jammed at the end of a long table in front of the windows, surrounded by several groups of teenagers and a family of ten all wearing matching ski hats.

Sophia insisted I keep her posted so I send her a text once we're settled at a table. *I am a smitten kitten.* I pop a fry in my mouth.

Blake rests his head on my shoulder and peeks at my phone. "Who are you texting?"

I jerk it away before he can see, but can't stop the blush that seems to be a permanent fixture on my face since we met. "Sophia. My best friend."

He raises his eyebrows but doesn't say anything.

"My dad says we're joined at the hip. She was supposed to come on this trip with us but her mom got upset at the idea of her being away from home for Thanksgiving and not seeing her grandparents so—" Blake's eyes grow wider and wider and I realize I haven't taken a breath. "Sorry. That's where you're supposed to say 'punctuation please.' It's a joke with my dad." *Oh my god, Cally, shut up.*

He smiles, and I let out the breath I've been holding. "So you're pretty tight with your dad?"

I lean back in my chair. "Yeah. After Mom died, me and Dad kind of became the two musketeers. Dad had always been involved in my life, but suddenly he was solely responsible for an eight-year-old. He made up this buddy system where we could call each other any time, any place, no matter what we needed, and that's what got us through those first months. The other stuff..." I hesitate, unsure if I should continue. Sophia's the only one outside the family who knows the rest of this story.

"What?"

I glance away for a second. "It's stupid."

His eyes search mine. "I'm sure it's not. Losing someone is hard." He pauses like he's going to say more, then he smiles and the moment passes.

I barely know this boy but something tells me to trust him. I take a breath. "I refused to ride on the left side of cars since that's the side Mom was on when she died. Technically, I still don't, but I don't tell people why. And when I'm with Dad he's driving so he doesn't notice."

Blake's lower lip pushes out ever so slightly, and I'm momentarily distracted. "I guess we all cope in our own way."

I force out a laugh. "Let's just say I got really good at calling shotgun."

He smiles. "And I'm guessing you're not in a hurry to visit England?"

"Or Australia or Ireland, or like half the Caribbean Islands." Part of me thrills that he put two and two together, but isn't making me feel weird about it. "Fortunately the places with snow all stick to the right side of the road. But enough about me..." I take a huge bite of my burger, making it impossible for me to say another word, and raise my eyebrows at him as I chew.

He pushes his fries around in the paper basket. "Let's see. I got my license in September, I hate sushi, and I don't normally drive that snooze-mobile—"

"Ooh, what's your car like?"

The dark expression from yesterday flashes over his face and I immediately regret asking.

"I don't mean that like 'ooh, what do you drive?' I'm just curious. I'm hoping Dad gets me a Wrangler for my sixteenth but he hasn't committed yet." I slap my hand over my mouth and point at him. *Hello, foot-in-mouth disease.* "You talk."

He takes a sip of his soda and clears his throat. "I didn't take it that way."

I don't believe him, but I keep my mouth shut.

"Actually, I have a Wrangler."

"For serious?!" I clap my hands and several people turn to stare. I give them a cheesy smile and turn back to Blake, my voice low. "Tell me what color." *If it's orange, it's settled. I'm having his babies.*

He takes a bite of burger and chews slowly, making me squirm in anticipation. "I'm kind of afraid to say now."

I shrug. "It's totally not a big deal."

He laughs. "Yeah, right. What color do you want yours to be?"

"Orange."

"Huh." He takes another bite and chews slower than a brontosaurus. Or stegosaurus. The one with the long neck that only eats plants. And now he's drinking again.

"You're killing me smalls."

"*Sandlot*. Nice."

That's it. I pick up a burned fry—I'm not wasting the good ones—and bounce it off his chest. "Why do you hate me?"

He winks, and my heart races. "I was just thinking how cute our matching Jeeps would be."

"It'd be borderline sickening." My smile fades. "But I have to get over the left-side thing if I ever want to drive one."

"When's your birthday?"

"Not 'til this summer. July."

"You've got time. Have you practiced at all?"

I shake my head. "Dad's forced me into the car a couple times but it didn't go well." To say that I had a meltdown would be an understatement. As soon as I put my hands on the wheel, images of Mom getting hit head-on filled my vision and I couldn't breathe. I couldn't move. According to Dad, I didn't stop screaming until he pulled me out of the car and dragged me back inside the house. That was two months ago. He suggested seeing a psychiatrist but I convinced him I'll be okay. "Maybe I need to move to a big city where driving isn't necessary."

Blake rests his elbows on the table and levels his gaze on me. "After the flip I saw you do, I have a hard time believing that you're scared of anything."

"Believe it."

"Okay, so no driving. But how do you feel about the left side of the tube?"

A shiver of excitement ripples through me at the thought of being close to him again. "That I can do."

***

At the top of the hill, I throw the tube on the ground and crouch behind it.

Blake squats next to me. "Headfirst?"

I raise a brow. "Chicken?"

"Hardly." He grips the tube, steadying it. "You first."

I rest my good knee on the edge and bounce a couple times before flopping onto my stomach. Between my snow pants and the ski jacket that hits my upper thighs, there's little chance Blake is able to check out my ass, but I can't help feeling exposed until he flops down next to me. I jostle into him—completely unintentional, I swear—and he pushes off with his feet.

I scramble for the handles as we rocket over the crest of the hill. "I wasn't ready!"

His arm clamps over the middle of my back, keeping me in

the tube but upping his chances of getting dumped on the first bump, which we're quickly approaching.

"You better hold on!" We hit the bump, catching a little air, and laughter bubbles out of me. Dad's called me an adrenaline junkie since I was a kid, and he's totally right. There's something about flying downhill on the edge of losing control while the wind blows my hair all over the place that makes me feel alive.

"Oh, shit," Blake mutters under his breath. He's still holding the back of my jacket and I tighten my grip to stay on the tube. We hit the ground with a thud. The toes of my boots slam into the packed snow and my teeth smack together. Blake manages to stay on without letting go of me, and he's definitely closer to my side now.

I'm still laughing. "You okay?"

"I didn't need that kneecap."

I glance at him to gauge if he's hurt, but his dimple is out in full force. He adjusts his position as we fly down the hill, and we pick up speed. He shifts again and the tube spins so we're sideways with his body closer to the bottom of the hill.

"What are you doing? You're going to make us—"

We hit the next bump and before I can say the word 'flip', the front of the tube dips faster than the back, sending me flying into the air. Blake pulls me tight against him and we land hard on the snow. Well, he lands on the snow. I somehow end up on top of him, chest to chest. His arms wrap around me as we come to a stop. My heart's pounding so hard I'm sure he can feel it through our jackets.

His eyes search mine. "You okay?"

I'm super aware of how close we are, is how I am. "I think we lost the tube."

He glances down the hill—the tube slides over the next bump and comes to a stop in front of two little kids, who look around before climbing in—then drags his gaze back to mine. They're so blue it's like the sky is reflecting inside them—or maybe the sky is so blue because of his eyes.

I move my arm so I'm leaning on an elbow and he rolls me so we're both on our sides. His dimple is still on display but I barely notice because his lips part and before I realize what's happening his head's leaning in and those perfect lips are pressing against mine. His touch is so soft I'm sure I must be imagining this, but no, Blake, the boy I met yesterday, is kissing me on the middle of a tubing hill.

My eyes close and my gloved hand drifts to his chest. His hand slides to the back of my head as his lips move against mine. I mimic his movement and wish there was a subtle way I could yank off my glove so I could feel his hair against my skin, but I don't want to do anything to distract him from kissing me.

But I don't have to worry. Shouts erupt from behind us and I open my eyes as Blake tucks me against him and rolls us down the hill. An overloaded tube lands where we just were and hits Blake in the back, pushing us into the snow.

A flurry of high-pitched squeals bombard us.

"Oh my god!"

"Are you okay?"

"Were you, like, making out?"

"They were totally making out."

I laugh against his chest. "Did that just happen?"

We push ourselves into a sitting position. Four girls my age stand in front of us, hands on their hips. One of them checks out Blake then catches my eye. "I'd make out with him in the middle of the hill, too. Nice work."

A fierce blush rips up my throat and over my face as the girls jump onto their tube and take off down the hill.

Blake grabs my hands and pulls me to my feet. "Either we jack a tube from the next people or it looks like we're walking."

I slip my hand into his and tug him down the hill. "Come on. We need to do that again."

His eyebrows pinch together like he's not sure which I mean—the kissing or the tubing—but as he walks alongside me, I don't care. I can't remember the last time I felt so happy.

six

"The tube landed on you while you were kissing?" Sophia's incredulous voice is mirrored by the look of disbelief on her face. Or as much of her face as I can see on video chat. When she gets excited she brings the phone closer to her mouth, which means right now I can basically see her lips, nose, and chin.

"Not directly on us. Someone yelled so Blake rolled us out of the way." Remembering his arms around me makes me warm all over and gives me goosebumps. Figure that one out.

"Best first kiss ever."

"I could have done without the group of girls. One of them gave me a verbal high-five for scoring Blake."

Sophia rolls her eyes. "I'm gonna need to see a picture."

"Tomorrow." My stomach does a little dance. Blake kissed me again when he dropped me off at the lodge, then invited me to go skiing.

"Ooh, another date?"

"He's taking me to another resort. Someplace less crowded."

She frowns. "I thought the ski patrol dude said not to—never mind, look who I'm talking to." Her eyes brighten. "They can't keep you off the slopes when it's only practice. There's no way you'd miss the chance to canoodle with a bo-o-o-o-oy." She flutters her eyelashes then presses the phone to her chest. Everything goes black.

"Stop hugging me."

Her eyes fill the screen. "I'm just super excited for you. I know how frustrating it was when Jake—"

"Let's not." Jake was new at school this year and I liked him right away. Unfortunately, my group of friends did too so before I could get to know him on my own, I was placed directly in the platonic category. "It's like they have some code that says no one's allowed to date me."

"That's why I avoid sports. Makes things *much* less confusing when it comes to boys."

"You make it sound so simple."

"Not simple, but not complicated. Look at how fast things have happened with Blake now that you don't have your posse hanging around."

I know she doesn't mean that the way it sounds, but sometimes I think Sophia wishes I wasn't friends with all the hot jocks in school. It's not like I'd ever stand in her way if she liked one of them, but since she's my friend, most of them avoid her romantically, too.

"You have a point."

She rests the phone in her lap so I'm looking up at her. "Have fun with this boy. Besides, it's not like you'll ever see him again, right?"

A knot of worry settles near my heart. Neither of us have said anything about what happens at the end of vacation, but it's stupid to think this could work. If I was eighteen and getting ready to go to college, maybe, but I'm only fifteen. A sophomore. Long distance romance is not in my future.

"Cally?"

"Sorry."

"You went inverted on me there."

I snort. "Introverted?"

She cocks her head. "Same difference. So I take it from your silence you don't think you'll see him again?"

"I don't see how we could. We live on opposite ends of the country. We literally could not live farther away from each other and still be in the US."

"There's always SnapChat."

I sigh. "He claims he doesn't believe in social media."

"What is it with boys?"

I shrug, and she waggles her brows. "Then I suggest you *really* have fun tomorrow."

"Ugh!" I slam my phone onto the bed—my version of throwing a pillow at her head—then pick it back up. "You're such a slut."

"You're such a prude."

A knock at my door startles me. "Dinner in five."

"Soph, I gotta go."

"I want every detail. And send a picture before I die of curiosity."

"Picture I can do. Details, we'll see."

"Prude," she repeats.

"Love you."

"Love you, too."

***

"You sure you don't want to come to breakfast?" Dad zips up his jacket and grabs his car keys. "I hate for you to be stuck here by yourself."

"I'm meeting Blake so I won't be alone."

Dad pauses. "You're spending a lot of time with him. Maybe both of you should come along so I can see for myself what's so appealing about him."

"Dad, no. We're just hanging out. Tomorrow we're both going back to our opposite ends of the country and I'll never see him again."

"Why do I get the feeling you're trying to get rid of me?"

I roll my eyes. "We're going to lunch, so I don't need to eat anything now."

His brows narrow for a second, then his face returns to its normal mellow expression.

I smile. "Go. I'll be fine."

I fight the urge to check the time on my phone until the door closes firmly behind him. Blake will be here in less than ten minutes. I rush to the bathroom to check my hair for the hundredth time, then slip on my snow pants, grab my skis, and head for the door.

The silver car from yesterday is already parked outside, and Blake climbs out when he sees me. A broad smile spreads across his face. "You look great."

I slowly look him up and down, exaggerating my movements to make him laugh, but instead I send my heart into overdrive. I know plenty of good-looking guys but this is the first time one has stared at me with such.... intensity. We lock eyes and my mouth goes dry. "You're not so bad yourself."

He winks and moves around the car to take my skis, but pauses before putting them in the trunk. "Are you sure this is a good idea?"

Cute boy. No parents. Yes, definitely a good idea. "The skiing?"

He raises an eyebrow. "What were you thinking?"

My cheeks grow hot and I smile up at him. "Skiing. Totally."

He laughs softly and slides my skis next to his snowboard. "So, food first, or should we go straight there?" He walks me to the passenger side and opens my door.

A girl could get used to this.

I'm not super hungry but most teenage boys I know need to feed every two to three hours. "Can we grab something on the way?" I climb in and reach for the door but he leans forward and brushes his lips over mine, lingering long enough for my hand to drift to the back of his neck and curl into his hair.

He mumbles against my lips. "What was the question?"

"I don't remember." I kiss him again, pulling him a fraction closer. Time seems to stand still. I'm always so focused on my goals—skiing, school, being a good daughter—that I rarely allow myself to fully let go. But this boy—I could get lost in him.

A low rumble sounds between us and I laugh against his mouth. "Food."

He pats his belly. "Yeah, it's been a couple hours since breakfast."

We go through the McDonald's drive-through and he's inhaling his egg and bacon sandwich before we're back on the road. My egg white sandwich still sits in my lap, unopened.

"That was impressive."

He crumples his empty wrapper. "Why aren't you eating?"

I fold the paper wrapper so I can hold my food without getting my hands greasy, but pause before taking a bite. I may hang out with boys, but I've managed to hold on to a few feminine traits. My teeth sink into the sandwich and I let out a groan. Okay, maybe I am more boy than girl. "How far is this place?" I ask, my mouth still full.

"Oh, uh... I looked it up. It's not too far. Maybe thirty miles. It's just on the other side of the mountain."

I study him as he drives. He hasn't checked his phone for directions, yet every turn he's made it's like he knows where he's going. "You seem to know your way around."

His eyes dart to me, then back to the road. "Yeah. We visit here at least once a year."

"That's cool." I lean my head against the seat and watch the mountains crawl by. We have mountains in Vermont but they're nothing like the Rockies. My whole life I've flung myself down icy, narrow trails. These wide, powdery Colorado slopes are like heaven. "What's it like in Tahoe?"

His fingers flex against the steering wheel. "Like this, but with a huge lake in the middle. You can see the water from the peaks. It's pretty cool."

"You really know how to paint a picture."

He shrugs. "You know how it is. When you live someplace you take it for granted." He nudges my arm with his elbow. "What's it like in Vermont?"

I smile. "Oh, you know. Snowy. Mountainous. With sunny days thrown in here and there."

He snorts. "Are you always such a smartass?"

"Yes." I take a sip of my drink and try to hold back a smile, but fail miserably.

He reaches for my hand and slips his fingers through mine. "I like it."

All witty comebacks flee my brain when our hands touch. I wish I could bottle the sensation of his skin on mine and how his heat crawls over me.

We ride in silence until we make the turn off the main road into the resort, and my knee starts throbbing like it knows I'm about to do something stupid. I slide my hand out of Blake's and slowly rub the tendons around me knee, hoping to be subtle, but he totally notices.

"Is it hurting?"

"It's all in my head. Either that or my dad and coach have it rigged to know when I'm breaking the rules."

"We don't have to go."

I level my gaze at him. "I didn't come to Colorado to ski ONE day. We're doing this."

"Okay." He holds up his hands in mock surrender. "But promise me you'll speak up before you do serious damage."

For a moment I'm left speechless because I was thinking the same thing about him. Blake's the perfect balance of cocky, sweet, funny, and hot, but worst of all, he lives a bazillion miles away from me so there's no way this is going to end well.

But there's no point in him warning me. My heart's already in this too deep—the damage is guaranteed.

seven

The edges of my skis cut through the snow and the scraping sound is like music to my ears. I shift my weight to my right leg and glide toward the tree line, then shift again and cut to the opposite side of the trail. Some people look at a snow-covered mountain and see nothing but frozen tundra—I see a blank canvas that's waiting for me to make my mark. I glance over my shoulder at Blake, who's boarding close enough that I can see the look of concentration on his face but not so close that we'll crash into each other.

He smiles when he sees me watching him and I crouch into a tuck to propel myself faster down the mountain. Tubing was fun, but nothing compares to flying down a hill with a couple pieces of fiberglass strapped to your feet. Or in Blake's case, one giant piece of fiberglass.

The swoosh of his board cutting through the snow gets louder, so I tuck my body even closer to my legs. Everything in my peripheral vision goes out of focus as I concentrate on the trail ahead of me—trees become a blur, there's a flash of neon blue and red as we pass a much slower couple, then the green of Blake's jacket as he passes me.

"Hey!" He must be hauling ass to pass me. I'm not going my absolute fastest, but not even Hunter can pass me on a board.

Blake banks hard and a spray of snow showers twenty feet past him as he comes to a stop. I lift my heels and twist my body so both skis slam hard into the side of the hill, covering the ground between us with snow.

He flips his goggles on top of his helmet and nods at my fresh powder. "You missed."

I return his smile and remove my goggles as I glide next to him. "I meant to."

"Aww, that's so sweet." He presses a gloved hand to his chest and pulls me to his side with the other. "How's your knee?"

I bend both knees and try to ignore the twinge that shoots up my leg. I clench my jaw. "Pretty good."

"Liar."

I turn my head so I'm looking into his eyes.

"I saw that look on your face. It hurts."

"Okay, maybe a little, but it's not like we're doing anything crazy. I haven't even tried to do a jump."

He pulls off a glove and touches his fingers to my cheek. The warmth is like a blast from the sun against my cold cheeks and my eyelids drift closed. *Is he going to kiss me again?* I feel his breath on my ear as he leans close. "I'm trying to spare you from another walk of shame."

My eyelids fly open. His smile is inches from my face but instead of kissing him, I push off his chest and turn my skis down the hill. "You'll have to catch me before I get on that sled again!" I tuck into my racing stance—skis straight, elbows in—and don't look back until I see the chairlift up ahead.

Blake comes to a stop next to me, off to the side of the line, and shakes his head. "I've never met anyone like you."

I don't know what to say to that. *Good? You must not get out much? Have you been hiding under a rock most of your life?* Because I may be a good skier, but I'm not all that.

He unhooks one foot and hop-slides over to me. He rests his hands on my shoulders and looks into my eyes. "I can't believe you're leaving tomorrow."

A lump catches in my throat. It's silly to get so worked up over a guy I barely know. "Aren't you going home tomorrow, too?"

His eyes cloud for a millisecond. “Yeah, first thing in the morning.”

“Maybe I’ll see you at the airport. We’re leaving pretty early because Dad’s worried about the time change and getting home too late, blah blah.”

“Oh yeah, maybe we will.” Something in his voice sounds off again, and this time I swear it’s not my imagination.

“Is something wrong?”

He blinks and the sparkling blues are back in full force. “It sucks we don’t have more time together.”

“I know.”

Before I can add anything else, he pulls me to his chest and lowers his mouth to mine. His lips are cold but soft, and they move with a gentle insistence that makes my insides turn to jelly. I slide my arms around his waist and lean into him, and he pulls me even closer.

A high-pitched squeal breaks the spell. “Ooooohhhh!”

I pull away and glare at a girl who looks old enough to know better than to interrupt a kiss like that. She skis after her friends, laughing. “We seem to have an issue with privacy.”

Blake kisses the tip of my nose. “Or I need to plan our next kiss better.”

My stomach does a somersault. Oh yes! Give me more of that! But in the meantime… “I know I said I can’t do any tricks, but this plain-Jane riding straight down is getting a little…”

“Boring?”

I laugh and fall against his chest. “Yes.”

“I have an idea.”

“Will it snap my leg off?”

“Not if we’re careful.”

“Then let’s go.”

Ten minutes later we’re standing at the top of the same hill as the last run. “How is this different?”

“Patience, grasshopper. We’re not going that way.” He nods at a narrow trail that cuts beneath the orange rope marking the boundary of the trail. “We’re going there.”

Excitement pulses through me. Trail skiing is no joke: there’s no path, the snow can get crazy deep, and there are trees everywhere. I push myself closer to the edge. “Is this legit?”

“Yeah, they let people—I mean, I heard some guys say these trails are killer.” He touches my arm. “Not actually killer. But, you know—”

“Yeah, I know what you mean.” I take a deep breath. “Lead the way.”

He lifts the rope so I can duck underneath, then drops to his butt to strap into his board. Once his feet are secure, he hops to his feet and plants a kiss on my lips. “We’ll go slow at first.”

A zing of electricity races through me. I know he’s talking about skiing, but for a split second, thoughts of what we could do if we DIDN’T go slow make me wish we weren’t on top of a mountain.

He nods at the trail. “Ready?”

What is it about this boy that makes my senses turn to mush? I laugh in an attempt to shrug off my momentary distraction. “You can’t go flinging kisses around and expect me to remember what you asked.”

His dimple creases his cheek as his eyes drop to my lips. “Sorry?” His voice is teasing, but his breathing is shallow, revealing that he’s as affected by me as I am by him.

His nervousness gives me courage and this time I press my lips to his. “I’d say don’t do it again, but I don’t really mean it.” Then before he can say anything else, I smack him on the ass. “Show me what you got.”

He stares at me for a second, a soft smile dancing on his lips, then hops forward and with one push disappears over the edge.

It’s now or never. I push forward with my poles until the tips of my skis are hovering over the edge. Blake is ten feet ahead, waiting for me to follow. With a quick nod, I lean forward, keeping my knees loose as the ground drops beneath me. Trail skiing is totally different from groomed skiing, and I feel a rush as I sink into powder halfway to my knees. I dig my poles into the ground and bend my legs and hop—kind of like a reverse squat—to move through the deep powder. My knee shouts in protest, but I'm going so slow that it's probably fine.

I continue the push-hop to gain momentum, and we fall into a steady rhythm, moving through the trees as if in slow motion. Sunlight filters through the branches, sparkling on the untouched snow and deepening the shadows beneath the evergreens. I inhale deeply, the scent of pine heavy in the air, and wish I could stay in this moment forever.

I shout to Blake. "Hold up."

He throws his arm around a tree branch to stop and looks up at me. "You okay?" He bends to unstrap from his board but I stop him from hiking to me.

"Stay there." I maneuver toward him, unable to suppress my smile. "This is so perfect." When I reach his side, I take off my helmet and toss it on the ground, then pop out of my skis and fall into the snow.

He tosses his helmet next to mine and flops next to me. We roll onto our backs, staring up into the trees and the blue sky high above.

"Thank you for bringing me here."

His coat rustles as he moves closer and loops his arm through mine. It's pretty much impossible to hold hands while wearing ski gloves, and I think I like this better because more of his body is pressed against mine. "Thank you for saying yes."

My stomach flip-flops, then tumbles into a knot. *I won't see him after today. He's perfect, and this is all we'll ever have.* The quiet and beauty of where we are combined with what I'm feeling nearly overwhelms me. Tears fill my eyes, threatening to spill. I wipe at my face with my free hand.

He clears his throat. "I gotta tell you, this vacation is way better than I expected."

I turn my head a fraction of an inch, just enough so I can see him without making him uncomfortable by looking right at him. "For the first time in my life I'm happy I missed a trick."

He turns his head and smiles his dimply smile. "Me too." He shifts so he's on his side and my heartbeat picks up speed. This boy-crazy side of myself is new territory, but I'm determined to go with it. I slide my hand over his side to his back, holding his gaze, ready for whatever's going to happen.

His teeth catch his bottom lip for a second, then he lowers his head until his mouth covers mine. The kiss starts out soft and timid like before, but one sigh from me and it's like I flipped a switch. His lips part and he nibbles the edge of my lip before gently sucking it into his mouth. I pull him closer, meeting his tongue with mine, and we sink into the snow, bodies entwined, completely lost in each other.

It takes a while, but the sensation of being half-frozen slowly works its way up my legs. "I think I'm turning into a Popcicle."

He tightens his grip on me and rolls so he's on his back and I'm lying on top of him. "Better?"

"Considering how many layers we're wearing, I guess it's the best I'm gonna get." His eyes widen and I clamp my mouth shut. *I can't believe I said that!* "I mean... umm..."

He buries his face in my neck and laughs. His warm breath makes me forget all about being cold. "I know what you mean. And Cally?"

I look into his eyes, amazed again at how blue they are. "Yes?"

"I wish we weren't wearing so many layers too."

I close my eyes and hide my face against his chest. "Oh my god. You like embarrassing me, don't you?"

"If it means you hold me closer, then yes."

I lift my head, surprised by how serious he sounds.

"I meant what I said before. I didn't think someone like you would ever look twice at me."

I snort. "Have you seen yourself?"

He rolls his eyes. "I'm trying to tell you something."

"I'm too young to get married."

He shakes his head, smiling. "Too bad. I was going to ask you to run away with me."

My heart pounds in my chest. We're obviously not running off anywhere, but just hearing him say that makes me happier than I ever imagined. "Or maybe we could just stay here forever."

His gaze flicks away from me and I can't read the expression on his face. He rolls me back to my side, then brushes a kiss across my forehead, down my cheek, finally landing on my lips.

A shadow falls over us and I open my eyes, expecting to see someone standing above us even though we're in the middle of nowhere, but it's just the sun ducking behind the clouds.

I shiver.

"You still frozen?"

"It's cold without the sun."

His arms tighten around me. He slips off his glove and trails his fingers down the side of my face, staring into my eyes for what feels like forever until he dips his head and buries his face in my neck.

Tears threaten but I blink them away.

He gently kisses my cheek.

"So that's a no on staying here?"

"I think your dad might have a problem with that."

I shrug. I don't particularly care what my dad wants right now. I want to stay here with Blake. I tuck my face into his neck and breathe in. He smells like soap and woods and everything I want in the world.

We lay like that until he starts shivering, then pick ourselves up and make our way back to the lodge.

eight

"Are you sure you have to leave already?" I rest my head against Blake's chest. We're leaning against his car in the parking lot of the ski place, stalling.

Blake sighs into my hair, his embrace tightening. "I wish I could, but my parents are really big on making sure we have enough family time."

My heart twinges at the mention of his parents. Plural. For a moment I wish I could meet his mom, to see what she's like—and what he's like with her—but it won't fill the emptiness I feel without Mom. "This sucks." The pressure that's been burrowed in my chest crawls its way up my throat, making it hard to breathe. I press my face harder against him. "Any chance you'll be visiting the East Coast?"

His voice is a whisper. "Do you want me to lie?"

I lift my face and look into his eyes, memorizing every detail. "Of course not."

His lips pull into a frown, but whatever he's thinking, he doesn't share. "Then no. I have your number. We can text and call..." he trails off. We both know this is where it ends.

"Right."

He traces his fingers down the side of my face, then cups my cheek in his palm. "Maybe... someday..." He bites his lower lip, then leans forward until his lips brush my forehead. He kisses my eyes, my cheek, and finally lands on the corner of my mouth.

I can't take it anymore. I don't care that we're standing in the middle of the parking lot. I slide my hands through his hair and pull his head to mine. Our lips part immediately—there's no time for gentleness—and we devour each other as if our lives depend on it. He turns me so my back is against the car and presses the length of his body against mine. A warmth spreads from my belly to other, less experienced parts, and I wish for the hundredth time that we were older, that we had more time, that we had someplace to go other than a parking lot.

When we finally come up for air, my breathing is ragged. A darkness clouds his eyes, like he's thinking the same thing I am about going somewhere more private.

But there's no time.

He kisses me once more, this time more gently, then takes a step back.

My gaze drops to the ground. I don't want to cry in front of him—again—but if I look at him I don't think I can stop it. The door creaks open and I slide inside.

The ride is too short. I feel like it's only been seconds when he stops in front of my condo.

His seatbelt clicks and I turn to face him. I try to speak but the lump in my throat is making it impossible.

"I guess this is it." He tries to smile but it comes out lopsided.

I unfasten my seatbelt and lean toward him. We meet in the middle, arms entwined, lips brushing over each other's face as if trying to memorize every detail.

He pulls away first. "I'll get your gear."

I meet him at the trunk and he props my gear against the side of the car.

"Text me when you land?"

I nod, still unable to find my words. I kiss him once more on the cheek. "Bye," I whisper, then grab my skis and hurry up the sidewalk. I don't want to look back, but I have to.

He's standing in the same spot, his gaze locked on mine.

I force myself to turn away. To open the door. To go inside

and close it. Then I run to my room, throw myself on the bed, and finally let the tears flow.

***

The doors to the airplane seal shut with a soft whoosh, but it's like a hammer to my chest. Even though we've been texting since last night, I'd secretly hoped Blake would be at the airport this morning, and when I didn't see him in security I dreamed that maybe he'd track me down at the gate, flowers in hand. A small flicker of hope burned that he'd force his way onto the plane, unable to go another second without seeing me, and kiss me in front of Dad and all the half-asleep people already in their seats. But that's not happening either.

The passengers around us are already in another world, eyes closed, some with earbuds firmly in place. Dad leans his head against mine, his leather brewery notebook in his lap, the faint scent of coffee lingering on his breath. "What's on your mind?"

He knows I'm sad to leave Blake—there was no hiding my red, swollen face when he got back from whatever he was doing yesterday—but he doesn't know that it feels like my heart's been ripped out and left in shreds on the terminal floor.

"Is it Blake?"

Okay, so maybe he has a clue. I shrug.

"Talk to me, Cally."

I take a deep breath and press my fingers to the corners of my eyes. It's like I have a bottomless cup of tears, ready to spew without warning. "It's not fair. I finally find a boy—a funny, beautiful, sweet boy—who sees me as more than just one of the guys, and he lives on the opposite end of the country."

"Do you have plans to talk to him after we get home?"

"Yeah, but what's the point? It's not like I'm ever going to see him again." With those words, another piece of my heart rips off and falls to the floor. At this rate I'm going to be dead before we land.

"You never know. The world works in mysterious ways."

I jerk my head to look at him. "Do you know something I don't?"

He holds up his hands. "No. But the world is a lot smaller than it was when I was your age. Can't you talk on social media and your video-chat thing?"

"He doesn't believe in social media." I don't know what it is but half my friends aren't into it either. Me, I love looking at everyone's pictures and seeing what they're doing—it's one of the few things that reminds the guys that I have two X chromosomes.

"Okay, then you're probably right. But I hate seeing you so upset." He fidgets with his seatbelt, eyes lingering on mine.

It's not like him to not say what he's thinking. "What's up?"

He flips the latch open, closed.

Open. Closed.

He's totally stalling. I rest my hand on his. "Dad."

"I have news, but I don't think this is the right time." He looks back and forth between me and his lap.

This isn't like him. My inability to keep a secret comes from him. "You can tell me."

"You're already upset. I don't want to make it worse." He looks in my eyes and my heart stalls.

Is he sick? He can't be sick. What will I do without him? "Dad, you're scaring me."

He takes a deep breath, then lays a hand on my leg. "This trip wasn't a vacation. It was a business trip."

Okay, so not sick. But this isn't a huge deal. He's been on plenty of business trips over the years so I don't know why this one is getting such a buildup. I watch him without speaking. If I interrupt he'll never spit it out.

He clears his throat. "You know that Calliope has been doing well. Really well."

Oh yeah, Dad named his brewery after me.

"Yeah. People love beer and yours is kickass."

He lowers his brow and I shrug.

"Or so I've heard."

I lean closer. "So business is good..."

"Henry and I have given it a lot of thought, and we've decided to open a second brewery." He studies me, face blank, like he's expecting a reaction other than excitement.

I get a sinking feeling in my stomach. Dad's never dramatic and this is definitely dramatic for him. "What's the catch?"

His eyes dart to his lap, then settle on me. "We've agreed that I'll be the one to open the new location. Get it going from the ground up. We're looking at a spring opening which means we break ground, so to speak, in less than a month."

There's something else. Something bad.

Dad moves his hand over mine. "Cally, the new Calliope Brewing is going to be here in Colorado. In Boulder."

Nausea rolls through me. "But—"

But we live in Vermont.

We don't live in Colorado.

My whole life is in our creaky old house with the bright purple shingles, curving wood banister, and the huge tree in the backyard.

But most importantly, our house holds my every memory of Mom. If we leave, where will she go? Another family won't know how much she loved that house, how we used to sit in the window seat facing the backyard, daydreaming about the future. How I still sit there with a blanket wrapped around me, pretending it's her protecting me from everything outside that window.

"Cally?"

"What about the ski team?"

A frown tugs at his mouth. "I talked to the school here but they've already got their team."

It's like he punched me in the gut. The plane isn't moving but I feel like the bottom dropped out from beneath me. "I won't be on a team?" No training. No competition. Nothing to keep me going every day.

I stare at him, unable to form a coherent sentence.

Dad squeezes my hand. "I didn't make this decision lightly. Everything else fell into place. Henry and I don't want to miss this opportunity."

A lump blocks my throat. I want to lash out, to scream that he doesn't care about me or my feelings or my life, but I know that's not true. Dad has always put me before everything else so if he's decided to yank me from my world, he has to have a good reason.

Dad moves his hand over my hair, settling on the back of my neck. The tears in his eyes mirror mine. "I promise I will make this as easy on you as I can."

"But no ski team." My voice is low. A statement, not a question.

"Not this season. I'm sorry." He closes his eyes and presses his forehead to mine. The gesture usually comforts me, but there are too many emotions swirling through me.

The overhead speakers ding. "This is your captain speaking. We're next in line. Flight attendants, please prepare for take-off."

Dad releases me and we lean our heads against our seats. He's still holding my hand and I cling to it like my life depends on it.

What started as the most exciting week of my life has turned into the biggest heartache I've ever known.

nine

ONE MONTH LATER

It's two days after the new year and once again I'm in a plane over Colorado, but instead of the despair I felt when Dad told me we were moving, a combination of heartache, anger, and what Dad keeps calling 'teen angst' swirls through me. I'm beyond pissed that Dad yanked me out of my life and expects me to start over, but right when I'm ready to lash out, sadness over everything I'm leaving sweeps through me and I'm reduced to a puddle of tears. Saying goodbye to our house was the hardest thing I've ever done and I'm terrified that we somehow left Mom behind.

My favorite is when the mood swings hit in public. One minute I'm scowling at the world—which Sophia informs me is not my best look—and then I'm pushing my hair in my face so no one can see my tears.

Which, if I'm honest, are usually for Blake.

I knew whatever we had wouldn't last beyond vacation, but a tiny part of me fantasized that we'd somehow end up together. I may have even suggested that Dad open the new brewery in Lake Tahoe instead of Boulder, but he shook his head and mumbled something about teenage love and not being ready for me to grow up.

Blake and I texted a handful of times, and while he was super sweet and flirty, the spark from the slopes wasn't there. I thought he'd at least sympathize about the ski team, but it's been radio silence ever since I told him we're moving.

Even my knee has healed. It's like the Thanksgiving trip never happened.

Slope Rule #4: Don't force it or you'll break something.

That rule's meant to protect your bones, but in this case it applies to my heart.

I swipe through the pictures from my going away party. Sophia and the guys took over one end of our favorite pizza place and we gorged ourselves until they closed. Hunter and Sam agreed that Blake's sudden change in attitude was weird, but seemed to have some guy-understanding that this is how things go. Personally, I think they don't want to think about me as a girl.

I pause on a pic of Sophia and Jake, my lip caught between my teeth. There was a time when he was, unbeknownst to him, the center of my universe, but we slid into friend-zone and there was no turning back. In this picture Sophia's smiling up at him like they're the only people in the room. And he seems just as into her.

I click off my phone and drop it in my lap. It's like they've already moved on without me. Sophia slept over after the party and we stayed up all night talking, but she never mentioned that she likes Jake.

A sigh escapes me and Dad nudges my elbow.

"Look out the window."

I meet his eyes and a pang of guilt twists my stomach. This can't be easy on him either. I lean over him to peer out the window and my breath catches. That's where I want to be. The sun's shining through a cloudless sky, reflecting off the snow blanketing the peaks of the mountains that seem tall enough to scrape the bottom of the plane. I stretch closer, drawn to the mountain like it's pulling me into its shadowy embrace.

Dad touches my cheek. "Maybe this won't be so bad, even without a ski team?"

I let out another sigh, not wanting to concede just yet. "It does have its perks. But explain to me why Henry couldn't move instead of us?"

Now it's Dad's turn to sigh. "Cally, we talked about this. Jenny's six months pregnant and all her family lives in Burlington. They'll need the help with a newborn." He pokes my side. "You're already self-sufficient."

I cross my arms and sink lower into my seat, the view of the mountains replaced with blue sky so bright that it reminds me of Blake's eyes, and I have to turn away.

Dad rests his head against the back of the seat and gazes out the window. I don't want to be difficult. We're in this together and right now he's the only person I know in the entire state of Colorado.

"Tell me what you're thinking."

"I'm angsting over my angst."

His snort of laughter breaks the tension.

"Forgive me for being a brat?"

His shoulder bumps against mine. "A. Always. And B. If this is the brattiest you get, I'm the luckiest father in the world."

The corner of my mouth turns up in a smile. "Remember that when I fall into a deep depression because I'm not on the ski team."

***

It starts to hit me that WE'VE MOVED TO COLORADO when we're driving on the stretch of highway that circles downtown Denver. There's farmland near the airport, then the suburbs begin, while the massive Rockies loom in the distance. It's really not that different from Vermont, except much, much bigger. And open. And, oh yeah, thousands of miles from everything I know.

"I thought we'd drive past the brewery before going to the house."

I'm grateful Dad didn't call it home. Not yet. "Sure."

"There won't be much to see. It's not scheduled to open until the spring, but I'm anxious to see how it's coming along." Dad's flown out here a couple times since we were here for Thanksgiving to sign leases for the brewery and this house that he assures me I'll 'learn to love.' If that doesn't sound ominous, I don't know what does.

He takes an exit for another highway and we speed toward Boulder. Soon we're turning onto a street lined with low brick buildings, their wide windows showcasing clothes and food and beer. Lots of beer.

"They seem to like their beer here."

Dad smiles. "There's a method to my madness."

My head swivels to take it all in.

Dad pulls to a stop in front of what looks like a Victorian house in the middle of the block of businesses. The familiar Calliope logo hangs above the window, the loops of the L's linking together, the E drifting off into a trail of stars. Dad commissioned the logo when I was heavy into my princess phase, and while I don't see any of that girl in myself anymore, I'm touched he's never changed it.

"What do you think?"

I take in the purplish-gray shingles, white trim, and dark gray shutters that flank the picture window and a lump catches in my throat. "It looks like our house."

Dad squeezes my hand and I press my sleeve to the corner of my eye.

"But it doesn't look like a brewery."

He shrugs. "Who's to say that? Calliope's never been one to blend in with the crowd. She deserves to stand out."

I meet his gaze and tears slide down my face. I'm not sure if he's talking about me or the brewery, or both. "I can't believe you did this."

"Henry and I agreed that since we're the newcomers, we need to make a statement. What better statement than a princess-themed brewery?"

My mouth falls open. "Dad, you are not!" An exterior color hinting at purple is one thing. But no one's going to—

"I'm kidding. It's more of a homey, living room atmosphere." He kills the engine. "Want to look inside?"

I scramble out of the car and follow him through the front door. An archway sweeps over the entrance, guiding us into the heart of the room. A hodge-podge of chandeliers dot the tin ceiling—some covered with sparkly tear-drop shaped glass, others more masculine metal and steel—while ornate crown molding edges the room and windows, and— "You put in my window seat?" I tip-toe over the tarp covering what looks like hard-wood floors, careful not to knock over the buckets of paint scattered around the room, and stop in front of a large bay window across from the bar.

Dad moves next to me. "It doesn't have the same view as back home, but I thought you could do homework here if you visit me after school."

Tears blur my vision. I can totally picture Mom curled up in the window seat with a book. "You didn't have to do this." I turn in a circle, waving my arm at the space. "But I love it."

He pulls me into a hug. "You don't know how happy it makes me to hear you say that. So," he pulls back to look me in the eye. "You ready to see the house?"

We backtrack through town, the happiness I felt at the brewery vanishing when he turns into a newer housing development. "Harmony Hills? Since when are we subdivision people?"

Dad doesn't answer.

We pass house after identical house, most constructed of pale brick and so large they'd cover half our block back home. A tree sits in the center of each yard, their bare branches reaching for the blue sky, and while the landscaping varies a little from house to house, there isn't a single personal touch on any of them.

"I'm guessing ours isn't purple?"

He winds through streets with names like Peak and Trail and Avalanche—Seriously? They named a street after a natural disaster?—and comes to a stop in front of the bazillionth white brick house.

He kills the engine. "This is it."

I lean my head against the seat. My arms and legs don't want to move. This can't be our new home. It's a fricking mini-mansion! We may have money but we are not the kind of people who throw their money in your face and make sure everyone knows exactly what they have—and what others don't. My friends know we're well-off but that's never been what I'm about. The rich kids have their own circle and I consider myself lucky that I don't have to hang out with them.

Dad touches my arm, snapping me out of my freak-out. "What are you thinking?"

I sigh. "Can I stay at the brewery?"

ten

Did you really think he'd let you stay at the brewery? Sophia texts.

No, but it was worth a shot.

The cookie-cutter feel continues inside the McMansion. Everything is beige or white, with the exception of dark hardwood floors that I admit are kind of cool, and every room looks the same. Worst of all, I can't feel Mom. The staircase railing doesn't have the nick from when Mom finally carried my first pair of skis downstairs after I insisted on sleeping with them for a month. The living room ceiling doesn't have spots of paint in the corner from the weekend we were snowed in and decided to repaint the walls. And the kitchen is missing—her. Even though it's been seven years since her accident, the scent of flour and vanilla and cinnamon enveloped me every time I opened a cupboard. This kitchen smells like bleach and lemon and emptiness.

I'm currently flopped on a double bed in the third bedroom from the stairs, but I could switch rooms and never know the difference.

It's like being inside a bran muffin.

Hope there's lots of bathrooms. When does your stuff get there?

I sigh. *Next week.* Thank god Dad packed sheets in his suitcase. It's bad enough we'll have to use someone else's dishes until our stuff arrives. I try not to think of the people who were in here before us.

Meet anyone yet?

My eyes flick over the stark white walls, and I roll onto my back to try to stop the sensation that they're closing in on me.

Just the ghost of Christmas future.

The house won't get the best of you.

I miss home.

I miss you.

Anything exciting happen since I left?

Texting with Sophia is rapid-fire, our replies coming as fast as we can type, so the pause now makes me sit up.

Soph?

Well...

Spill.

I get the feeling this will be about Jake, but part of me hopes it isn't.

I sort of had a date today. With Jake.

Even though I saw it coming, my stomach drops. I don't like Jake like that anymore and I love Sophia and want her to be happy, but it's like a punch to the gut.

Cally?

I swallow the bitterness lingering at the back of my throat.

I had a feeling he liked you! How was it?

I can feel her exhale from halfway across the country. We've never kept secrets from each other so I'm sure that was as hard for her to write as it was for me to read.

Amazing. We met for coffee, then window-shopped downtown.

Did you kiss?

Not yet, but it's coming.

I smile. I've always worried that my friendship with the guys kept them from asking her out, so if me moving helps Sophia with Jake, I can add one positive to the list.

I want to hear all about it.

Deal.

Love you.

Love you too. Gotta go. xoxo.

I drop my phone on my chest. I should probably unpack or see if Dad needs help, but exhaustion tugs me into sleep before I can even turn off the light.

***

The next morning, after taking a minute to remember where the hell I am, I throw on my sneakers and grab a sweatshirt before heading downstairs. Dad's scribbling in his notebook on the kitchen counter while sipping from a Starbucks cup. He nods his head at an identical cup next to him.

I inhale, letting the cinnamon and vanilla worm their way into my brain. "Thanks."

"Going somewhere?"

"I thought I'd check out the neighborhood."

He smiles from behind his cup. "I was afraid you'd lock yourself in your room in protest."

The corner of my mouth lifts. "Don't think I didn't consider it. But I can only stare at white walls for so long—and I need some fresh air."

"We should probably hit the grocery store at some point, but do you want to go skiing later?"

I laugh. "Duh."

He quirks a brow. "You're okay renting?"

"Just this once."

"I need to go into town for a bit. How about I pick up lunch on the way back, then we'll head out?"

I take another sip. "Perfect."

Shortly after he leaves, I slip the house key in my pocket and step into the brisk morning sunshine. The brochures weren't kidding when they said it's sunny almost every day. I shield my eyes as I make my way down the driveway and nearly collide with an elderly woman walking a droopy-eyed Basset Hound.

"Good morning! You must be our new neighbors!"

I position myself so I'm not facing the sun and smile as her face comes into focus. Tight gray curls frame a face swirling with wrinkles, but it's clear from her grin the lines are from years of laughing. Her head barely reaches my shoulder and she seems even shorter because of a slight hunch. If she laid down next to the dog he'd probably be bigger than her.

I hook my thumb over my shoulder at the house. "Yeah, my dad and I moved in yesterday."

She touches her finger to her lips. "I didn't see a moving truck. Ernest and I always notice things like that."

I bend forward to scratch the dog's ears and am thanked with a tongue to the face. I wipe off the slobber with my sleeve. "You must be Ernest." He bays, a low echoing sound that I feel in my chest.

Her laughter makes me look up. "Oh, heaven's no. This is Cooper. Ernest is my husband." She holds out her hand. "I'm Eleanor Sherman."

"Cally. Cally Clarke." Just call me double-oh seven. "My dad's Tom. Our stuff is supposed to get here next week, so we—"

With zero warning, Cooper lunges down the sidewalk, jerking his leash from Eleanor's hand. I catch her arm to keep her from falling as Cooper gallops around the corner onto the next street.

"Oh dear. I'll never be able to catch him."

I squeeze her arm. "I'll go. You wait here." I sprint down the street, praying Cooper didn't go past the next street or I might never find my way back.

I round the corner as Cooper's tail disappears in a row of bushes along the sidewalk at the end of the block. "Cooper!" I wrap an arm around my chest to keep the girls from smacking me in the face. A bra would have been a good decision before I left the house. There's no sign of Cooper behind the bushes, so I hurry through the yard around the side of the house and slam directly into a chest.

"Oof!"

"Sorry!"

He catches me as I start to fall, but my momentum topples us both into the grass. I'm pretty sure my knee lands in a place I've only dreamed about touching and his elbow catches me in my very bra-less chest. A boy around my age with short black hair and warm brown skin is smiling at me.

I scramble to my feet, and only then do I notice the pair of bright green eyes locked on mine. You'd think those would have been the first thing I noticed. They pierce right through me, jump-starting my heart and causing a blush to creep up my neck.

A slow smile lights up his face, all white teeth and full lips and holy crap I haven't brushed my teeth or brushed my hair and what the hell must I look like? His smile deepens and he nods at my arms, which are clamped over my chest. "Are you okay?"

My face reddens. There's no way he can tell I'm not wearing a bra, but I feel exposed anyway. "Yeah, sorry. Did you see a Basset hound gallop this way?"

"Cooper?"

"You know him?"

He rubs a hand over his hair. "Yeah, but Dolly knows him better."

I raise an eyebrow.

"My lab." He nods his head toward the backyard. "Follow me." He leads me alongside the house and I follow him over the stone path, staying a few feet back so my breath doesn't knock him out. We round the corner and—

"Dolly, no!"

"Cooper!"

Mrs. Sherman's floppy-eared dog is going to town on Dolly, who, from her half-closed eyes, doesn't seem to mind. "Cooper!" I sprint across the yard but he doesn't stop.

I'm mortified. Beyond embarrassed. But despite the absolute humiliation, a giggle escapes. Mr. Hottie Green Eyes smirks, and we bust out laughing. "What a stud," I say.

Cooper starts to do his thing again and he grabs Dolly's collar. "I better put her inside."

I slip my hand into the loop of Cooper's leash. "I should probably get him home. Sorry for knocking you over." I tug at the hem of my sweatshirt, wishing for the fiftieth time that I'd put on a bra. Or deodorant.

"Is Mrs. Sherman your grandma?"

"No, my neighbor."

He smiles, and I swear his eyes brighten. "You live here?"

I check my non-existent watch. "For almost eighteen hours."

Yes, his smile is definitely bigger. "Junior?"

Disappointment pricks my chest. "Sophomore."

"Me too."

"I'm Cally." I hold out my hand and his warm hand covers mine.

"Evan."

Cooper tugs me toward the sidewalk, no doubt ready for a cigarette and a nap. "Mrs. Sherman is probably worried."

Evan squeezes my hand once more, then lets go. "You going to Monarch?"

I nod.

"Then let me be the first to welcome you."

"I guess I'll see you around." I lift my hand in a half-wave and turn to go. I'm almost to the sidewalk when he calls out.

"Hey, Cally."

I turn back.

"Do you ski?"

I smile so hard the sun's probably glaring off my teeth. With a quick nod I say, "Yep," then follow Cooper back to Mrs. Sherman, my heart lighter than it's been in weeks. If there are more kids like Evan at this school, how bad can it be?

eleven

You met a cute boy within 24 hours. The first day of school will be cake.

As long as I don't knock anyone else over. *You think Evan will talk to me?* I haven't seen him since the Cooper sex-show and the boost of confidence over knowing someone in my new school has fizzled as the first day grew closer.

He practically felt you up. He'll talk to you.

Easy killer. I'm not ready to go there yet. Broken heart, remember?

So don't give him your heart. But your number...

I smile. Sophia makes it sound so easy. *Gotta finish getting ready. Love you.*

Good luck! xoxo

I tug at my sweater, but it doesn't magically make me look any different than I did five minutes ago. I shove my phone in my back pocket, take a deep breath, and make my way to the car where Dad's waiting, engine running.

"You'll be fine."

"Yeah, yeah."

"Remember, no matter how good or bad your day goes, it'll eventually end, just like every day before it."

I level my gaze at him. "Are you reading daily affirmations again?"

A smile touches his lips. "I'm just trying to help."

"Thanks, but no more inspirational quotes."

He nods, and pulls out of the driveway.

Any qualms I had about not fitting in ease the moment I step through the front doors. It smells like every school I've ever been in: a combination of musty desperation and bleached anxiety with a dose of stale hormones. Several kids smile as I pause inside the main entrance, and a scrawny girl with a mop of curls on top of her head helps me find the office. An aide brings me to my first class, where the warm fuzzies continue.

I text Sophia as I'm heading to lunch. *People are oddly nice.*

Pleasantville nice?

It's weird. I expected at least a couple bitches.

School sucks without you.

:(

I pause outside the cafeteria and take a deep breath. As awkward as it is being the new kid, classes are easy because the teacher tells you where to sit. Lunch is a free-for-all.

The line snakes along the back wall, giving me a chance to survey the room. The jocks are easy to spot, but after that it's harder to determine the pecking order. Laughter rings out from a table near the windows, drawing the attention of half the room. Two blond girls and another with a sleek, dark ponytail giggle over their trays, smiling at Evan.

Evan!

I'd begun to wonder if I'd imagined him, but there he is, his smile doing things to my pulse from across the room.

"What can I get you?"

I start to turn around, then do a double-take at a boy walking toward the exit. There's something familiar about the way his hair falls in his face, but half the boys my age have that haircut.

"Miss?"

I shake my head. "Sorry." I point at a piece of pizza, then grab an apple juice from the case near the cashier. I look back but the boy is gone. I must be imagining things.

"Cally!" Evan's standing halfway between me and his table. "Over here."

Relief floods through me. I don't have to sit alone. I follow him to his table but as we get closer, the nerves return in full force. It's not that I don't get along with girls—Sophia is proof of that—but they can be judgmental and catty and—

The girls swivel their heads in unison, matching smiles lighting their flawless faces. "Hi, Cally," says the model-hot blond in the middle. "I'm Brianna. This is Mikayla," she gestures to the other blond, who's junior-varsity attractive compared to Brianna, "and Kenzie," the dark-haired girl who, now that I'm closer, I realize is a stunning combination of Pacific Island exoticness. "You know Evan. The other guys are Reece and Austin. Welcome to Monarch." Reece and Austin are built for outdoors and equally hot—I'm sensing a pattern with Brianna's friends—but pale in comparison to Evan.

"Uh, thanks." There's no way I'm going to remember all that. I pull out the empty chair, feeling immensely inadequate. Did I somehow end up at the School for the Future Models of America?

"How do you like Boulder so far?"

"Are you from the East Coast?"

"Is it true your family owns that new brewery downtown?"

I meet the blond's eyes who asked the last question. "Brianna, right?" She nods. "Yeah, that's ours."

One of the guys laughs. "What kind of a name is Calliope?"

"What's with the purple?"

"I think it's cool!"

Evan smiles at me. "It's named after you?"

My cheeks redden. I've heard all this a million times, but I still get sweaty and tingly when people ask me about the name. "Yeah." I shrug. "My dad was feeling sentimental. But the one in Vermont isn't purple."

Brianna leans forward, eyes sharp. "So it's a chain?"

I suddenly feel like I'm facing a firing squad. I sit up straight. "No, just the two."

"Bri's family owns Mischief, the monstrosity the next block over," says Reece. Or is it Austin?

Brianna gives him a look that wipes the smile from his face and the pecking order becomes clearer. Brianna is definitely their leader. And she doesn't tolerate bullshit.

He holds up his hands. "The highly successful and dope monstrosity." The look on his face—a hint of apology mixed with cockiness—reminds me of Hunter, who's more likely to blurt out whatever he's thinking and deal with the consequences—in this case, Brianna's anger—later.

She rolls her eyes away from him and smiles at me, but the warmth from before is gone. "Do you ski?"

"Yeah."

The blond on her right perks up. "You should come with us Saturday!"

Brianna cuts her a look that I can't decipher, but it's replaced with a smile so wide my own cheeks hurt. "We hit Eldora every weekend. Can you make it?"

On the surface the invitation seems friendly enough, but I can't shake the feeling that I'm stepping into a viper pit. Never mind that this will be the first time I've hung out with more than one girl outside of the ski team since I was ten years old. "Sounds like fun."

Evan smiles at me again. "Can't wait to see what you've got."

Okay, if the guys will be there this won't be too bad. But our gear better be there when I get home—no way in hell I'm using rentals with these girls.

***

After lunch, I'm grabbing books for the second half of the day when my stomach lurches and I drop one on my foot. Hallucinations aren't really my thing but I swear that was Blake who walked by.

"Stop it," I mutter to myself, shaking my head. I slam my locker shut and hurry in the direction I've been told is my English class. The bell rings and kids scatter. One of the blond girls at lunch—Mikayla, who insisted I call her Mike—offered to draw me a map, but I shrugged her off. Now I'm alone in the hallway, clutching my class schedule.

By the time I find the classroom and open the door, the teacher has already started. Dressed in skinny jeans and a long sweater, she greets me with a warm smile. "You must be Cally." I nod and she points to an empty desk against the far wall.

I'm just settling in when the door opens again.

"Sorry, Ms. Simpson."

My head snaps up.

That voice.

I know that voice.

My heart stops and I can't seem to catch my breath. His head is lowered so his hair falls in his face but my body seems to register what's happening before my mind fully comprehends who's walking toward me.

"Blake, I'd hoped we'd get started on the right foot this semester."

He turns down the aisle before mine and sits in the second-to-last desk.

I whip my head forward before he catches me staring.

Did he see me?

Does he know I'm here?

Why is HE here?

I force myself to face the front of the room, but the urge to peek at him is so strong I can almost feel a hand on my head forcing me to turn around.

Ms. Simpson continues the lesson, but I don't hear her.

When the bell rings an eternity later, the back of my neck is on fire. I don't know if he was actually staring at me but it feels like it. I grab my books and follow the other kids to the door, unable to decide if I want him to see me or not. *Did he know he'd be here when I told him I was moving? Why didn't he say anything?* My stomach plummets to my shoes. *Or is this why he stopped texting?* I make it to the front of the room with my eyes glued to the girl in front of me, but a shout in the hallway makes me look up. Blake's a few feet away, eyes on me. The lopsided half-smile flits across his face for a second, but then it's gone so fast I think I imagined it and he's walking out the door ahead of me.

What the hell was that?

Once in the hallway, I take a deep breath and before I can change my mind say, "Blake!" The desperation I've felt over the past month fills that one word and while it's not loud enough to be a shout, his slight pause tells me he heard. He turns enough to lock eyes with me again, but this time he doesn't smile.

Just as my heart's about to get trampled by the kids swarming around me, an arm loops through mine and tugs me down the hall.

"Please tell me you're not friends with *Blake*." Brianna says his name like he's not worth her breath. He turns down a hallway and my body wants to follow, but there's no escaping Brianna.

"We met—"

"Listen to me. Don't waste your time with a Ski Bum. Sure, he's easy on the eyes, but how far will that get you?"

What the ever-loving cluck is she talking about? I glance at her from the corner of my eye. Pointing out that I'm fifteen and am not exactly concerned with where dating a boy will get me beyond, I don't know, making out in his car, doesn't feel like the right thing to say.

She stops and faces me, her sharp eyes focused on mine. "I'm trying to help you, Cally, and I don't help everyone. Eating lunch with us put you on the right track, but Blake and his friends..." she shakes her head. "Let's just say, they're no Moguls."

I wait for her to laugh, but the determined look on her face doesn't waver. "Should I know what that means?"

"Evan. Austin. Reece. The Moguls."

Laughter bubbles inside me but I bite my cheek to keep it in check. "They have a name? Like a gang?" I've wandered onto the set of a teen movie.

She rolls her eyes. "Not a gang. More like a club. They're the Moguls and me, Mikayla, and Kenzie are the Snow Bunnies."

A snort escapes before I can stop it. I cough into my hand, hoping she didn't notice.

She raises an eyebrow, assessing me. "If you ski with us this weekend, your social status is locked. And," a smile softens her features, "I'm sure Evan would be more than happy to keep your mind off what's-his-nuts."

"Evan?"

"I saw the way he looked at you at lunch and I know you met over break. Now I'm not saying you have to date him, but it'll help your standings to date a Mogul while you're going through initiation."

"Initiation?" And now I'm a parrot. Just because I don't hang out with many girls that doesn't mean I'm intimidated by them, but this has gotten so bizarre it's like I've forgotten the basic conversation skills I learned in kindergarten.

Her jaw drops for a mili-second. "To be a Snow Bunny." She lets out a dramatic sigh. "Just do what I say and you'll have your pick of guys by the end of the month." The bell rings and she plasters on a bright smile. "See you later!"

I watch her sashay down the hall, more confused than I was when Blake ignored me.

twelve

As part of initiation I have to go out with a Mogul.

My phone rings and Sophia's face fills the screen.

I smile.

"Initiation?" Sophia's mouth hangs open.

"To be a Snow Bunny."

"Snow Bunny." Her mouth opens wider.

I give myself bunny ears and waggle my brows.

"And what the hell is a Mogul?"

"Close your mouth before you swallow your phone."

"You are in Pleasantville!"

"Moguls are the rich ski boys. Or boarders. Apparently I'm only allowed to date them. Guys like Blake are considered beneath me."

"What does Blake have to do with this?"

In an effort to keep my head above water and not sink back into the semi-depression I went through when Blake first stopped texting, I sort of pushed the fact that HE'S IN MY ENGLISH CLASS, and oh yeah, MY NEW SCHOOL, out of my head. And while I know I shouldn't keep things from my best friend, I hadn't planned on telling her until I'd had time to wrap my brain around the fact that I'M GOING TO BLAKE'S SCHOOL.

I sigh.

"Cal?"

"You ready for this?" I tell her about English class and him being weird in the hallway. Sophia's eyes get wider and wider as

I talk. "And that's when Brianna made me swear a blood oath to join her gang."

"What the hell crazy-ass town did your dad drag you to?"

"I thought I was off to a good start meeting Evan last week, but I can't figure out why the rich girls have adopted me as their new plaything."

"Evan's cute, right?"

"If you like beautiful skin, clear green eyes, gorgeous smile, all in a six-foot tall package..."

"Ooh, tell me more about his package."

I snort.

"So maybe this gang thing isn't all bad. At least until you've made more friends."

"You want me to swear a blood oath?!"

She stops smiling. "Wait, there's really a blood oath?"

I wink.

"You brat."

"I'll remember you said that when I become a Mogul Bunny."

"I don't even want to know what that means."

My phone buzzes with a text from Dad.

"Soph, I gotta go. Time for dinner."

"Pee monster's growling anyways."

I snort. "God, I miss you."

"Love you!"

I stare at my phone, not wanting the conversation to be over. It felt good to talk like normal after worrying all day about saying the wrong thing and casting myself as a freak on my first day of school.

Something niggles the back of my mind, and I scroll through my contacts to Blake's name. When we met over Thanksgiving, he put his number in my phone and saved it under his name so I never actually looked at the number. Not like I knew the area code for Colorado or Lake Tahoe, but he made sure I wouldn't look. I tap his name and the number pops up.

303.

Colorado.

***

By the end of the week, I'm remembering people's names and don't feel as lost as I did on the first day, but I can't stop wondering why Blake lied. What difference did it make if he lived here or in Colorado? If he was worried about me wanting a relationship, he already knew I lived in Vermont. But he stopped texting when I told him I was moving here. So maybe that was it. He only wanted something over vacation and when he found out I was coming here, he didn't know how to tell me that I didn't mean anything to him.

And the tears are back. I swore I was done crying over Blake, but this new realization stings worse than those first days of silence because back then I thought I'd never have to see him again. Now I have to get over him knowing I could run into him when I least expect it.

"You okay?" Mike nudges my arm. It's Saturday morning and we're in the back of Brianna's 4Runner on our way to Eldora. I wipe the corners of my eyes with my fingers, expecting her to roll her eyes or say something snotty, but she looks at me with concern.

"Yeah, I guess I just miss my friends back home, you know?"

"I get it. I moved here in sixth grade and it took a while to get used to... things." She glances at the front seat but I can't tell if she means Brianna and Kenzie, or Boulder in general.

"What are you two whispering about?" Brianna's voice is light, but I catch her watching us in the rearview mirror.

Mike laughs. "Just how awesome our new outfits are!"

I raise an eyebrow, afraid to ask. "Outfits?"

Kenzie looks over her shoulder at me and grins. "You'll see."

Brianna smiles. "The guys are gonna love 'em."

"Do you all ski together?" I ask. Back home, Hunter, Sam, and I usually stuck together on the terrain park, but every so often I'd break off on my own to fly as fast as I could down the mountain. They could spend hours perfecting a trick but I'm a well-rounded adrenaline junkie—I like speed and aerials.

Brianna's still watching me in the mirror. "We meet up with them in the lodge once they're done throwing themselves in the air." She rolls her eyes and I decide now's not the time to mention that's what I plan on doing, too.

When we get to Eldora, we bypass Pleasantville and stumble head-first into future Stepford Wives of America. Forget Future Models, these girls are full-on crazy pants. They prance out of the locker rooms in matching non-matching outfits: form-fitting ski jackets—each in a different bright color—with tight-fitted pants that show enough of their bums to get attention, plus headbands, goggles, and matching ponytails. Brianna's smile fades when she sees my navy blue snowboarding pants and jacket. The lime green racing stripe hardly compares to her neon-pink ensemble.

"I won't lose you, that's for sure."

She eyes the helmet looped over my arm. "A helmet? Seriously?"

I shrug. "You don't?"

She lifts a shoulder and rolls her eyes at Kenzie. "We don't fall."

I can't tell if the attitude is directed at me or the world in general, but I'm too excited to ski to worry about what's going on inside Brianna's head.

Once we're strapped into our skis—I'm shocked they haven't color-coordinated those—I trail behind them to the chairlift. Eldora isn't as big as the other resorts surrounding Denver, but the powder is just as good. Brianna and Kenzie pair off for the chairlift so I wait next to Mike. The chair swings around, scooping them up, and we slide into position. As soon as we're in the air and out of earshot of Brianna, I take a deep breath.

"So what's with the outfits?"

Mike's is bright blue. She rolls her eyes and lets out a small laugh. "Don't let Bri hear you say that."

I let out a breath I didn't realize I was holding. Maybe they're not as Stepford as I thought. "So the Queen Bee dictator thing isn't an act?"

Mike runs her gloved hand over the bar holding us into the chairlift. "She's one-hundred percent diva."

"Why do you put up with it?" The few times I've talked to Mike she seems nice, normal. Very unlike Brianna.

"Like I said before, it took a while for me to make friends when I first moved here. Middle school was a fresh start and for whatever reason, Bri latched onto me. I've been friends with her and Kenzie ever since."

"But..." I hesitate. I'm not even sure I want to be friends with these girls, but I don't want to make enemies after my first week. "Maybe I shouldn't say this, but it doesn't seem like you like her that much."

She shrugs. "What am I supposed to do? Bri doesn't let people go. If I don't do what she says, she'll destroy me. The rest of high school will be torture."

Following Brianna around for two and a half more years sounds like torture. "She's like your pimp, except she's not forcing you to sleep with anyone."

Mike quirks an eyebrow.

"What?! I was kidding!" My shriek echoes off the mountain and Brianna and Kenzie look back at us. We wave, fake smiles plastered to our faces.

Mike laughs. "Not sex, but she pushes her opinion about who I should or shouldn't date."

"So it's like a prostitution ring without the prostitution."

"Ha, a little."

"Mike, that blows."

The top of the mountain arrives too soon and we're swooshing down the ramp to where Brianna and Kenzie are waiting.

Brianna adjusts her goggles. "It's no Switzerland, but it'll have to do until spring break. Ready girls?" Without waiting for an answer, she pushes over the lip of the hill and carves a perfect arc across the powder.

Kenzie and Mike follow, their movements mirror images of Brianna. The three of them curve gracefully around a bend, their neon outfits glowing against the snow like that stupid tracker they use on TV to help spectators who can't track a ball or puck.

I adjust my goggles, push off with my poles, and lower into a tuck. My first love is moguls but flying downhill as fast as I can is a close second. I catch up to them at the next bend and shift my lower body to slow down.

"There you are." Brianna smiles. "I was worried this hill was too much for you."

I bite back a snotty comment. *Be nice, be nice, be nice.* "Just admiring the view."

She tosses a glance over her shoulder. "Try to keep up!" She crouches into what I guess she thinks is a tuck and goes a little faster down the hill. The girls mimic her and I feel like I'm trailing after a psychedelic rainbow.

"Try to keep up. Are you kidding me?" I resist the very strong urge to whip past them, instead hitting the brakes every few turns to keep from plowing them over.

When we reach the bottom they glide into line for the same chairlift.

"Do you want to check out any other runs?" *Like maybe something with some jumps or a double in the name?*

Brianna flips up her goggles and levels her perfectly mascaraed gaze at me. "We do Hornblower and International first, then take a break in the lodge, then we go to Powderhorn and Sunset." The other girls giggle.

Okay, then.

I ride next to Mike again, but she's quiet this time.

I nudge her with my elbow. The fabric makes a rustling noise. "Hey, I'd never repeat what you said."

She studies me. "Thanks."

"You're the first normal person I've talked to. Why would I want to piss you off?" Her lips curl into a smile and I laugh. "But that doesn't mean I'm following her around all day."

After two more runs I'm itching to find more difficult terrain. I don't want to ditch them, especially Mike, who seems pretty cool, but when a little girl points at us and squeals, "Pretty!" I decide I've had enough of the 80s vacation brochure.

"Hey, Mike, I'll catch up to you later."

She glances at Brianna as if to see if she heard me, then gives me a sad smile. "See ya."

I push down the seed of guilt that blooms in my chest and cut down a narrow trail to the right. The canopy of trees block out the light and for a moment I'm transported to my last day with Blake. The guilt over leaving Mike hardens into a lump in my throat. I stop along the edge of the trail and push up my goggles. Tears burn my eyes, making it hard to see.

Slope Rule #5: There's no crying in skiing.

Sure, Tom Hanks said that about baseball, but blurry eyes can mean a broken neck when you're flying over the hard-pack. Especially if you're inverted.

I yank off my glove and wipe my eyes. A group of snowboarders races past but no one looks back at me. A breeze rustles the trees high above me, filling the air with snow. I lift my face, eyes closed, and take a deep breath as another pack of boarders zooms by.

I run my hand over my head to try to push Blake out of my mind, then snap my goggles back in place.

A solo boarder coasts by.

This must be the right direction.

I race after the gray figure, feeling lighter in my boots. We round a bend and burst out of the trees and it's like the heavens open up and angels are playing their harps because there, finally, is the terrain park.

thirteen

A boarder in bright yellow glides up the incline of the halfpipe, then crouches into a jump, grabbing the back of his board as he soars ten feet over the lip. His arms extend as the board reconnects with the snow, then he repeats the same maneuver on the opposite side. Over and over until the end of the run.

Beyond the tube, pipes and walls and a couple fun boxes jut out of the hill, the snow around them spray-painted bright blue to keep people from accidentally slamming into the obstacles. Everywhere I look, boarders are twisting and flipping and landing on their asses.

Heaven.

I skate to the crest of the hill. There doesn't seem to be skiers here, but I've never let that stop me. A couple of younger kids are waiting their turn at the top of the big jumps, so I slide behind them.

One boy looks at my skis, then lifts his gaze, doubt clear on his face.

I scowl at him—I'd glare but it loses its effect through my goggles—and sneer at his board.

His friend wipes out on the first jump and I swallow a laugh. "Why don't you worry about yourself?"

He rolls his eyes and hops forward to gain momentum down the hill. To his credit, he lands the jump—if you can call six inches a jump—and pumps his fist in the air.

My cue to go.

My knee is healed from the fall over Thanksgiving, but I haven't hit any real jumps since then so I need to take the first couple slow.

Slow, Cally.

Take it easy.

I laugh. Who am I kidding?

I soar past the boys, who are camped on the side of the hill, no doubt anxious to watch a chick skier bite it on the jumps. I resist the urge to flip them off and concentrate on staying loose when I land.

By the time I reach the bottom, my adrenaline's so jacked my heart's practically thumping out of my chest.

"Nice air."

I turn around. A girl my age in head-to-toe gray gives me a thumbs up. She's already got her back foot unstrapped from her snowboard and is shuffling toward the chairlift.

I join her in line. "Thanks."

"Not many skiers over here. Especially—"

"Girls?" I laugh, and she smiles.

"Yeah. But it's cool." The chair swings around and we lean back as it lifts us into the air. "I'm Amber."

"Cally."

"You new around here? I spend most of my time on this run and I've never seen you before."

I lean over to watch a boarder do a three-sixty off the second jump. "This is my first time. We moved here a couple weeks ago from Vermont."

"Welcome to Colorado, Cally from Vermont."

Something in her tone makes me question if she's actually being nice, but when I meet her gaze, she's smiling. I shake my head.

"What?"

"Nothing. I'm just..." I shake my head again. "I'm terrible at meeting new people." I've already spent too much time with Brianna if I'm doubting the sincerity of every person I meet.

Another boarder sails through the air alongside us and I bounce in my seat. The chair can't get to the top soon enough.

We slide down the ramp and turn toward the top of the run. While she clamps her boots into her board, I toss my poles against a rack and scan the terrain. I can ride the rails and table, but my body's itching to get some serious air. If Amber thought my plain-Jane jumps were impressive, wait until she sees me flip.

She stands and brushes snow off her butt. "Ready?"

I nod at the jumps. "After you."

"Okay, but don't go 'til I'm at the bottom."

"Deal."

She takes the first jump pretty safe—a one-eighty with her hand on the back of the board—but the next two are so high even the other boarders stop to watch.

Adrenaline pumps through me. It's not the same as a true competition, but it's close.

I hop over the edge and tuck low to gain speed. As my skis cross the blue spray paint marking the lip of the first jump, I push from my crouch, twisting my torso. I complete a full rotation seconds before hitting the ground and bend my knees to cushion the impact.

The next jump is already here.

I crouch again, but this time when I push off I bend my knees so my skis are vertical behind me and grab my bindings with one hand, the other straight out to keep me balanced.

I've barely made contact with the ground when I'm soaring up the third ramp. I push up with my legs and arch my back, keeping my legs straight as they flip over my head. Snow is replaced with blue sky, then very quickly snow again. I brace for the landing, arms extended to the sides. I come to a sharp stop next to Amber, whose mouth is hanging open.

I can't wipe the grin off my face. "That felt good."

"I'll say." She laughs and shakes her head. "We're gonna have fun today."

Slope Rule #6: A little confidence can go a long way.

We spend the next hour flipping and twisting and trying to one-up each other, and by the time we head into the lodge for a break I'm so happy I feel like I'm still flying through the air. We grab a couple sports drinks from a cooler and find a table.

I twist off the cap and take a long drink. "You on your school's team?"

"Me? Nah. Too much political BS involved. Besides," the corner of her mouth turns up in a smile, "I don't do well following orders. What about you?"

My light mood cracks ever-so-slightly. "I was. Back home. But I missed tryouts here and the team is already set." Tears threaten and I take another drink to hide them. I wish I didn't care so much, but I do.

"What school are you at?"

"Monarch. In Louisville. Outside of Boulder."

She nods. "I go to Nederland, just down the road. Our teams are joined so kids from Monarch compete with us, and because so many people want on the team, it's all juniors and seniors. Did anyone tell you about the competition at the end of the season?"

It's like she dangled catnip in front of me. I sit up straight. "I live for competitions."

She laughs. "Yeah, I picked up on that. The Eldora Dash is here in March and the top skier and boarder—guy and girl—from our schools automatically get spots on the team. This is where the team practices so even though anyone can enter, it's unofficially our race."

I set my drink on the table. "Seriously?"

"Why would I lie?"

"Sorry, the girls I'm here with are a bit... manipulative. I guess it's making me question people's intentions."

She holds her hands up, palms facing me. "No ulterior motives here. The top guy and girl are guaranteed a spot. It's all downhill—no moguls—but if you can race like you flip, it's pretty much yours."

The adrenaline from earlier pumps through me. If I got on the team in the spring I could train with them all summer. I'd only miss a couple months of competing.

My phone buzzes against my chest and I dig it out of my inside jacket pocket. Fifteen missed texts, most of them from Brianna and a couple from Mike. "Uh oh, I think I'm in trouble."

Amber leans forward to look at my screen. "Your mom?"

My heart twinges at the common assumption, but I let it slide. "Worse. The girls I'm here with." I reply to Brianna. *In the lodge. I'll come find you.* "I better go. But give me your number so we can meet up here next week. If that's okay?"

She enters her number into my phone, sends herself a text, and hands it back to me. "It's a date."

"Thanks Amber. This was awesome." I wave as I walk away, guilt weighing me down with each step. Part of me wants to tell Amber to come with me but I can't see her getting along with the Snow Bunnies. She's too normal.

I spot them near the fireplace looking as airbrushed as they did when we arrived. The guys' hair is sticking all over the place—they wear helmets—but the group of them still looks like an ad for a ski resort.

"Hey, Cally!" Evan waves me over. "Where've you been?"

I point out the window in the direction of the terrain park. "On the jumps."

His eyes lock on mine and his smile widens. A tiny flutter swirls in my stomach. He really is cute. "I'm sorry I missed it."

"There'll be plenty of chances for that." The words are out of my mouth before I have time to think about them. I meant that I plan to spend the rest of the day on the jumps, but based on his smile and the shoulder punches he gets from the guys, my comment came out dripping with innuendo. I lower my gaze, but not before I catch Mike's tight lips and narrowed eyes. Her shoulders tense so she's sitting ramrod straight.

What's that about?

Evan reaches behind him and grabs a chair from the next

table, swinging it around so it faces the table. "Have a seat."

I try to catch Mike's attention but she's suddenly very interested in the lift ticket dangling from the zipper of her jacket pocket. If she has a thing for Evan there's no way I'm going near him. Aside from Amber, who doesn't go to my school, Mike's the closest thing I have to a friend. I move the chair a fraction away from Evan and sit.

Brianna's talking about her ski trip to Europe. Again. "Only losers stay here on break."

The others smirk—everyone except Mike.

Evan leans close. "Do you want a hot chocolate or something?"

My gaze drifts to the sports drink in my hand. Hot chocolate sounds amazing but I don't want to encourage him. "Nah, I'm okay. But thanks." I look up and the hair on the back of my neck prickles.

Brianna is watching me. "Cally, we obviously don't mean you since you, like, moved here over break."

Is she still talking about how rich she is? "Yeah, and I vacationed here over Thanksgiving. Talk about lame." Her eyes narrow for a split second, picking up on my sarcasm. So she's not a complete airhead.

Evan shifts in his chair so he's facing me. "Where'd you ski?"

I fill them in on the vacation that was actually a business trip—leaving out all details of Blake. "So I had a month back home before we moved."

Brianna leans back in her chair. On the surface she looks relaxed but she's like a cheetah, waiting to pounce. "Right. The brewery."

The conversation grinds to a halt. I'm not sure what kind of reaction she wants from me, but I'm not taking the bait. I scan their faces. "Any of you on the ski team?"

Austin stretches his arms above his head. "Competition is tough. It's almost impossible for sophomores to make the team."

Brianna rolls her eyes, and Mike and Kenzie imitate her. "Regardless, I'm not getting up at five AM to go skiing unless it's at St. Moritz."

I can't stop my eyes from rolling into my skull. I doubt that's the reason. The thought of her breaking a sweat or listening to anyone—especially a coach—tell her what to do is about as ludicrous as this conversation.

Brianna slaps her hand on the table. "What? You don't like Switzerland?"

I refocus and dig my fingernails into my palm to stop the laughter bubbling in my chest. The angrier Brianna gets the funnier this whole situation seems. "I prefer Germany. You know, beer country."

"Whatever." Her shoulders relax and she turns away from me to whisper something to Kenzie. I'm beginning to think Snow Bunnies isn't completely accurate. More like Snow Bitches.

Before I have time to dwell on it, the guys start challenging each other to race when they get back on the slopes.

And Mike refuses to look at me.

fourteen

I've already pissed off the popular kids.

Did you really think you'd be BFFs with a group of girls?

It's Sunday night and I'm texting Sophia instead of reading about the civil war.

No. But one seems semi-okay. And I met a cool chick from another school.

And the boys...?

Evan is cool but I think Mike likes him.

Cally we talked about this. No crushing on gay guys.

Mike—Mikayla. She's the semi-okay girl.

Why can't people have normal names?

I smile. Sophia would devour Brianna.

I wish you moved with me.

xoxo.

***

There's a special kind of suckiness to waking up on Monday morning and dreading going to school for more reasons than simply because it's Monday. I haven't heard from Brianna or Mike since they dropped me off Saturday evening and my stomach's in knots. I hope they decide to ignore me, but Brianna strikes me as the kind of person to make my life a living hell. "It was nice while it lasted," I mutter as I head downstairs for breakfast.

Dad's leaning against the counter, pen in one hand, coffee in the other. A half-eaten granola bar is on the counter next to his notebook and tablet. "Good morning."

I nod at the tablet on my way to the pantry. A day like today calls for Cocoa Crispies. "What's new in the world?"

He takes a sip before swapping the coffee for the granola bar. "Oh, you know. War, poverty, a new brew for the opening."

I stop with my hand midway to the box of cereal. "You finished it?"

"We transfer to the secondary today."

"Dad, this is huge. You said it might not be ready for another couple months." Calliope Brewery doesn't release new beers very often—maybe once every couple years—and it has such a devout following back home that people skip work to be one of the first to try it.

He smiles, the skin around his eyes crinkling. He looks tired, but happy. "We sampled it yesterday. I wasn't sure how it'd turn out—you know how the first few batches can go."

Yeah, terrible. For my thirteenth birthday, Dad debuted a raspberry wheat—because I'm so sweet, ugh—but they didn't get it right until six months after my birthday. Nailing a new recipe in time for the opening is like kicking the winning field goal of the SuperBowl with no time left on the clock.

I set the cereal on the counter and give him a hug. "I'm proud of you."

He squeezes back.

If only being the most beer-informed fifteen-year old in the world can carry me through whatever's in store today at school.

***

The Snow Bunnies either decided to let my transgression slide or it didn't bother them as much as I thought. They were their normal Queen-Bee selves—smiling to those they felt worthy, ignoring or rolling their eyes at those deemed beneath them—

and over the next few weeks, I slipped into their routine. I've met up with them each weekend to ski, but I always duck away to hit the terrain park with Amber.

One month into my new school and I finally feel like I belong.

Sort of.

Even though I'm hanging out with the Bunnies, I refuse to become one of them. I won't be mean to anyone just because Brianna tells me to, and there's no way in hell I'm wearing the stupid tracksuit thing Brianna keeps texting me to buy, no matter how cute she thinks I'll look in the teal version. And I've started running after school. I may not be on a team but my body doesn't need to know that, plus the exercise keeps my mind calm.

Mike hasn't opened up to me since that first day skiing. I can't figure out if she regrets spilling her guts to the new girl or if she's decided she doesn't like me, but either way, I'm bummed I haven't seen that side of her again. The normal side.

And I'm still not over Blake. I've become a master at watching him out of the corner of my eye, gathering intel about him whenever I can. I know he's best friends with Luke, the skinny guy from English class, and I think he works at an Italian place near the pedestrian mall downtown. And I know he's still curious about me because I catch him looking at me at least once a day. But every time I try to talk to him his face becomes ice and he walks away.

It's torture.

I carry my tray to Brianna's table, second-guessing my choice of a shrink-wrapped turkey sandwich, when Brianna looks my way and smiles.

"Hey, Cally."

I take the empty seat across from her between Evan and Mike, nerves on edge, and pick up my sandwich. "What's up?"

Brianna exchanges glances with Kenzie. "Well...." she draws out. "We were just talking about you."

Color me shocked. Brianna always starts conversations this way and there's no telling what's coming next. I glance at Evan, who lifts his shoulders and shakes his head. No help there. "And?"

Brianna nudges Kenzie, who picks up the conversation. “Since you’re new and still meeting people, we thought you should have a party!” Kenzie’s voice lifts at the end, like she rehearsed this.

“A party?”

“Yeah,” Brianna says. “My mom and I toured the new houses in Harmony Hills last fall and they’re absolutely gorgeous.”

Kenzie smiles at me and bobs her head, a shining example of the Snow Bunnies’ group dynamic. Brianna is the lead bitch and not to be trifled with, and Kenzie is her errand girl—but I haven’t figured out where Mike fits in. She already confessed she doesn’t like Brianna, but there must be a bigger reason than social suicide keeping her around.

Evan bumps my tray with his. “So whaddaya say, Cal? Party at your place?” His eyes lock with mine and I straighten my tray.

“I’ll have to talk to my dad.”

Brianna props her elbows on the table and rests her chin in her hand, not a care in the world. “Text him now.”

“What’s the urgency?”

“I like to have my calendar locked at the beginning of the week.”

My traitorous eyebrow shoots upward before I can stop it but at least I keep my eyes from rolling back. “I’ll ask him tonight. He’s got a big day at work and I don’t want to bug him with something silly—”

“Oh? What’s going on?”

The shift in conversation makes me pause. Since Brianna’s dad owns one of the established breweries, anything I say might go straight to him. It’s like she’s been steering me to talk about the brewery since I sat down. Really, since I met her.

I shrug. “You know. Chair delivery. Glasses. That sort of thing.” I force a smile. “It’s really coming together.”

Disappointment mars her face, but is quickly replaced by a smile. “Text me as soon as he says yes.”

My instincts are humming. She’s up to something, but I need someone who knows her better to figure out her motives. I face

Mike, who hasn't said a word, and lower my voice. "Do you want to get coffee after school?"

She looks at me but her eyes blank. It's like she never confided in me on the chairlift.

Kenzie pipes up. "You should! Maybe you can convince Cally that this party will be beneficial to her social standing."

Seriously, who talks like that? The warning in Kenzie's voice doesn't escape me, but I refuse to let them bully me.

Mike shrugs. "Sure, why not."

We make plans to meet at my locker at the end of the day, and the boys take over the conversation, talking about the upcoming ski meet this weekend. Just because they aren't on the team doesn't mean they aren't obsessed with how the team is doing.

In English, I hustle to my seat, careful not to look at Blake, but he's not there. I get out my notebook and assume my lecture-listening position—legs crossed at the ankles, one arm on the desk, my pen in the other hand—when he breezes through the door.

A few people glance at him as he makes his way to his desk, but he's so gorgeous I don't understand how every girl isn't staring. His perfectly mussed hair screams for fingers to run through it and his lips make me ache to kiss him. I shift in my seat, feeling suddenly warm. His gaze lands on me, just for a second, but it's enough to send my pulse through the roof.

I look away first and stare at the whiteboard until he's out of my peripheral vision.

Get a grip, Cally.

***

Mike's waiting for me at my locker after the last class, but she doesn't look happy about it. "Do you mind if we take the bus?"

Sophomore year is weird because kids start driving throughout the year and you never know who's sixteen yet. I guess Mike is still fifteen like me.

I smile. "Aside from my dad, it's my most reliable form of transportation." And it's a lot easier to avoid the left side with all those extra seats. I grab my coat from my locker and we fall in step toward the exit. I wait until we're on the bus to bring up the fact that the cool girl I met on the chairlift seems to have vanished. "Did I do something to—"

She abruptly turns to face me. "I haven't been fair to you." Her gaze dips below my chin like she doesn't want to look me in the eye. "You walked into a crapload of drama."

"Evan?"

She presses her lip together and her eyes start to water. "Yeah."

"I thought maybe you liked him."

She tilts her head back and looks at the ceiling of the bus. "Oh god, is it that obvious?"

I shrug. "I don't think it is to him. But if you like him, he's all yours. I've been here two seconds and would rather be friends with you than—"

"That's the thing. I HAD him, but we broke up right before break."

"Oh." That makes a little more sense.

We're silent until we step off the bus at the fringe of a cobblestone pedestrian mall. Wrought iron benches line the center path, spaced between metal sculptures of frogs and toads and a woman reclining on a swing, and we pass through a large rock that's had the middle cut out. A pang of longing grabs my heart when we pass a pair of mothers with strollers, but I brush it off by opening the door of a children's boutique for them. Mothers shopping with their children, especially teens, always makes me sad. When we reach the coffee shop on the next block, we hurry past a man playing a violin with an open case at his feet and step inside.

I place my order first, grab a table in the back corner, and settle in. Mike waits at the counter for our drinks and when she sits next to me, I shake off the nostalgia the mothers sparked and lean toward her. "Seriously, I know we barely know each other but I don't do drama and I definitely don't chase after guys who my friends like."

A smile lifts the corner of her mouth when I call her my friend. "I'd forgotten people like you exist."

I drop my gaze, unsure how to respond without saying something about Brianna that I might regret. "Besides, I'm not exactly a dating phenom. Back home I only had one female friend, Sophia. The rest of my group was all guys and none of them were interested in me." Jake flits through my mind and I feel a twinge of regret laced with guilt. I should be having this conversation with Sophia.

Mike sips her latte. "I find that hard to believe. I mean, Cally, have you looked in a mirror?"

My cheeks warm. I pull a strand of hair across my face to shield myself from the compliment. "Okay, there's one boy who liked me, but that's not gonna happen."

"Because he's in Vermont?"

I snort and roll my eyes. "Worse." And I tell her about Blake.

Her eyes get wider and wider. "And he knows you moved here?"

I nod, and my head feels like it weighs a thousand pounds. "We have English together." To get through the day I banish all thoughts of Blake, but now the frustration and hurt from the past two months washes over me.

"What a dick."

"That's about as far as I've gotten, too."

"So you don't like Evan?"

I shrug. "He was the first person I met here. He's a nice guy and," I smile, "he's not so bad to look at."

She smiles, but she looks sad.

"But I just like him as a friend. Besides, I can't be interested in anyone else while Blake is still rattling around in my head."

Mike lifts her cup. "Here's to not understanding boys."

I touch my cup to hers, then take a sip.

She traces her finger around the rim of her cup. "You really haven't talked to Blake?"

"I tried my first day, but he gave me a weird look and walked away without saying anything."

"Ouch." She pauses. "What if you invite him to the party?"

My mind jumps back to lunch. "What's with Brianna pushing that on me?"

She rolls her eyes. "Just what she said. Her stupid social calendar, blah blah. She had a party at the end of break so her parents won't let her have another one until later this month."

"Good thing I came along."

"I get not wanting to have it just for her, but it'll be a good way to meet people. She can be a bitch, but she does draw a crowd."

"I guess it wouldn't be a bad thing to make more friends."

Mike smiles for real this time.

"Brianna's already warned me off Blake. What's she gonna think if he shows up?"

"You think he will?"

"If I knew what that boy was thinking we wouldn't be having this conversation."

"Good point." She shrugs. "What's the worst that can happen? Brianna's head explodes and life as we know it ends."

I laugh. "When you put it that way."

Now to figure out how to get the boy who's ignored me for months to not only talk to me, but show up at my house. Maybe he'll talk to me outside of school and I can finally get some answers about why he lied.

But not until I clear my conscience with Sophia.

fifteen

I owe you an apology.

I am still pissed you abandoned me.

I'm serious. I never ask you about Jake.

Oh.

So what's happening with Jake?

Are we doing this? I thought...

I wait while the bubble showing that Sophia's typing bounces at the bottom of the screen.

I didn't know how to bring him up because of... before.

I fire off a series of one-line texts. *I know. I haven't been fair to you. He didn't like me back. Nothing happened. I live halfway across the country. I need to get over myself.*

You are pretty self-centered.

So. Jake?

He's awesome.

My chest tightens, like it's too full. *It's because I'm happy for her*, I tell myself. My screen fills with details of their latest date and how he kisses and basically how perfect life is. *I'm not jealous. I won't be jealous of Sophia.* Her happiness leaps through the screen and it strikes me again what a horrible friend I've been for making her think she couldn't talk to me about him.

I'm glad you're happy. He sounds perfect for you.

The bubble bounces on the screen, goes silent, then bounces

again, like she keeps changing her mind about what she wants to say. Finally the message comes through.

And what's your boy situation?

I decide to leave out the Evan and Mike situation and jump straight to my biggest problem.

I convinced Dad to let me have a party Friday and I want to invite Blake.

But you haven't talked to him.

Correctamundo.

You need to step up your game. What have you been wearing?

I look down at my standard uniform of jeans and a sweater.

Ball gowns.

Maybe try a dress?

It's winter.

You have cute boots. I packed them myself.

The boots in question peek at me from the back of my closet, where they've sat since I unpacked.

Okay, boots. What else?

Skinny jeans.

Ugh.

You're not supposed to wear boyfriend jeans unless you actually have a boyfriend.

There's incentive. Can I still wear a sweater?

Anything but that holey knit thing you love.

I pick at the hole on Old Faithful's sleeve. *It's not so bad.*

Cally.

Fine.

I want a picture before you leave.

Okay mom.

There's another pause. I don't throw that phrase around lightly, and I want Sophia to know I'm grateful for her help. There are some things Dad just can't do.

Love you.

xoxo.

***

Tuesday I squeeze into a pair of dark skinny jeans—I own several pairs thanks to Sophia, but I never wear them—and toss Old Faithful, my favorite sweater, on the floor of the closet. "I'll see you after school." Smoothing the aqua fabric of a Sophia-inspired sweater over my belly, I contemplate the boots. Sophia's always going on and on about fashion over comfort, but my sneakers are beyond comfy. "Fine." I huff as I carry the boots to my bed and yank them up to my knees.

Okay, these are more cushiony than I remember. Maybe this won't be so bad.

Dad's waiting for me downstairs. "You look nice. What's the occasion?"

I need to catch myself a man! "Nothing. Just thought Old Faithful could use a break." I pour my cereal and slide into a chair at the table. "So you're sure you're okay with me having a party?"

He tilts his head. "Having second thoughts?"

I sometimes forget how well he knows me. "No, I just..." This is when it'd be really helpful if Mom were here. "Remember Blake from Thanksgiving?"

"How could I forget? Have you heard from him?"

I brace myself. I haven't told Dad that Blake goes to my school because if I did, then it'd feel more... I don't know... real. "He goes to my school."

Dad chokes, spraying coffee across his notebook and all over the counter. He presses a towel against the pages, then wipes his mouth.

"Yeah, that was pretty much my reaction."

"You don't seem happy about this."

"He won't talk to me."

"Ahh."

"And I want to invite him to the party."

He gives my outfit a once-over and raises an eyebrow.

"Yes, I have ulterior motives."

He crosses the room and plants a kiss on my forehead. "You look great. And as your father, I'm grateful that whatever you have planned doesn't require skimpier clothing." He tousles the back of my head. "Good luck."

I don't feel lucky at the end of lunch. My feet move slower than normal and the slice of pizza I ate is churning in my stomach. My hand slips on the doorknob to English class, so I wipe my hand on my jeans, adjust the hem of my sweater, and try again.

He's already sitting at his desk. I duck my head and make my way to my row, but it's impossible not to stare at him. I slide into my seat and risk what I hope is a subtle glance.

My stomach flips.

He's staring back at me.

My legs go all wobbly just thinking about the chance at time alone with him.

But first I have to figure out how to get him to A) talk to me, and B) come to my party. Does he still have feelings for me? I believe he really liked me over Thanksgiving, and that doesn't just go away, right? I peek at him again.

He's still looking.

Heat flushes through me and I tug at the neck of my sweater.

Ms. Simpson rises from her desk and faces the whiteboard, marker in hand, and writes the word EXPERIENCE in large letters.

Several kids snicker, but I'm pretty sure she's not talking about that kind of experience. At least I hope not. I open my notebook to a fresh page and scribble it across the top, then rest my head on my fist to stop myself from looking at Blake. At the moment, ninety-nine percent of my experience has been with him and I'm sure he can feel the heat rising off my body from the next row.

Ms. Simpson faces us, hands clasped against her belly. "Our experiences make us who we are. Good, bad... each thing that happens to us builds upon the last thing, forming the way we think, how we react, and ultimately, who we become."

"Woah, that's deep," says a boy from the back of the room.

She shrugs, a smile playing on her lips. "I minored in psychology. Anyway, right now, the things in your life feel massive. Each slight is monumental. A pleasant surprise can make you feel higher than a kite."

More snickers. "Or as high as Durbin."

I turn to see Luke shove Blake in the arm.

"Boys, quiet. I'm trying to make a point."

They settle down and she paces the length of the board. "Over the next month we'll be studying memoirs, an account of one's personal life and experiences, also known as an autobiography. They're usually written as a narrative—like a novel—but are entirely true."

A girl across the room raises her hand. "Like the Diary of Anne Frank?"

Ms. Simpson nods. "Yes, exactly. You don't have to be famous to write a memoir. All it takes is an interesting story."

"Then how did Bieber get one published?"

She laughs. "Money does have its advantages."

"Then I'm screwed."

I barely heard it over the laughter, but I still hear Blake's voice in my dreams and I swear that was him who said it. I risk a glance at him. He's staring at his desk, the light mood of the class unable to penetrate the barrier that seems to have gone up around him.

Ms. Simpson clears her throat. "Your first assignment is to read a couple passages from well-written memoirs. I'll email the links to you by the end of the day. Then you'll write your own."

"A freaking memoir?"

"An essay. Five hundred words on the best day of your life. Due at the beginning of class on Monday."

Easy. The first time I nailed the inverted iron cross. How I'm gonna put that in five hundred words, though, I don't know.

"We'll follow that up with the worst day, the most memorable, then end this unit with the event that most changed your life."

Memories of Mom rush through me like a tsunami, leaving me gasping for breath. Usually I have a minute to prepare myself—Dressing rooms are the worst. Do you know how many kids call for their mom in there?—but this catches me off-guard.

"What if the most memorable is also the best?" the girl behind me asks.

"That's why I'm telling you all four assignments now. Take some time to reflect on your topics."

Worst Day.

Most Memorable.

Event That Changed My Life.

Mom. Mom. Mom.

Ms. Simpson begins reading aloud from a book on her desk and my head sinks lower down my arm. I can't write about her for all three, but nothing else compares. I could include the move here, but it feels weak in comparison.

When the bell rings I'm no closer to figuring out my topics and the excitement I felt earlier about Blake has deflated like a limp balloon. Cute outfit or not, I'm no longer in the mood to chase him down.

I step into the hallway, eyes on the ground.

"You okay?"

My heart flips. His voice hasn't been this close since—

"Cally?"

I meet Blake's blue eyes and everything around us drops away.

He holds my gaze for a moment... two... then his brow furrows.

A strong case of word vomit is coming, but all the things I've wanted to say get caught in my throat.

"You seemed upset when Ms. Simpson talked about the assignment. I figured you were thinking about your mom."

He was watching me? My voice comes out small. "You remember that?"

His voice is equally soft. "I remember everything."

My insides go all gooey and I start to step toward him, but a rush of anger stops me. "Then why have you gone all Jekyll and Hyde on me?"

He rubs his hand over his face, then up through the hair that hangs near his eyes. "What does it matter now? You're all tight with the Snow Bitches."

"Wait, people actually call them that?"

"I do."

See! We're meant to be together!

"The first time I saw you Brianna dragged you away. You haven't said anything to me since then so I figured you know the truth about me and that was that."

"So you're accusing me of being judgmental—which I'm not—when really you're the one who's judging me."

His lips tighten and I'm distracted by the line of his jaw. It seems like a dream that my lips once trailed over—

He waves a hand in front of my face, scowling. I seem to be the only one affected by our proximity. "I just wanted to make sure you're not upset."

"But just about my mom. Not you or the fact that you act like we never met." I lower my voice as hurt and anger roll over me. "That nothing happened between us."

His face pales and his jaw clenches. "Do we have to do this now?"

I cross my arms over my chest to keep myself from running my fingers through his hair and shaking his head until he says something that makes sense. "Come to my party." The words escape before I can think about it.

He cocks his head. "What?"

I wave my hand at the kids around us. "I don't want to do this where everyone can watch. Brianna convinced me to have a party Friday—" more like forced, but whatever, "—and I thought maybe, if you're not busy..." I trail off. Heat flushes my cheeks and I can't meet his eyes. This is why I don't go on dates. THIS—asking boys out—is mortifying.

His finger touches my cheek and I startle. He's leaning close, his face inches from mine. "I'd love to."

The warning bell rings and we jerk apart. He hikes his backpack higher on his shoulder and the corner of his mouth lifts in a smile that melts my heart. "Until then."

I float to my next class, not quite sure that actually happened. I text Sophia as I slide into my seat. *Party invitation accepted.*

Emotional whiplash has completely drained me. It seems like he's still interested, but has he been reliving our time together the way I have? Sometimes I can still feel his arms around me, can taste him on my lips, but I can't tell if he's affected the same way.

As I replay our conversation in the hall, one thing keeps getting stuck: *I figured you know the truth about me.*

What is he hiding?

sixteen

You're acting like you've never had a party before.

It's just that I don't know what to expect.

Do you think Blake will show?

Hard to say.

Other than saying hi before class, we haven't talked since Tuesday. I've caught him looking at me in class and at lunch, and I haven't stopped secretly staring at him, but I have no idea if he's planning to come. Part of me is scared that he will. I'm still not recovered from the first time he broke my heart and I'm not sure I can go through that a second time.

You still have his number?

Have you ever known me to throw anything away?

Text him.

What if he doesn't reply?

There's a beat before Sophia replies. *Then at least you know.*

I lean back on my bed and sigh. At least Amber said she's coming. I'm not sure how she'll get along with the Snow Bunnies, but she's the most normal person I know here and I'll need that if I'm going to get through tonight.

I gotta run. Jake's picking me up soon.

Ooooooohhhhh. Have fun! xoxo

I stare at the ceiling for another minute before rolling off the bed and trudging downstairs. Dad helped me clean during the week and I've already put out chips and cookies, so there isn't much to do except watch the hands on the living room clock crawl in a circle.

My phone dings at five after seven.

I'm here.

I fling open the front door, expelling a rush of air. Amber's standing on the porch next to a girl with long dark hair but I can't stop staring at Amber. I've never seen her without a hat or her helmet and I didn't expect a mass of red curls.

"Your hair is gorgeous!"

Amber blushes and hooks a thumb at her friend. "This is Bethany. Are we the first ones here?"

I'm half a foot taller than them but I'm too relieved to worry about looking like the Jolly Green Giant. "Yeah, but I'm glad. I've worn the varnish off the floors waiting for people to show up." I step aside and they follow me into the foyer. We stop in the kitchen and I point at the fridge. "Help yourselves." They each grab a can of soda and I lead them to the living room. "Now we have time to catch up. We haven't talked since last week."

Bethany nudges Amber but doesn't say anything.

"Or do you want a tour?"

Amber cracks open the can and sips the fizzies off the top. "Sure."

I lead them through the kitchen, across the living room, and down a hallway. "My dad's office is down here. He ran out to pick up some food but he'll be back soon." The door's open a crack, allowing a glimpse of his battered wooden desk and shelves filled with books.

Bethany peeks through the opening. "He must read a lot."

"More like drinks a lot."

Uncertainty darkens their faces and I realize I never told Amber what he does.

"He's a brewer. Most of those are beer cookbooks, plus more History of Beer books than any one person should really own."

Bethany smiles. "My dad's an accountant. His books would make your eyes bleed."

Amber laughs as I close the door. The click of the l atch catching echoes in the empty hallway. “You said you moved here for his job. I take it Boulder will have another brewery soon?”

I lead them to the stairs. “Yep. Calliope Brewery is ours.”

“Ooh, the purple one?”

Amber rolls her eyes at Bethany.

Bethany laughs. “What? I like purple.”

I step into my room and wave an arm at the purple bedspread and curtains. “Me too.”

Amber laughs. “I didn’t take you for a girly girl.”

“I’ve got to balance aerial maneuvers with something more feminine. I don’t do dresses, so purple is it.”

Amber studies me for a beat, then she smiles. “You skiing tomorrow?”

I smile back. “Is that really a question?” I nod at Bethany. “What about you?”

She laughs. “Let’s just say I’m Amber’s feminine balance.”

Amber shakes her head. “Your house is cool.”

I gaze at the plain white walls and beige carpet, longing for the archways and scuffed floors from Vermont. For the cinnamon and vanilla. For Mom. “It’s not home. This is a rental. Dad says we’ll look at houses once Calliope opens.”

The girls fall silent. I need to lighten up or people will leave before the party gets started. I could really use Sophia right now.

“Come on, let’s go back downstairs.”

We’ve barely settled onto the couch when the doorbell rings. I leave them in the living room and nerves propel me to the front door. I know Bri and the girls are coming, plus the guys, but beyond them I have no idea who to expect. I’ve met a lot of people but talking in the halls or saying hi in class is different than being in my house. Taking a deep breath, I yank the door open.

Dad smiles at me, his hands weighed down with plastic bags.

I exhale. “Why didn’t you come through the garage?”

He winks. "I know how much you hate the unexpected, so I thought I'd burst your anxiety bubble. Now get out of the way, these are heavy."

A laugh rolls up my throat and my shoulders relax. I'm shutting the door when someone calls my name. I open it again.

Evan's walking up the sidewalk, Reece and Austin a few steps back. He's holding a small white box with a yellow ribbon. "This is for you."

"You didn't have to bring anything."

His eyes crinkle as he smiles. "I know."

I take the box and usher them inside. "Thanks. The girls aren't here yet, but my friend from Eldora's in the living room."

Austin laughs. "Bri won't be here for at least an hour."

Panic chokes my throat. "But I don't know half the people who are coming!"

Evan slides his arm over my shoulder as we enter the living room. "You'll be fine."

Amber stops talking, hand in the air, when she sees us.

I shrug off Evan's arm. "Guys, this is Amber and Bethany. I met Amber at Eldora last month."

Evan moves to the chair closest to where she's sitting. "Snowboarder, right?"

She nods, uncertainty clear on her face.

Austin sits next to Bethany on the couch, eyes on Amber. "You're the first chick I saw go inverted."

Reece snorts. "I doubt that."

"I mean on snow."

I sink into the chair opposite Evan, leaving Reece standing in front of the coffee table. "And this is Austin and Reece."

Reece continues. "You've probably done more on snow than most guys our age have—"

Austin cuts a glance at Bethany. "Dude, chill."

Yeah, Reece is definitely just like Hunter. I lean back in the chair, letting their banter settle my nerves. This is the closest to home I've felt since moving here. Austin's asking Bethany about her classes when my gaze lands on Evan. He's talking to Amber, describing some kind of aerial move with his hands. His lips look fuller when he laughs and a small flutter stirs in my belly.

No. You're not going there—for so many reasons—starting with Mike and ending with the fact that Blake will hopefully make an appearance.

But I can't resist joining the conversation. I mean, I'm the host. It'd be rude not to talk to him.

I lean forward. "So Evan, how's Dolly?"

He tilts his head, thinking, then a broad smile brightens his face. "I can't believe I haven't told you."

All eyes are on him as I ask, "What?"

"Cooper knocked her up!"

My mouth falls open. "You're not serious."

"Totes."

The girls' heads swivel between us. "Who are Dolly and Cooper?" Amber asks.

I cover my face with my hands. It's not like it's my fault, but the fact that Evan and I were there during the deed feels strangely intimate.

"Dolly's my hussy of a yellow Lab and Cooper's the Basset Hound from across the street."

"Omigod!" Bethany slaps a hand over her mouth, eyes wide.

"That's how Cally and I met. She was chasing Cooper for the old lady across the street and—"

"And we practically got to third base before we said hello."

Now all eyes are on me.

Evan holds up his hands. "Not like that. She ran so fast around the corner that we slammed into each other." He looks at Reece. "Get your mind out of the gutter."

Reece laughs. "Impossible."

I smile at Evan. "I'll have to tell Mrs. Sherman she's gonna be a gramma. I usually see her when I'm out on my afternoon run."

"Ask if she wants a puppy."

Austin nudges Bethany with his shoulder. "You know what else is impossible? That I've never seen you at Eldora."

She rolls her eyes, but a smile tugs at her mouth.

I laugh. "Barf."

Reece looks at me. "Drinks are in the kitchen?"

I stand. "I'll show you."

Evan starts to get up but I wave him off. "I'll grab stuff for everyone."

Once in the kitchen, Reece leans against the counter. "So... you and Evan?"

I raise an eyebrow. "What, are we in seventh grade?"

He smiles. "He didn't tell me to ask, I just see what I see."

I grab sodas and set them next to him on the counter. "We're just friends."

"Friends who give friends presents?"

Oh yeah. I set the box on the table but never opened it. "Yes. Friends."

"Mm-hmm."

"No, seriously. And please don't encourage him. I know—" I take a breath. I don't want to betray Mike by telling Reece that she still likes Evan, but I need to put a stop to any rumors. "I know he and Mike dated and I don't want to get in the middle of anything."

A mischievous smile spreads across his face. "Sometimes that's the best place to be."

I snort. "Is that all you think about?"

"Pretty much."

I laugh, and it feels good. Of all the guys here, Reece is the most like the guys back home. "I'll keep that in mind."

The doorbell rings. I shove the cans into his arms but Brianna, Kenzie, and Mike are already walking through the foyer by the time I get to the door. A combination of excitement and dread rush through me. This party will be easier with them here, but I can't shake the feeling that Bri has ulterior motives—beyond needing to fill a slot in her social calendar.

"Hey, lady." Bri drops a kiss on my cheek as she breezes by, and Kenzie does the same.

Mike pauses next to me and rolls her eyes. "I must have missed the we're-still-in-Europe memo."

I laugh, and Bri turns around. "You coming?"

"Yes," Mike and I say. We follow her into the living room, where the conversation has stopped. Amber's eyes widen when she sees Brianna, and Austin shifts slightly away from Bethany.

Brianna pushes her shoulders back. She's been in the room for two seconds and is already in control.

"You guys want something to drink?"

Brianna's face lights up. "Can we sample your dad's brew?"

"Uhh..." I scan their faces to gauge how many of them are going to pressure me for beer. "My dad's upstairs so that's probably not a good idea."

She lifts a shoulder. "Just a sample. We'll be done before he notices."

I step forward, jaw clenched. "Not this time."

An awkward silence hangs over the room and I'm on the verge of doing backflips to break the tension when Brianna narrows her gaze at Amber. "Do I know you?"

Amber sips her soda before answering. "Doubtful."

Brianna's eyes become slits. "So why are you here?"

Amber's mouth falls open and I move next to Brianna. "We met at Eldora and I invited her. I didn't realize I had to get my guest list approved."

She lets out a huff of air. "I'm just trying to help you, Cally."

Maybe Brianna's the one I should have thought twice about inviting. I lock eyes with Amber and mouth sorry.

The doorbell rings again so I duck out of the room, hoping someone changes the topic. Before long the living room and kitchen are full and based on the noise level, everyone seems to be having a good time. Dad winds his way through a couple times to make his presence known, kisses the top of my head, then points at me and heads back upstairs.

Amber finds me in the kitchen. "I can't believe you're friends with those bitches."

"Friend is a strong word."

"They're mean, boring, and terrible skiers. And with all that makeup they're not even attractive, unless you're into that kind of thing."

"That's a bit harsh."

"But it's true." She crosses her arms, seeming more upset now than she did when Brianna made her introductions. "I didn't figure you for a follower."

I straighten my back. "I'm not! Mike is cool. And the guys are normal. It's just Brianna and Kenzie…" I trail off and shake my head. She's right. Since when do I let mean girls tell me what to do? "Being friends with guys is so much easier."

"Not all girls are asswipes."

A weak smile lifts the corner of my mouth. "I know. My friend Sophia from back home is amazing. We text all the time but it's hard not having her around."

Amber studies me for a moment, then nods toward the living room. "What does she think about them?"

I laugh. "She thinks I need to get my head out of my ass and not let them push me around."

"See. You know how to pick good friends. Let's call this momentary weakness because you're at a new school. Could happen to anyone."

I raise my soda to hers and we clink cans. "To not being a pansy pushover."

She smiles, but it's cut short by a huff in the doorway.

"Cally, you're needed in here." Brianna's eyeing Amber like she's a piece a gum on her shoe.

A rush of heat pushes me forward, but I stop after two steps. This is not the time for a confrontation with Brianna, no matter how badly she needs to be knocked down a few pegs. I swallow past the anger and force my voice to stay level. "What's going on?"

She narrows her eyes. "In. Here." Her gaze skates over Amber, dismissing her.

I lean against the counter. "Give me a few minutes."

Brianna rolls her eyes and turns back to the living room. She murmurs, "hopeless," over her shoulder.

"I'm leaving anyway."

"Amber, don't go." I take a step toward her. "What happened to not letting her push me around?"

She lifts a shoulder. "What can I say? I'm a hypocrite."

"Please stay."

Her eyes soften and for a moment I think she's considering it, but then her jaw clenches and she shakes her head. "I get enough crap from the mean girls at my school and blondie in there takes what they've got to a whole new level. This was fun but I have a thing about self-preservation." She pulls out her phone and types a message.

"I'm sorry."

She touches my arm. "Don't apologize for them unless you become one of them."

Her words hit me in the chest like a physical blow. I've barely been here a month and I'm somehow getting dragged into the bitchiest clique at school. This is not who I am.

Bethany appears in the doorway to the kitchen. "Ready?"

Amber nods. "Walk us out?"

"Sure."

They follow me to the door, where I face Amber. "I wish you could've stayed longer."

"Next time. Ten tomorrow?"

A smile spreads across my face, one that reaches my heart. Skiing fixes everything. "I'll see you there."

Bethany hugs my shoulders. "Thanks for inviting us." She's sweet, and I'm glad Amber has a friend like her. Amber hugs me, then I reach for the door.

It swings open and I freeze, mouth open.

Blake's standing on the porch.

seventeen

Amber and Bethany smile at him as they step outside, but I can't make my mouth work. As much as I fantasized about him coming, I didn't think he'd ever be here at my house.

The girls are on the sidewalk before I realize he's with two friends: Luke, the skinny guy with close-cropped hair from our English class, and a boy I've seen but haven't met.

Luke steps forward. "Cally, right?"

My voice seems to have left with Amber, so I nod.

Luke hooks a thumb at the other boy. "This is Ian."

Ian pushes his shaggy brown hair out of his eyes and smile. "Cool place."

"And I believe you know Blake."

Blake hasn't taken his eyes off me since I opened the door and I'm having a hard time looking anywhere but his eyes. And his lips.

"Sooo..." Luke clears his throat. "We'll just let ourselves inside."

I move out of the way to let them pass and hear the door click shut behind me.

Blake moves forward until we're practically toe to toe, eyes still on mine. A breeze swirls around us, blowing his hair in his face, and I wrap my arms around myself. The cold air on my neck brings me back to Thanksgiving and the memories of us together make it hard to see straight. I shiver.

"You cold?" His voice is low and soft and I feel myself leaning toward him before I realize I'm doing it.

I shake my head.

He smiles that lopsided smile and my heart somersaults. "You gonna say anything?"

My voice comes out thick. "I can't believe you're here."

He breaks eye contact, looking at the ground between us. "That's what I've been thinking for the past month."

I stagger back a step. I didn't expect him to acknowledge things so quickly. "Then why..." The hurt from the past month rushes back and I press my hand against my throat, unable to get the words out.

His gaze follows my hand, lingering on my neck. I brush a finger over my skin, imagining it's his lips.

"I know I owe you an explanation. I just..." He shakes his head, sending his hair over his eyes. "Can you forgive me?"

I don't want to give in too easily but something about this boy makes me want to screw the rules and jump into his arms. "That depends."

He watches me, not saying anything, and I scramble to think of a condition. Sophia's voice echoes in the back of my head. "This hot and cold thing's gotta stop." Although technically it's been all hot, then all cold. "I won't let you hurt me again." Which is a lie. Just talking to him now has the potential to crush me if things go back to our new normal on Monday.

He pales. "Again?"

"Did you forget that you suddenly lost my number?"

He looks down again. "I'm sorry."

Laughter from inside carries through the door and I'm pulled out of my Blake-induced haze. "I don't want to get into all that right now, but—"

He reaches forward and grabs my hand. His skin is warm despite the cold air and heat races up my arm, jolting me in the heart.

I'm screwed.

"I promise I'll explain. But for now," he smiles that lopsided grin, "it's really good to talk to you."

Dear lord, I'm beyond screwed.

"Should we go inside?"

I lift a shoulder and smile. "I guess."

He opens the door and I drop his hand. As much as I've dreamed of the day that Blake and I are an actual couple, I don't want to be the center of rumors this soon in my new school.

We find Luke and Ian in the living room with everyone else. "You get lost?" Luke asks, winking at Blake.

"She was showing me the landscaping."

Reece chokes on his soda. "I bet she was."

Heat flames my cheeks and I search the room for a distraction, any distraction. Evan's studying Blake like he's gauging unexpected competition, while Mike smiles and gives me a thumbs-up. My gaze stops on Brianna, who's sitting on Austin's lap. I'd begun to think she was too good for high school boys, but from the way his hand's trailing up and down her back, I'd say I was wrong.

Brianna narrows her eyes at me.

What did I do now? Whatever's got her pissed off can wait. I smile at Blake. "Drinks are in the kitchen."

He and Ian wander off and Luke nudges me. "Nice to see that you can actually talk."

Just when I thought I couldn't blush any more. "I was surprised to see him—you guys. But I'm glad you came."

The slip didn't get past him. "I figured. I had to convince him to come."

"What?" My stomach drops. *Blake doesn't want to be here? Then what the hell was that outside?*

Luke leans closer so the others can't hear. "He knows he's been an ass but he's so stubborn he'd rather be miserable than try to fix it."

"Oh." *Jesus, Cally. Calm down.*

"Lucky for you, he's friends with me."

I study him, rewriting the slacker impression I'd formed in English class. "So he told you?"

He nods. "You were all he talked about after Thanksgiving."

And just like that butterflies whip through me, releasing the doubt and anger from the past month.

"What are you two whispering about?"

Even his voice makes me weak in the knees.

Luke's smoother than me. "Skiing. Cally was telling me about her sick flips."

I tilt my head, mouth open. Since I haven't told him anything about myself, he must have heard it from Blake.

Blake smiles, eyes on mine. "They are pretty spectacular."

I shake my head to clear the dancing hearts. "You're not so bad yourself. On the slopes, I mean."

Luke punches him in the arm. "Ooh, burn."

Blake pushes him back and I step away before I become a casualty of their boy-wrestling. Brianna's still giving me the evil eye but I'm too happy to give her resting bitch-face much thought.

I head to the kitchen to get myself a drink and chat with two girls I recognize from history, but my gaze keeps returning to the living room. I can't see Blake, but I know he's there, looking way too delicious for his own good. Hopefully Brianna doesn't scare him away before I get more time with him.

A prick of jealousy makes me flush at the thought of him talking to another girl, even Brianna. I roll my eyes and the girl I'm talking to tilts her head. "Sorry, not you. I'm being stupid in my head."

She looks even more puzzled.

"I'm gonna check on people in the living room."

"Okay, see ya."

In the living room, Austin and Brianna have snuggled closer and she looks the closest to relaxed that I've ever seen. Kenzie, Reece, and another boy are crammed on the couch with them. Mike and Evan are still in opposite chairs, but the longing on her face is so clear they may as well be the only people in the room—except he's oblivious.

She looks my way as I approach her. "Having fun?"

My gaze lands on Blake, who's leaning against the wall listening to a very animated Luke tell what—based on his arm gestures—can only be a snowboarding story. I sink onto the armrest, taking in the people around me—*my friends*, a little voice tells me—and smile. "I am."

She pokes my side and laughs. "It's about time."

"What do you mean?"

"I don't know. You always seem tense, like you're waiting for something bad to happen."

I nod in Bri's direction. "Can you blame me?"

She snorts. "No. I guess I don't ever fully relax around her either."

A balled up napkin lands in my lap. I look up and meet Kenzie's glare.

"What are you two whispering about?"

I don't miss a beat. "I was just saying what an honor it is to have you here."

She rolls her eyes. "I'm sure."

I nudge Mike and she coughs into her hand, stifling a laugh.

Kenzie straightens, her eyes narrowing into a look I've seen on Brianna's face. I guess when Bri's busy, Kenzie steps up as head bitch. Her smile becomes a sneer and she points at Blake and his friends. "If you're so honored, what are they doing here?"

I glance at Blake, who meets my eyes, but it doesn't look like he heard her. "Uhh... talking?"

She leans forward. "No. Why are they here? I know Bri told you to stay away from him."

"Are you—" I look from Mike to Kenzie to Blake. "Are you serious?"

Kenzie stares at me, lips pursed in an expression she MUST practice in front of a mirror. "Do I look like I'm kidding?"

Much to my delight, Brianna looks up from whatever Austin was whispering in her ear and aims her glare at me.

Anger pushes me to my feet. "You know what? I'm beginning to regret inviting YOU tonight." Kenzie's mouth falls open and my voice rises. I glare at Brianna. "First you chase away the nicest girl I've met since moving here—" I glance at Mike and she shrugs. "And now you're telling me I can only be friends with your pre-approved list of boys?"

I've definitely got Blake's attention now. Luke has stopped talking and literally every eyeball in the room is focused on me. I take a deep breath.

Slope Rule #7: Go big or go home.

"I think you should leave."

Brianna launches to her feet and I take a step back, straightening my shoulders. I hadn't planned on saying that but I'm not backing down now. I've faced much worse than her in the starting gates.

"I don't know who you think you are, but you just ruined your life. I was trying to be nice and—"

"This is nice? I hate to see how you treat people you don't like." Except I already have.

She points a finger at me. "You're finished."

My stomach twists but I roll my eyes. "Whatever."

Brianna steps over Austin's legs and stalks past me, Kenzie close on her heels. She passes Mike, then turns to look at her when she doesn't stand. "What are you waiting for?"

Mike hesitates. Could this be the moment she finally breaks free from Brianna? She catches my eye for a moment, then drags her gaze to Brianna, who looks ready to yank Mike out of here by her hair. She closes her eyes for a moment, then stands. "I'll text you later," she says as she walks by. "Good luck with Blake."

My cheeks flush. I'd been so focused on Brianna that I forgot he's standing five feet away.

Austin and Reece trail after the girls, but Evan pauses next to me. "I'll stay if you want me to."

I smirk. "Aren't you worried about Bri's wrath?"

"She doesn't control me."

My brows shoot up. "Dissension in the ranks?"

"No. I think for myself." He lifts a finger and touches my cheek. I'm dying to turn around to see if Blake's watching. Instead I move my head enough that he drops his hand.

"You should probably go."

His smile falters for a moment. He glances over my shoulder, then back at me. "See you tomorrow?"

Tomorrow? Oh, skiing. Right. "Sure."

He smiles and nods over my shoulder. "See you Blake. Luke."

He walks away and I turn around.

Blake's watching me with an amused expression on his face. "That was almost better than watching you ski."

I press my hands to my belly to calm the mix of emotions churning my stomach. I hate confrontation, but I hate getting pushed around even more.

His eyes follow my hands and his smile fades. "You okay?"

The front door slams and I jump, but no one else seems to react. In fact, no one seems to care that Brianna and her minions have left. Drama at a party is expected and an early exit from the queen bitch doesn't mean the party is over.

I smile at Blake. "I am now."

eighteen

Where's Sophia when I need her? Blake's standing a foot away, eyes on me—exactly what I've wanted for months—and my brain has forgotten how to form words.

Smile! I can smile!

I smile.

He smiles back, that adorable half smirk that shows his dimple.

Okay, this is good.

His smile grows.

Pull it together, Cally! I glance at his empty hands. "You need something to drink?"

"Nah, I'm good."

Luke elbows him from behind and Blake stumbles toward me. His gaze drops. "Can we... uh..." He looks me in the eye. "Can we go somewhere and talk?"

Not in my room, Dad would kill me. But it's too crowded down here. I'm not expecting anything to happen but I don't want an audience for whatever he's planning to tell me. "Outside?"

"Sure."

We find our coats and step outside into a brisk wind.

"Over here?" He's looking around the corner to the side of the house.

I take a deep breath. *Pretend he's any other guy. Hunter. Or Sam. Not someone who broke my heart and has the potential to do it all over again if he keeps looking at me that way.* I follow him into the darkness.

It takes a moment for my eyes to adjust, and when they do, I need another breath. Blake's standing close enough that our shoulders brush. He's not facing me, but my heart doesn't seem to care. It's thumping so loudly it drowns out everything else.

He clears his throat.

But doesn't say anything.

The front door opens and sounds from the party drift outside. "Cally?" a girl calls.

I turn my head in her direction but don't move.

Blake's hand slides down my arm, stopping briefly at my fingertips—the heat from his hand sending tingles up my arm—then his hand falls to his side.

The front door closes and the quiet night falls around us.

Just a guy...

He opens his mouth but I interrupt him.

"Are you entering the Dash?"

He tilts his head. "The competition at Eldora?"

"Yeah."

"I wasn't planning on it."

"Why not? I've seen you shred a mountain better than anyone else here."

He shrugs. "Not my scene."

"It's totally your scene."

He looks away. "You haven't been here long enough to understand."

I touch his arm and he meets my eyes. "What's there to understand? Competition. You're an amazing boarder. End of story."

"Maybe where you came from, but not here." He nods at the side of the house in the direction of the living room, avoiding my eyes. "I'm not one of them."

Brianna's warning to stay away from Blake rings in my ears. Nothing about him sets off warning bells and it seems like he likes me, but he must have some big secret I don't know about. Why else would he act so weird?

"You're no different from Evan and those guys. I mean, you're hotter, but..." I trail off, cheeks blazing.

The corner of his mouth turns up and his eyes soften for a moment. But the smile fades. "It's easy for you. Your dad, this house... you've got everything they do."

"Not everything." My voice comes out a whisper. I hate throwing my mom into the conversation, but she's never far from my thoughts.

"But you have enough. In their eyes, you're one of them. I'm surprised they didn't give you a matching uniform."

The bitterness is his voice is unmistakable and the pieces start to fall together. "Let me get this straight. You think that because my family has money I think I'm special? That I wouldn't be friends with someone who doesn't?"

Oh. That is it.

"That's how the rest of them are."

"And you just assumed I'm the same?" He shrugs and I want to shove his shoulders, but I cross my arms over my chest instead. "Is that why you lied?"

Our eyes lock but his expression is unreadable.

A moment passes. The silence is killing me but I'm done making excuses for him. I need to know why—

"I didn't mean to." His voice is so low I almost don't hear him.

I take a deep breath, fighting back the anger that's ready to explode all over him. "How do you accidentally lie about where you live?"

He takes a small step back and runs his hands through his hair before stepping closer and resting his hands on my shoulders. My breath catches at his sudden closeness. He dips his head so he's staring directly into my eyes. In the darkness his light eyes are dark, but you'd have to be a complete moron to miss the intensity in them. "I don't know why I lied to you. When you asked where I lived..." he shakes his head. "It just came out."

"But you didn't even hesitate. It's like you had the lie ready in case I asked."

His hands slide over my shoulders, down my arms, until he catches my hands in his.

I want to pull back. I don't want to make this easy on him after the months of torment he put me through, but his touch feels so good.

"I was staying at the resort with my aunt and uncle and cousins. They're from Tahoe."

"So you decided to adopt yourself into their family?" I regret the words as soon as they leave my mouth. I don't know anything about his family and for all I know he IS adopted. "I'm sorry. I didn't mean it like that. But you have to understand why I'm hurt, right?"

He frowns. "I didn't mean to hurt you, Cally. You're the coolest chick I've ever met."

My heart does a flip-flop but I force myself to keep quiet now that he's finally talking.

"You see how Bri and her bitches are. I figured—"

"Mike's not like that." So much for not interrupting.

"Okay, she's not bad. But I figured anyone as hot as you wouldn't talk to me for more than five minutes once you found out I wasn't part of a jet-setter clique."

"I couldn't care less about that."

He lifts his hand and trails a finger down my cheek. "I realized that once I got to know you. But what was I supposed to say? 'Oh, hey, I'm not really from California.' I was having a great time with you and since I didn't think we'd ever see each other again, I figured the truth didn't matter."

I take a step back. "So you just wanted to see how far you'd get on vacation?"

He matches my movement, once again closing the distance between us. "Do you really think that?"

I shake my head. He could say the same thing about me. We both went into whatever this thing was between us knowing we only had a few days together. I'm as guilty as he is.

Except I didn't lie.

"So you were staying with your aunt and uncle?"

"Yeah."

"Why weren't your parents there?"

"They couldn't leave the restaurant. My dad's brother brings his family here over one of the breaks every year and they usually invite me to stay with them. I work at the restaurant a couple nights a week so my parents gave me the time off. It's as close to a vacation as I'm gonna get."

Bits of our conversations over Thanksgiving come back to me. Suddenly the small hesitations that I figured were nerves are starting to make sense. "So whose car were you driving?"

"My dad's. Mine was in the shop for a couple days. It took everything I had to convince him to let me borrow it." He touches my cheek again, but this time he doesn't pull away. "I'm really sorry I lied."

My body sways toward him, but I pull back. There's still more I need to know. "I understand—sort of—why you lied about where you live, but why did you freak out when I told you I was moving here? And why have you acted like I don't exist for the past month?" He's close enough that I can smell his body wash but I can't ignore the hurt and frustration that's creeping over me. I'm grateful for the darkness because tears are burning my eyes and I don't know how long I can keep them from falling.

He looks away and takes a deep breath. "I'm sorry."

A lump catches in my throat. "That's—that's not enough."

His eyes return to mine. A gust of wind blows the tree branches above us and light from the streetlight brightens his face. His eyes shine in the faint light. "I don't have a good reason. Like I said, the girls here—"

This time I do push his shoulder—just as the front door opens. "I'm not like the girls here!" Music and laughter spill into the night air, colliding with my anger.

He watches me, jaw clenched. "Cally, I know I screwed up. And I don't have a good excuse. I wish I did, but I don't. Can we—"

"There you are!" Luke and Ian stumble around the corner, laughing.

Ian shoves Blake's arm. "I told him you left."

Luke winks at me. "And I told him you snuck off with Cally."

Heat flushes my cheeks. There are so many emotions bubbling inside me that I'm ready to burst, but I don't want to embarrass myself in front of Blake's friends.

Blake covers for me. "We were just talking."

Ian points at my face. "I dunno, bruh, she looks a little flushed."

I push through them. "I'm going back inside."

"You sure you don't wanna stay?"

I turn around to see Luke waggling a joint between his thumb and forefinger.

"What the hell are you doing?"

Luke shrugs. "Relaxing?"

"You can't smoke that here!" I look at Blake for backup but he doesn't seem concerned. "Blake, tell him."

I don't know what Blake's thinking after where we left off, but he does what I ask. "Dude, lay off. She doesn't want you to."

Luke flips the joint into his mouth. "You know it's legal here, right?"

"It's—what?"

Ian pumps his fist in the air. "The people have spoken!"

Blake smiles, but it's not condescending the way Brianna's is when she knows something I don't. "Colorado legalized marijuana. It's easier to get than alcohol anyway."

"But if you really don't want us to, we'll wait." Luke rolls the joint between his fingers. Back and forth, back and forth. Energy seems to course through him, like he couldn't stand still if you paid him.

I release a breath I didn't realize I was holding. This would have been a fight with Bri. "Thanks. I don't mean to be a goody-goody, but I'm so used to getting drug tested for skiing that..." I trail off as a sadness I thought I'd gotten past rolls over me. I'm not on a ski team. No one cares if I smoke pot. I could light up every night for the next month and it wouldn't make a difference. Well, Dad would probably lose his shit and I'd probably fail tenth grade, but other than that...

Luke throws his arm around my shoulder. "No worries. I'm not so bad that I can't wait until later." Blake snorts and Luke smiles. "But we're leaving soon, right?"

I burst out laughing, and it's like months of tension and stress fade away. Hanging out with the Snow Bunnies is okay but I can never relax. But these guys—Blake and his friends—they're like my friends back home. No pretense, no worrying about what anyone else thinks, they're just being themselves.

Blake nudges my side with his elbow. "That looks good on you."

I tilt my head in question.

"Your smile."

Ian jumps on Luke and puts him in a headlock. "I don't think we're needed here."

Luke's voice is muffled through Ian's sleeve. "See ya, Cally! Thanks for the party!"

They stumble around the corner to the front of the house, leaving us alone. My nerves come back in full force. *Is he gonna kiss me?* He hasn't finished explaining but he looks so good and he's so close and—

"I should probably get going."

The butterflies come to a screeching halt, slamming into my chest. "Does he really need to smoke that bad?"

He looks at the corner of the house. Sounds of them wrestling in the front yard drift toward us. "Nah, but there's another party they want to go to." He pauses. "I made them come here first."

I drift closer to him. "I'm glad you did."

He clears his throat and his voice is suddenly hoarse. "Me too." He takes another step closer and I'm in his arms, my face buried against his chest.

This feels so right. Why have we waited so long?

Oh right. Because he's ignored me since I've been here.

As much as I hate to, I pull away.

"See you tomorrow?"

Did I miss him asking me out? "Uhh..."

"You're going to Eldora, right?"

"Oh, right. Yeah." I'm supposed to be riding with the Bunnies, but I'm guessing that's not happening.

His mouth opens as if he's going to say something, but then he closes it.

"I usually meet up with Amber at the terrain park after a couple runs."

"Cool. Maybe I'll see you there." Not exactly the profession of love I was hoping for, but it's better than where we were twelve hours ago. He pulls me against his chest and holds me for a moment before brushing his lips against my cheek. "Bye, Cally."

I'm still standing in the dark long after he's gone, arms wrapped tightly around myself.

When I go back inside, almost everyone is gone. "How long were we out there?" I mutter to myself. The few kids left in the living room stand when I enter. "Thanks for coming, guys." Before long the house is empty and I'm still reeling from my conversation with Blake. This is what I wanted but I'd begun to think it was never going to happen.

I bend over to pick up trash off the floor and my bladder screams at me. "I can do this later." I head to the bathroom but pause in the hallway. The door to Dad's study is open a crack. "I thought he was in the basement." I stick my head inside.

He's not there.

I whip around toward the living room, but nothing has changed from two seconds ago.

Who was in here?

I step inside and look around. Nothing looks different—notebooks balance on one corner of the desk, magazines on the other, and an old hoodie hangs from the back of the chair—but I never pay enough attention to notice if anything's out of place. His leather-bound notebook with all his beer recipes is the only thing that's always with him and—

My stomach drops to the floor.

It's not on his desk.

I scan the bookshelves, the floor, the stack of boxes in the corner, but it's not there. Sweat beads on my upper lip. It's got to be here. But it's not.

Maybe he brought it downstairs.

I close the door firmly behind me and gallop down the basement stairs.

Dad's stretched out on the beat-up leather sofa watching a movie. "Miss me already?"

I take a deep breath. "Do you have your notebook?"

He twists into a sitting position and rests his feet on the floor, face serious. "No."

My skin goes clammy. "Are you sure?"

"What's going on?"

"The door to your office was open a crack and when I went to say hi you weren't there and I didn't see your notebook."

He stands and rests a hand on my arm. "I'm sure it's fine. I put it in a drawer before your friends got here."

I'm halfway up the stairs before I hear him behind me. I race down the hall, fling open the door, and yank open the top drawer. Then the next. Then the drawers on the other side.

No notebook.

Dad moves next to me, his hand hovering over the open drawer. "It was here." The color drains from his face and his mouth sets in a firm line.

My heart beats erratically. I run my hands through my hair, scanning the room for the hundredth time.

"How well do you know the kids who were here tonight?"

"I've been here a month."

"Who would want to take my notebook? How would they even know what it is?"

My breath catches. "Brianna."

"Who?"

"Her dad owns Mischief."

His hands go to his hair, gripping like it's the only thing keeping him under control. "And you're friends with her?"

A horrible, sinking feeling makes me sway on my feet.

Social calendar my ass.

My voice is a whisper. "The party was her idea."

nineteen

Did she take it?

She's the only person with a reason.

It's after midnight—two A. M. Sophia's time—but there's no way I could sleep without talking to her. I pace my room, mind scrambling for an explanation other than Brianna, but nothing else makes sense. Yes, she's a royal bitch, but I didn't figure her for a thief.

Do you think her dad put her up to it?

No way she did it on her own.

That's messed up.

I can't imagine Dad ever asking me to do something like that. Half the time he feels guilty that I spend as much time in a brewery as I do—there's no way he'd recruit me to be his spy.

I flop facedown on my bed. He didn't lose the recipe since he's already brewed the first batch, but what if Mischief somehow comes out with it first? A fresh wave of panic rolls through me. How many other brewery secrets are in there?

Yawn.

Sorry. I'll let you go.

Wait! What about Mr. B man?

Blake. I'd almost forgotten about him. Anger at Brianna bubbles hotter for ruining my good mood.

He came. We talked. He hugged me. Twice.

Sounds hot.

I remember how cold it was outside and giggle. *Totally G-rated.*

Next time?

Fingers crossed. He said why he lied but I feel like there's more he's not telling me.

But at least you talked...

Yeah.

And he's still smoking hot?

If I close my eyes I can almost feel his arms around me. *Mm-hmm.*

Colorado is good for your game.

I snort. We'll see.

Passing out. Keep me posted.

Night.

xoxo.

***

The next morning I'm a jumble of nerves. Dad's waiting for me in the kitchen with a cup of coffee in his hand, the lack of a notebook by his side like a missing limb.

I hang my head. "Morning."

He takes in my long underwear and moisture-wicking shirt. "Are those girls still picking you up?" The distaste in his voice when he says 'those girls' makes me cringe.

"Doubtful."

"I could bring you."

"Dad, you're not driving me halfway across Colorado." I sit in the chair across from him.

"It's half an hour away."

"Still. I'm sure I can get a ride from someone else." I scroll through my phone, but my list of Colorado friends is sadly lacking. I hesitate over Evan's name. I don't want to encourage him, but he lives right around the corner...

I fire off a text before I change my mind. *Got room for one more this morning?*

He writes back almost immediately. *For you, anything.*

So much for not encouraging him.

Dad takes a sip of coffee. "I don't like you being friends with girls like that."

I smile weakly. "If it helps, I don't think we're friends anymore."

"This could have serious consequences for Calliope. I'm planning the opening around this new beer and if our debut looks like a rip-off of the local competition, no one will take us seriously." He levels his gaze at me. "We have a lot invested here and I don't want to have to go back to Vermont with my tail between my legs."

Go back to Vermont? A thousand thoughts leap to mind. I could go home. To Sophia and my friends and the ski team and our house and–

But the expression on his face tells me to swallow all that. "Is that really a possibility?"

"Nothing in business is ever guaranteed. Henry and I felt like the time was right but negative press can undo even the best laid plans."

"Well, shit."

"You said it."

I stare at my hands, sorting through my thoughts. As much as I'd love to go back to my old life, it feels like that's already in the past. Of course Sophia will always be my best friend, but the rest of it... I'm not so sure. I may not have things figured out here but Boulder is my world now. Amber is cool, and if I keep working on Mike I bet I could convince her to break away from the Snow Bunnies and things would be almost okay.

One final thought bumps against my heart.

Blake.

Moving back to Vermont now that we're finally talking could shatter my heart even worse.

Dad opens a drawer and pulls out a pen and notepad and sets them in front of me. “Can you write down the names of the kids who were here last night?”

“Like a suspect list?”

He shrugs. “I’m not going to call any parents—yet—but Google should help me narrow down who could have taken it.”

As much as I’d love for it to be someone random, in my heart I know it’s Brianna.

I write her name at the top of the list.

***

An hour later I’m crammed in the backseat of Evan’s SUV. I figured I wouldn’t hear from Brianna, so I was surprised when Mike texted me to give me a heads up.

He catches my eye in the rearview mirror. “You sure you’re okay back there?”

“Just perfect.” Reece is in the front passenger seat, so I’m wedged between Austin and Evan’s younger brother Andy.

Evan tried to make Andy ride bitch, but I convinced him that since I have the shortest legs it made more sense for me to be in the middle. Over the years I’ve gotten so good at avoiding riding on the left side of the car that people don’t even realize I’m doing it.

Andy was happy to keep his seat and I was a little embarrassed to admit that I didn’t even know Evan had a brother, although I recognize him from school. And he, apparently, has noticed me. Every time we hit a bump he not-so-accidentally brushes his arm against me. He’s managed to hit my boob three times and as I lock eyes with Evan I decide that if Andy does it again he’s gonna accidentally get my elbow in his nose.

“Andy, lay off my girl.”

His girl?

Andy tucks his arm closer to his side and gives me a crooked grin. They’re only a year apart but I get the feeling Andy’s going to pass Evan in the charm department. As soon as he learns to control his elbows.

Reece turns around to face me. "I told you the middle is the best place to be."

I roll my eyes and nudge Andy. "So I hear you're going to be an uncle."

Andy looks at me in surprise, then realization dawns on his face. "Ha, Dolly. That dog almost gets more action than I do." He nudges me on purpose this time. "Almost."

I roll my eyes.

When we arrive at Eldora, only the first few rows of the parking lot are full.

Andy groans as he opens the door. "I told you it's too early for this."

Evan glares at him in the rearview mirror. "You wanted to come."

Andy rolls his eyes and hops out.

I follow him and shut the door, coming face-to-face with Evan, who's smiling down at me. "Sorry about him. He thinks he's a ladies' man."

"You're just jealous!" Andy shouts from the back of the SUV.

Color touches Evan's cheeks.

Is he actually blushing?

"Anyway, are you gonna stick with us today?"

I shrug. "Sure." Amber texted that she's running late and while I don't mind skiing by myself, I miss showing off with guys.

He touches a finger to my chin. "Don't sound so excited."

I force an overly cheesy smile and punch him lightly in the arm. "I'm super-duper excited!"

He laughs, and before I know what's happening he's pulling me against his chest and squeezing.

Two things make me push him away: the memory of Mike's sad face from last night and the fricking gorgeous specimen that is Blake. Evan's cute, but just the thought of Blake gets my heart thrumming. I need to keep Evan strictly in the friend zone. "We gonna stand here all day or hit the slopes?"

The guys are already halfway to the lodge, but Evan pauses as we pass Brianna's car and gives me a mischievous smile. "You wanna leave her a love note? I really have to piss. I could..." he trails off, hand on his zipper.

I swat at his arm. "No! God no. Just—just keep it in your pants." I instantly blush, and I shove him forward to cover my embarrassment. He half-stumbles, laughing. We're almost to the lodge before I ask what's been in the back of my mind. "Isn't she, like, your leader or something? That's the second time in two days you've made a comment like that."

"Bri's a bitch and we all know it."

"So why do you hang out with her?"

He shrugs, and I suddenly realize I've ventured into Mike territory.

"Never mind, forget it."

"Nah, it's cool. Austin has an on-again, off-again thing with her, plus our parents are all friends. You know how it works." His assumption that because I'm a quote-unquote rich kid I automatically understand the intricacies of extreme wealth makes me feel a little dirty. We may have money, but I'm not one of them.

"Sure, I get it." I adjust my skis on my shoulder and spit the rest out before I can change my mind. "But isn't it... isn't it weird hanging around Mike?"

His head swivels toward me, surprise on his face, but he recovers quickly. "She told you?"

"Yeah." We're already at the lodge but it's now or never. "And I gotta tell you, as the new girl, I'm not big on getting in the middle of whatever was or is going on there."

He rests his gear against the racks and holds the door open for me. I set mine next to his and head inside. Austin, Reece, and Andy already have their street shoes off and tossed in a cubby. "You gonna talk all day or what?" Reece shouts over the heads of people putting on their gear. I grab an open spot on a bench and quickly change into my ski boots and set my everyday boots near the guys' and follow them outside.

The sun's still making its way through the crisp morning sky. The air is still, and I know I'll be sweating after a couple runs.

Evan maneuvers so we're on the chairlift together but doesn't answer me until we're fifty feet in the air. "I didn't know you knew about us."

Us. "She told me a couple weeks ago." I slide my gloved hands back and forth across the safety rail. "You're a really cool guy and all but—"

"You that worried about what Bri would say?"

"Brianna? No. She actually encouraged me to—" I shake my head. "Never mind. I'm worried about Mike. She's my only friend at school and I don't want to jeopardize that since—" I stop. He doesn't know Mike still likes him and while I'd love to play cupid, it's not my place to butt in.

"Since what?"

"Nothing."

"Is this about Blake?"

My head whips to face him and I blurt "What?!" before I catch myself.

He smiles, eyes not meeting mine. "Just curious."

Heat goes beyond my cheeks and runs straight to the tips of my toes.

"Blake's a good guy. I mean, he's not me, but you could do worse."

Never in a million years did I imagine I'd be on a chairlift with Evan talking about Blake. Isn't there a rule about your crushes—or past crush and love-of-your-life—not knowing about each other? Or at least not openly acknowledging the whole feelings thing?

"Brianna warned me away from him my first day of school."

He snorts. "Figures."

I cock my head.

"She had the hots for him back in middle school but he blew her off. I never knew exactly what happened but one minute she was following him around like a lost puppy and the next he was at the top of her shit list."

"Huh." So maybe Blake's wrong about the whole money thing. Maybe Brianna's just holding onto the world's longest grudge.

"I don't let her dictate who I'm friends with." He shrugs, then finally faces me. "And you shouldn't either."

"Did you just give me your blessing?"

A huge smile spreads across his face and he rests his hand over mine. "I must be delirious. Forget what I said. Go out with me tonight."

I laugh. A few lazy butterflies kick around in my belly, but they quickly settle down. "Save it, Romeo." Being friends with Evan will be so much easier without the uncertainty of what might happen between us.

We're nearing the top of the lift when Evan leans toward me. "I thought I was the first person you met here. So I gotta know. How did Blake slip by me?"

I adjust my goggles and scoot to the edge of the chair, ready to push off. We may have moved into the friend zone but no one else needs to know about how Blake and I met.

We glide to where the guys are sprawled, fastening their bindings to their boots. I slide past them and stop at the top of the run. Adrenaline shoots through me and I bounce my knees. "You boys ready?"

Before they can answer, I hop to the edge and plunge straight down.

twenty

The air is so still I can feel Mom all around me. I take a deep breath, holding her as tightly as I can as I slice through the snow. The first jump is a hundred feet away and it's early enough that there's not a line so I don't have to wait. I crouch into a tuck, picking up speed. Sunlight catches the top of the jump, calling to me, daring me to go faster. I crouch lower, my fists balled, until I'm at the lip of the jump. I straighten my legs and twist my core so my entire body spins to the right. In that split second I see the guys at the top of the hill, a little kid watching me, the line of trees where the chairlift is, then the bottom of the hill comes back into view.

I relax my knees as my skis hit the snow, then resume my tuck for the next jump. I'm on it in seconds, soaring through the air. This time I keep my legs tucked up, arms against my legs. I land harder and a flash of worry darts through me, but my knee is fine. It's been okay since Christmas.

I smile as I approach the third jump. I usually save big tricks until I've had a few runs, but between the fight with the Snow Bunnies and the talk with Blake and the missing notebook I have too much energy telling me to go for it.

I arch my back as soon as my skis hit the jump and my legs flip over my head.

Sky.

Snow.

The base of the hill, where two people in jeans and out-of-date winter coats are leaning on their poles.

"Oof." I exhale as I land, then quickly do a side stop to avoid the couple who decided the bottom of the jump is a good place to stand. The tranquility I felt from Mom evaporates. I don't spray them with snow like I want to, but stop close enough for them to hear me. "You need to move. That's not—"

The guy smiles at me. "That was unbelievable! I didn't know you could do that on skis!"

"Um, thanks. But you really need to move." Austin is already on the second jump and since the third is the biggest his air could land him right where they're standing.

The woman points at the hill, oblivious to what's about to happen. "This is so amazing. We don't have snow like this where we live. I never knew you could do things in the air like that."

Speaking of air, Austin's in it now, heading straight for us. I whip my head between him and the couple, and it's like everything moves in slow motion. The couple finally realizes what's about to happen just as Austin sees they still haven't moved. His body does a weird twisty thing to try to avoid them and he lands hard on his side.

I hurry to him. "Austin, are you okay?"

He flips onto his back, legs bent. "What is wrong with you people!" His shout carries through the morning air.

"Omigod, are you all right?" The woman shuffles toward Austin but I stop her with a glare.

"You need to get out of here before someone else gets hurt."

Austin lifts his head. "And don't hang out at the bottom of the jump!" He looks at me. "Dumbasses."

They finally get a clue and shuffle away.

I lean forward. "Are you okay?"

"My ass is gonna have a bruise the size of my face, but yeah, I'm okay."

"There's a visual I didn't need."

A piercing whistle makes us turn. Reece pinwheels his arms backwards as he soars toward us in an attempt to slow himself down. He lands a safe distance away but doesn't slow down until he's practically on top of us. He throws his weight to one side in a hard stop, covering us with powder.

Austin wipes his face with his sleeve. "Asshole."

Reece flips his goggles onto his forehead. "You break a nail?"

I laugh. Most of the snow missed my face. "More like his ass."

"Even better."

Evan whoops from the top of the last jump and we all take cover. He lands short like Reece did and, like Reece, sprays us with snow. This time I get covered and I shake out my ponytail, laughing. Some girls complain that guys our age are too immature but that's what I like about them. They don't care what they look like or what anyone who might be watching thinks—they live for the moment and do what comes naturally. Girls like Brianna and Kenzie spend so much time overthinking things that they never relax and have fun.

Austin throws a snowball at Evan but he still hasn't gotten up. As a recent veteran of a faulty landing, I recognize a diversion when I see one.

I tap his board with the tip of my ski.

He meets my eyes, jaw clenched.

"You okay?" I mouth.

He gives his head a quick shake. "Can't believe I'm out after the first run."

Evan hops closer to Austin. "Oh shit, are you really hurt?"

Austin brushes snow off his board, stalling. "My hip's jacked, but I'll be okay."

Reece winks at him. "Text Bri. She'll make you forget all about your broken hip."

Austin throws a handful of snow in Reece's face. "Help me up, asshole." He unhooks one foot from his board, then Evan and Reece each take an arm and haul him to his feet. He tests his weight on the bad leg before nodding.

I glance longingly at the line to the lift. In another hour it'll be twenty people deep, but right now there's only a handful of people. "You guys care if I get another run in before..." I have no intention of joining them in the lodge if Brianna's going to be there, but I don't need to say that to them. They were at the party.

"Yeah."

"Sure."

"See ya later."

They push-slide toward the lodge and I skate back to the lift, ready for some serious runs. I've been skiing every weekend since we moved here, but that's nothing compared to what I'd be doing if I was on the ski team. If I have any chance at winning the Dash at the end of the season I need to up my game. Aerials are cool, but like Coach Brown always said, showboating doesn't win competitions. If I want to win, I need to put in time on the moguls and straight runs, too.

I take the same lift up but cut over to the next run. Double black. My breathing slows as I survey the bumps. From up here they look like gentle slopes, but once inside the crevices can be as deep as I am tall. I bend at my waist until I feel the stretch in the back of my legs, then push myself over the edge.

Moguls are a completely different animal than jumps, but it's equally hard on your knees. If not harder. I fall into a rhythm after the first couple bumps—bend, push, bend, push—shifting my weight with each new obstacle. I've taken this run a couple times but today's different. Coach Brown's instructions ring in my ears. *Those knees need to be locked together. Every second counts. Don't look anywhere but eight feet in front of you.*

I never understood why eight feet and not five or ten, but eight feet is just enough distance to see the next bump while your body's reacting to the one you're still on. Instinct is crucial in slope-style and I'm lucky enough to have it.

My legs burn as I push through the final dip. A smaller jump lies where the bumps smooth out and those instincts tell my body to tuck. I'm preparing for another flip when the little voice in my head says maybe I should go easy and not bust my knee on the second run of the day. I twist my torso, settling for a simple three-sixty, and land easily at the base of the jump.

I touch my knee on reflex. The familiar ache is back. I tell myself it's because of the moguls, but a harder landing could have been bad.

I take the lift up the same run and go through Coach Brown's drills, skipping the jump at the end. After an hour I'm sweaty and ready for a break. And I'm itching to end with an aerial. I go easy on the bumps, letting my legs react but not pushing for time, saving my energy for the jump. When my skis hit the paint marking the edge, I tuck into a ball and twist to the right, flipping my body into a corkscrew somersault. It looks harder than it is and is easier to land because my feet stay underneath me, but this time something's wrong.

When I finish the rotation I'm too close to the ground.

I brace myself for the impact and land hard on my side. My skis pop off and momentum carries me into the deeper powder at the edge of the run.

I come to a stop on my side but roll to my back to remove pressure from where I landed. I let out a groan and lift my head. My skis are close to where I landed, fifty feet up the hill. I drop my head back into the snow. I'm gonna have an Austin-sized bruise on my ass.

Clouds drift overhead and I allow myself a minute to catch my breath. I know I shouldn't have tried that trick, but at least it wasn't my knee.

Slope Rule #8: Listen to your instincts.

The sound of a board cutting through the snow gets louder. "You okay?"

I turn my face, shielding my eyes.

Blake's standing over me, backlit from the late morning sun. It's eerily similar to the first time I saw him.

"What are you, my knight in shining armor?"

"That was a pretty spectacular fall."

"And I was worried no one saw it." I prop myself up on an elbow as he squats next to me. Bits of hair stick out from his helmet and—why is he touching my leg?

"Seriously, are you okay? You haven't moved."

I glance at my knee, not wanting to tell the truth so he doesn't stop touching me. Although if he's touching what hurts... "It's not my knee. I landed on my side."

His gaze travels up my leg. "You broke your ass, didn't you?"

I smile. "It seems to be the theme today. Austin did the same thing on the first run."

His eyes cloud over. "You're here with them?"

"I needed a ride. We got one run in before he got hurt and they went back to the lodge." And Amber's still MIA. "Can I ask you a favor?"

He raises an eyebrow.

"Can you clean up my yard sale?"

His face breaks into that adorable half-grin. "Be right back." He releases his feet from his board and runs up the hill toward my skis. When he reaches my side, he jams each ski into the snow and leans them against each other, forming an X. Then he sinks into the snow next to me.

"Wasn't sure how long you need." He meets my gaze, then looks away and fidgets with the lift ticket hanging from the zipper on his pocket.

He's nervous.

Which makes me nervous. It's last night all over again—when I found him on my front porch—and I've forgotten how to talk. I wiggle into a sitting position and just happen to slide a little closer to him in the process. We're not touching, but we're close.

He drops the ticket and rests his hand on mine. "Can we—"

He stops.

Can we what? Make out? Roll around in the snow for a bit? My body warms at the last thought. There's still so much I need to know, but I can't seem to resist him. I dip my head so I can see his eyes.

"Can we start over?"

His words set my nerve-endings zipping every which way. I turn my hand in his so we're shaking hands. "I'm Cally."

twenty-one

He moves closer until our sides are touching. "I haven't stopped thinking about you since Thanksgiving. I've tried, but it's no use."

I bite the corner of my lip. I'm ready to forgive him but I still want to know why he's put me through hell for the past couple months. And that he's not gonna do it again. "I haven't either. But I don't understand why you acted like you didn't know me."

He releases my hand and wipes it over his face. "I wouldn't say that."

I have seen him watching me, so I guess that's true. "But you haven't talked to me. Or even been nice to me." That last part is what hurts. Having him watch me from a distance has been torture.

His eyes widen. "I haven't been mean to you!"

"Well not mean, but definitely a jerk."

He leans his head until his forehead's on my shoulder and his helmet is pressed against the side of my face. "I'm sorry. I thought Brianna filled your head with her BS and since you didn't talk to me after that first day, I assumed we were over. Especially since I stopped texting you."

I'm glad he can't see my face right now. Hearing him acknowledge that he ignored me doesn't feel as good as I thought it would. Instead it brings back all the sadness and frustration I felt before I moved, and then every time I've seen him at school.

He lifts his head and looks me in the eye. "I'm sorry I reacted that way. I don't know why I didn't just talk to you and find out for myself what you were thinking."

My stomach sinks as I remember the humiliation I felt that first day after English when I called his name in the hall and he barely responded. "That would've been a lot easier."

He lowers his gaze. "Can you forgive me?"

I already know that I will, it's just a question of when. My pride won't let me stand up to Brianna one minute, then roll over—literally!—when a cute boy treats me like crap. Even if we do have a connection unlike anything I've ever experienced.

His glove touches my chin. "Cally?"

I meet his eyes and my heart does a somersault. It's not like I forgot he has incredibly gorgeous blue eyes, but seeing them this close—with the bright sky making them seem almost inhumanely clear—makes all logic evaporate from my brain.

"You're killin' me smalls."

I smile, and before I can think about what I'm doing, I lean forward and kiss him. "Yes," I whisper against his lips.

He pulls me closer and all thoughts but him are gone. His lips are soft and his kiss is gentle and unhurried, like the first time we kissed, and I guess it's kind of like our second first kiss. He tilts his head and our helmets clink. He laughs gently against my cheek. "Yes?" he asks.

I inhale deeply, the memory of how he smells updating with the sensations that sweep over me now. "Hmm?"

"Are you saying you forgive me?"

Oh right. "I suppose."

He pulls back so he can look in my eyes. "That doesn't sound very convincing."

I lift my hand to touch his cheek but it gets caught on his helmet and I end up poking him in the eye. "Omigod! I'm sorry!" I try to rub it but just poke him again.

He bursts out laughing and leans his head back, away from my gloves of doom. "Okay, okay! It's good enough."

I press my hand against his chest and lean closer. "Did I blind you? Can you see?"

He blinks several times and looks all around like he can't focus. "Cally, is that you?"

"Oh, stop it." I push his chest and in the blink of an eye he wraps his arms around me and pulls me against him. My breath comes out all fluttery but then our helmets smack again and I giggle. "This seems to be a recurring problem."

He hesitates and I wonder if I pushed it too far. It's one thing for him to apologize for being a dick but another to talk about what happened between us over Thanksgiving. He presses a kiss to my nose and I relax. "You have a point." His hand slides over my side until he reaches my hip. Then he pats my butt.

He actually touched my butt. Through fifteen layers of clothes and snow pants and gloves, but still.

"Do I need to call Ski Patrol to get your broken ass down the mountain?"

"There's no way I'm doing that again."

"Then let's go." He yanks my skis out of the snow and lays them perpendicular to the slope of the hill. We both push to our feet and I test my weight on my bad side. "Okay?" he asks.

I nod. "I've had worse."

He touches my cheek, and I like the fact that he can't seem to stop touching me. "I remember."

I step easily into my skis and let gravity pull me downhill. We're nearing the lodge when the rumble of an approaching snowmobile makes me stop. "You didn't call them."

He stops a few yards ahead of me, eyes on the Ski Patrol. "No. They've already got someone."

It's coming from the terrain park.

The snowmobile races down the hill, one person driving, the other sitting backwards on the seat to watch the person strapped into the sled. I can't see the person's face, but it's clear it's a kid.

Blake's face goes white.

I slide next to him and touch his arm. "Can you tell who it is?"

He shakes his head. "I think it's one of the Half-Pipes."

"The Half-Pipes?"

"A bunch of middle school kids that I help with tricks and stuff. They wanted a nickname to be like the Moguls and weren't too happy when that one stuck."

I narrow my eyes, trying to see a face as the snowmobile nears the lodge. "Are you sure it's one of them?"

His eyes are locked on the sled, which is getting smaller by the second. "Only one way to find out."

I tug at his arm. "Then let's go."

He looks at me for a second, seeming confused.

I soften my voice. "Come on." I push past him and head for the lodge, glancing back to make sure he's following. When we reach the med station there's already a crowd of people near the door. We ditch our equipment against the building and push past several familiar faces.

Two boys who look eleven or twelve are pressed against the wall of the small room, staring at a closed door.

Blake mutters under his breath, then locks his hand on mine and leads me to them. "What happened?"

Four wide eyes look up at him in terror, then slide back to the door.

Blake rests a hand on the smaller one's shoulder. "Joey, tell me what happened."

He hooks a thumb at the kid next to him. "Ben and I were practicing that back grip you showed us and Andrew decided to add a three-sixty." Blake's jaw clenches but he doesn't interrupt. The corner of Joey's mouth quirks. "It was more like a two-sixty the first time, so he wanted to do it again."

Ben clears his throat. "And that's when he fell. We fall all the time so we didn't think it was a big deal, but he wasn't moving."

Blake's head jerks to the door, then he rests his other hand on Ben's shoulder. My heart clenches at how much he clearly cares for these kids. "Did you text his parents?"

"Ski Patrol said for them to meet him at the hospital."

Blake looks at me, eyes wide. "I… I don't know what to do."

I lock my arm against his side. "Do you want to go to the hospital?"

"But what—"

The door swings open and a Ski Patrol guy stops in the doorway. He looks between the boys and us. "You're his friends?"

We all nod.

"An ambulance will take him to the hospital. Are your parents here?"

They shake their heads.

Blake drops his hands. "I can bring them."

Ski Patrol nods. "Okay. Now I need everyone to clear out of here so we can take him outside."

We step backwards in unison. Ben bumps into a desk, breaking the spell that's transfixed him since we arrived, and leads us outside.

Red lights bounce off the snow. A Ski Patrol woman is clearing a path for the ambulance, but people stay pressed close, wanting to see the action.

"People, I need you to back up! This isn't a joke!"

Two men carry a stretcher out of the door and Blake's grip on my hand tightens. I've never met Andrew, but he looks tiny strapped to the board. His eyes are closed and a neck brace prevents his head from moving.

"Are you sure you're okay to drive?"

Blake nods once and mumbles, "Yeah."

I look him in the eye. He seems completely rattled—more than he should be over a boarding accident, even if it is bad enough that a kid's going to the hospital. "What's going on?"

His gaze focuses on mine and he takes a deep breath. Opens his mouth like he's going to say something, but then closes it. He presses a kiss to my nose instead. "Not now."

A million questions race through my mind, but this isn't the time. "Please be careful."

"Do you want to come with us?"

"I don't want to intrude."

"You're not."

I mentally tick through my options. If I stay, I need to ride back in Evan's cramped car and possibly have to deal with the Snow Bitches until they're ready to leave, but if I go with Blake I could be at the hospital until Dad is done at work and can come get me.

"Blake, let's go." Joey and Ben have their boards slung over their shoulders and are heading toward the parking lot.

"Maybe it's better if I don't go." I don't know these kids and it would be weird to be at the hospital with Andrew's parents. I hate to see Blake go now that things finally seem to be okay, but he needs to help them right now. "I can ride home with Evan."

"You sure?"

"Text me later to let me know how he is."

"I will. Text me when you get home."

I smile. It feels like my heart is trying to crawl out of my chest. "I will."

He pulls me against his chest and holds me for not nearly long enough, then steps away. "I'll see you later."

I watch until he reaches the parking lot, then haul my skis onto my shoulder and trudge back to the lodge. Inside, all the tables near the fireplace are taken so I weave through groups of people toward a spot near the large window. Snow pants and helmets creep beyond the tables like long tentacles, threatening to trip me. My hip feels a little better—sitting in the snow for as long as we did probably helped—but my legs tremble from exhaustion. I collapse into a chair, shed my gear onto the table, and pull out my phone to text Evan when a sinking feeling makes me pause.

What if they've already left? I probably should have checked before I told Blake to leave without me, but Evan wouldn't leave me here. Would he?

Still here?

I rest my phone on the table. It could be half an hour before I hear from him. I try to distract myself with the people flying down the mountain in front of the lodge, but all I can think of is how Blake reacted to that kid getting hurt. He seemed scared, almost panicked, and the look on his face reminded me of how I feel when I come anywhere near the wrong side of a car. Like there's not enough oxygen in the world to make the ache in my chest go away.

I send him a text. *Any word?* Then I settle back in the chair. This could be a long wait.

My attention jumps between the slopes, the people around me, and my phone. I'm beginning to get dizzy when my phone vibrates.

Still here. Where you at?

Evan.

In the lodge. I'm done for the day.

Need company?

Nah, I'm good. Just don't leave me here. :)

Did you hear about that boarder who broke his neck?

What?! *He broke his neck?*

That's what I heard.

It's a kid. Blake knows him.

Oh shit. One of the Half-Pipes?

Yeah.

Couple more runs and I'll meet you?

Ok.

I've barely set my phone down when it vibrates again.

The doctors won't tell me anything.

Are his parents there?

Not yet.

I have no idea what to say. I fight off the instinct to tell him that I'm thinking of him and I wish I was there. That's what a girlfriend would say, and I'm most definitely not his girlfriend.

At least not yet.

I settle for lame instead. *Sorry.*

He doesn't write back, and I tell myself not to read into it because A) he's got more important things on his mind than my neurosis, and B) he's a guy. Once they've said what they want, they stop talking. It's really an amazing concept, something I'm determined to try someday.

I rest my phone on the table again but I need a distraction. I text Sophia.

News flash.

It takes sixty excruciating seconds for her to reply.

Go.

I kissed Blake.

Woah. YOU kissed him? Where?

On the mouth.

eyeroll

Skiing.

You two and the snow.

Tell me about it.

Did you talk?

A little. Enough.

So it's back on?

I think so. His friend got hurt so things got cut short.

Otherwise you'd be giving me a different news flash?

Ha, hardly. While I'm nowhere near ready for sex, that doesn't stop my imagination from rolling us off the slope and into the trees where no one would see us.

Soon enough.

"You're blushing. This must be good."

I lock my screen as Evan leans over my shoulder. "Not a chance."

"Come on, give me a hint." He drapes himself into the chair next to mine and bumps my knee with his.

I shake my head, willing my cheeks to return to their normal color.

"You're no fun."

I roll my eyes.

He pokes me in the side. "Okay, so maybe a little fun. Possibly really fun but you don't seem to want me to find out." He winks. "You ready to go?"

"Only if you promise to stop asking me out."

He presses a hand to his chest and flops back in his chair.

I laugh, but my smile doesn't last. "I mean it."

He holds out his hand for me to shake. "I'm just giving you a hard time."

As if on cue, my phone vibrates. I totally left Sophia hanging.

Sorry, my ride's here. Talk later. xoxo.

Fiiiine. xoxo

And now I left Evan hanging. I shake his hand, then pick up my helmet.

"I mean, yes, you're gorgeous, but I get it." He smiles. "Are we cool?"

I nod. "Where's everyone else?"

"They're meeting us at the truck." He stands and holds out his arm like some character from a Jane Austen book. "Shall we?"

I slip my arm through his and follow him through the mess of people, just as Mike comes out of the bathroom. Her mouth falls open when she sees us and I jerk my arm away, which only makes me look guilty.

Evan stiffens, which surprises me. But maybe our talk about her earlier got him thinking.

Mike hustles around the corner and is gone before we reach her, and I make a mental note to text her on the way home. I know the girl I met on the chairlift is trying to come out and maybe this will be the push to make it happen.

The guys are waiting in the car—gear loaded, radio and heat cranked—and my breathing becomes more shallow as we get closer. Every time I make a stink about riding on the left side of the car, the sooner someone realizes what I'm doing and my secret's out.

But I exhale as we get closer. The front seat is empty.

Evan leads me to the passenger side but pauses with his hand on the handle.

"What'd you have to promise to arrange this?"

He shrugs. "I merely pointed out that I've been driving them here all season and have yet to see any gas money."

Not that he needs it, I'm sure. I climb in and twist around to say hello. Austin's directly behind me with his shins pressed into the seat. "How's your ass?"

"Superb."

"Wanna switch?"

"Nah, I iced it so long I can't even feel it. But thanks."

I settle back into my seat. I don't mean to close my eyes, but the heat blasting from the vents relaxes my exhausted body and the next thing I know we're pulling into a driveway. For a second I have no idea where I am or why I'm here, then I see Evan smiling at me and it all clicks back into place.

Cold air swirls through the interior of the car as Austin gets out. They do their goodbye thing then the door closes. The headlights light his way as he hobbles to the front of the house, then we're back on the road.

"Your phone's been blowing up."

"Blake!" But first I need to text Mike. I ignore the unread texts and write her instead. *Can we talk? Not what it looked like. Things finally on with Blake.* My stomach flips at the admission. Technically I don't know what we are, but I need to convince Mike that I haven't lied to her.

Reece leans between the seats. "Any news?"

I scroll through my texts from Blake.

Still haven't seen him.

His parents here.

Neck not broken. Concussion.

I let out a breath.

They're making us leave.

Talk later?

I blush at the last one. Fortunately it's too dark in the car for them to notice. "He's got a concussion but his neck isn't broken."

Evan visibly relaxes.

"I didn't realize you know them."

"We're not exactly friends, but we see them every weekend. Besides, you never want to see someone get hurt like that."

I know that, and I'm a little irritated that he thinks I don't. "Blake was pretty freaked out."

"Well, yeah. After his brother," Evan says.

"He has a brother?"

"Had."

"What?"

"He hasn't told you?"

I shake my head. Blake had—HAD—a brother and that's why he was freaking out? What happened to him? Each question launches fifty more that won't be answered until I see him again. If he tells me then.

"I'm sure he will."

Reece slides his hand under my arm and pokes me in the armpit.

"Hey!" I squeal, twisting away from him.

"So you and Blake, huh?"

The heat from my face could set the car on fire.

He pokes me again and I smack his hand away. "He's a cool guy. No reason to be embarrassed."

I eye his hand, which is still within reach of tickling me. "I know, it's just... I'm not usually the one with a boyfriend or whatever. Guys don't see me like that."

Evan snorts. "Are all the guys you know blind?"

"Ha, ha."

"No, really. Either they're blind or they're gay, because—"

"You're kind of smoking hot, Cally." Reece interrupts.

"Oh, shut up. Now you're just teasing."

"Teasing, sure." Evan says. "Lying, no."

"And I know hot girls." Reece manages to poke me again and I jump forward, slamming my knee into the dashboard.

"Okay, stop!" I push his hand away and punch Evan's arm for good measure. "Can we talk about something else?"

My phone dings and they burst out laughing. "It's not him."

It's Mike. And she wants to meet.

twenty-two

I've never been this nervous to meet a girl before.

Relax. You said she's cool.

I hate that she might think I went behind her back.

But you didn't.

You and your logic.

It's Sunday afternoon and I'm meeting Mike for coffee in half an hour. Her reply last night gave no indication as to what she's thinking. She suggested coffee and I said yes.

For the millionth time I text *Wish you were here.*

Me too. xoxo

Dad drops me off in front of the coffee shop that's a block away from the brewery. We didn't talk about the stolen recipe—in fact, we really haven't talked since yesterday morning. When I got home from skiing he was on his laptop and I was so tired I passed out right away. I want to ask what this could mean for the business but I'm terrified to find out.

The warm aroma of coffee and fresh pastries greets me when I step inside, but I don't see Mike. The tables along the windows are all taken so I wind toward one in the back corner, which is probably better for talking anyway, and drape my jacket over one of the chairs before heading to the counter to place my order. While the foam machine spurts to life, my gaze drifts out the window to a car double parked in front of the shop. Mike's blond ponytail catches the sunlight as she leans over to kiss her mom on the cheek, and everything inside me goes still. My skin burns, tears sting my eyes, and my breath is lodged somewhere in the lower part of my lungs where it's completely useless to me. It sometimes surprises me how physically acute my longing is to have Mom back. To have the all-encompassing grief replaced with my friends' casual confidence that their moms will be here tonight, tomorrow, next week.

"Miss?"

I startle at the voice from behind the counter.

The barista is holding out a cup. "Your order?" She says it in a way that tells me I was so zoned out I didn't hear her the first few times.

I take the coffee. "Sorry. Thanks."

She smiles and turns her attention to Mike, who's walking through the front door.

"Hey, I'm over there." I point at the corner table.

She glances at the table, but doesn't smile or do anything to indicate that she's happy to be here. "'Kay."

Okay then. I return to the table and stir the whipped cream into my coffee until the liquid is an acceptable shade of light brown. I straighten when Mike sits. "Hi."

"Hi."

We stare at each other for what feels like eons, a thousand starts to the conversation storming through my mind, all of them stupid. I take a deep breath. "I don't really know what to say so I'm just gonna word vomit on you."

The corner of her mouth quirks.

"I don't know why we haven't talked—like, really talked—since my first week here, but I think you're really cool and I thought we could be friends. I meant it when I told you nothing would happen with Evan. Nothing has happened. Blake and I are finally talking and yesterday we kissed."

She raises an eyebrow.

"I know. Evan actually knows about Blake, although not the stuff from before I moved here. And," I pause. She's being so quiet

I have no idea how she'll react to this next part, but if I'm being honest, I need to go all in. "I told him I knew about you two—that you dated—and that I consider you a friend and won't go there."

"You told him that?"

I nod.

Her expression is wary. "I'm almost afraid to ask, but what did he say?"

"I didn't tell him anything about what we talked about, but he seemed surprised. Then when we saw you yesterday when we were leaving he almost acted like he felt guilty."

"Interesting."

"I don't want to make a big deal out of nothing, but I got the feeling that us talking about you has him thinking about you."

She takes a sip of coffee and is quiet for a very long minute. "That would be an improvement." She studies the foam on her coffee. "Do you think he might still have feelings for me?"

Truthfully, I do, but I don't want to get her hopes up in case I'm wrong. "He definitely seemed concerned about you. I say you talk to him. See where it goes."

She stares at her cup without saying anything.

I'm beginning to wonder if I imagined the connection we had. It was one day and I haven't seen a glimpse of that side of her since then. Just when I'm considering abandoning my coffee and going home to work on my English paper, she sighs.

"I'm sorry I've been so distant since..." she waves her hand. "I guess since your first week, huh?" I nod. "It's just, I've been so locked into Bri's world that I stopped trying to be my own person. The whole reason Evan broke up with me is he said I acted too much like her. He wanted the real me, but she's had me so brainwashed that I don't know who that is anymore. When you and I talked that was the first time I felt like myself in months, but Bri put a stop to that. Again." She picks up her cup but sets it back down without drinking. "I hate that she has that kind of control over me but I'm scared what will happen if I actually stand up to her."

My stomach cramps at the memory of standing up to Bri at my party. I'm glad I did it and I'd do it again, but confrontation makes me squirmy. "Have you ever tried?"

She shrugs. "Here and there. Just over stupid stuff, like not going to a party or wearing an outfit."

I shake my head. "Her and those coordinated outfits."

A smile brightens her face. "I know, right?" Then the smile fades. "She's controlled my life for so long that I can't imagine anything else."

"That's depressing."

She stretches out her fingers, studying the cuticles. It feels like she's avoiding looking at me. "I hate feeling like a victim."

I lower my voice. "Is it really that bad?"

Her eyes redden as she nods. "I feel so stupid that I've let it go this far." She looks up and tears shine in her eyes. "I swear I used to have a backbone."

A protectiveness I haven't felt since Sophia got pushed down on the playground in fourth grade pulses through me, heating my skin and making me sit up straight. "I'll help you."

She looks startled. "What do you mean?"

I'm not really sure but words fly out of my mouth. "I'll help you break free from Brianna. I'm fairly confident that after Friday she hates me more than the fact that they don't have class-segregated bathrooms, so now's the perfect time."

She raises an eyebrow. "How so?"

I'm a little surprised she hasn't jumped up to join the revolution. This is uncharted territory for me but I'm so amped I'm ready to rally everyone in the coffee place behind our cause. *Viva la Brivolution!* "Her foundation's crumbling. She'll let you go without much of a fight in order to save face to the rest of the school."

"Appearance is critical for her."

"So it's settled."

"Not so fast."

I lean forward, arms on the table, until my hands are right next to hers. I hesitate at making contact. *What have I got to lose?* I grab her hands and squeeze. She jumps at my touch but doesn't pull away. "The longer you let this continue, the harder it will be."

She takes a deep breath. "So how do we do this?"

I break into a smile. "Really?!"

"I'm glad you're excited." The sarcasm is so thick I can almost taste it.

I need to break her out of this funk. I pump our hands in the air and she laughs. It's a start. "I haven't exactly done this before, but the first step is telling Bri no. You don't have to make a big show of it, but if she tells you to do something you don't agree with, don't do it."

"You make it sound so easy."

I've never really thought about it, but I guess I've always done what I wanted. Maybe it's because Sophia and the guys don't play stupid mind games and have always been there for me, or maybe it's because I learned at a young age that there are more important things in life than earning the approval of a self-involved drama queen. But still, I couldn't imagine cutting myself off from my friends—even though that's basically what I did when we moved here. "It's time you put yourself first. High school is horrific enough without a power-hungry mega-bitch making it worse." I release her hands and take a long drink of my coffee. "I can't promise it won't be awful at first, but how great would it be to spend the next two and a half years doing whatever you want?"

She gets a wistful look on her face and I wonder if she's thinking about Evan. If what she said about the reason for their breakup is true, maybe that can change, too.

After two more cups of coffee and countless scenarios of how the breakup with Bri will play out, we head outside to catch the bus home. We're still debating whether or not Bri's head will spin around on her neck or pop completely off when I get two texts: one from Amber apologizing for not showing yesterday and asking if I can night ski sometime this week, and the other from Blake, asking me on an actual date.

I reply to Amber first. *I'll check with my dad.* I'm staring at my phone, unable to formulate a response to Blake that's more than OMG SQUEE when Mike pushes the button for her stop.

"Everything okay?"

I snap my head up. "What? Oh, yeah. Have you been skiing at Eldora at night?"

"Every now and then, sure. But that's not what's turned you into a pile of mush."

I can't fight the smile that spreads over my face. "I don't know what you're talking about."

The bus slows and she sways with the movement. "I think I've earned the truth."

She's right. I hounded her for an hour—the least I can do is open up about what's going on. "Blake asked me out."

She jumps up and does a little dance as the bus jerks to a stop and she almost falls over. "Cally, that's great!"

"I haven't replied."

The doors swing open. She steps outside but holds onto the railing. "Do it now. That's an order." The doors swing shut and she smiles at me through the glass. Self-esteem looks good on her.

Too bad mine has vanished.

I wait until I'm safely in my room, English paper pulled up on my screen, before writing him back.

A real live date? Sophia would be appalled at my lack of charisma.

I'm finishing describing the inverted iron cross—and trying not to let thoughts of Mom distract me—when he finally writes back.

Is there another kind?

I smile. This isn't the time to confess that I've never been on an actual date. Group dates and hanging out after school, sure. As of right now the only time I've ridden in a car alone with a boy was with him.

What do you have in mind?

So that's a yes?

OMG I haven't said yes. *Yes!*

Dinner? A movie?

Sitting in a dark room with Blake for two hours sounds amazing. *Movies are cool.*

Friday?

I flip onto my back and kick my legs in the air. Then I count to ten. *Cool.*

:)

How's Andrew?

He went home today. Nothing's broken but has concussion and sprained neck. No boarding.

I'm relieved, but I also feel bad for him. It sucks to be out of commission. *I'm glad he's okay.*

Me too.

Did you write your paper?

Writing it now.

See, we're meant to be. And it has nothing to do with the fact that it's due tomorrow and we're teenagers so of course we waited until the night before to write it.

What's your topic?

The day I got my Jeep.

His Jeep! HOW did I forget he has my dream vehicle? And I'm going to ride in it on Friday! I drop my arm over my face. I know he can't see me but I feel like if I don't calm down my crazy excitement will somehow go through the airwaves and freak him out. I take a deep breath. *Nice. Mine is the first time I nailed the inverted iron cross.*

I'd like to see that.

That reminds me. *So you're really not entering the Dash next month?*

No.

Why?

Not my thing.

But you're so good. You'd crush those other guys.

There's a pause before his reply comes through.

I'm not like them. My life is about more than living on the slopes.

Irritation pricks at the back of my neck. Skiing is my life. If I could be out there every day, I would. Does he think he's better than us? *What's that supposed to mean?*

Other responsibilities. Can't do practice during the week.

My anger deflates. *Oh.*

So there's no point.

Not even bragging rights?

:)

You should at least enter.

I dunno.

We'll see. I'm not sure what's taken over me since moving here, but I'm filled with a determination to make him enter. Between him and Mike it's like I'm the Florence Nightingale of teenage self-esteem. *I should finish my paper.*

Me too. See you tomorrow.

I toss my phone onto my pillow and stare at the ceiling.

A real date.

With Blake.

My belly flutters and I flip back over, burying my head in my arms. Five more minutes of fantasizing about next Friday and then I'll get back to work.

***

I hit snooze for the third time and pull the blankets over my head. As excited as I am to see Blake, I dread seeing Brianna. Maybe Mike will stage her revolt first thing in the morning and she'll forget all about me.

You're terrible, I scold myself. Mike is my friend and I promised to stand beside her. If it means I take the brunt of Bri's wrath, so be it. I'm not the one choosing to further disrupt my social standing and possibly lose all my friends. But I don't think everyone will abandon her. Bri and Kenzie will, but the guys don't seem to care about the social hierarchy. Who knows, maybe Evan will give Mike another chance when he sees that she's trying to change.

And while I'm wishing for things, maybe Brianna will hand over Dad's notebook with a little note that says 'My Bad' taped to the front.

The halls at school are unusually quiet. It's like the student body recognizes something big is about to happen and they don't want to disrupt the balance in the force.

Either that, or they want to hear the explosion when it happens.

I find Mike at her locker before the first bell. "How're you doing?"

She shakes her head, her face oddly pale. "I think I might throw up."

I touch her arm. "You're doing the right thing. She's one person. And no one but you gets to control your life. It's time she realizes that."

Her lower lip trembles. "I'm not so sure."

"What happened to what we talked about yesterday?" She can't back down now! And I swear I'm not thinking that because without Mike I won't have any friends. I truly want her to be happy. "I promise I'll back you up."

"I'll try." The corner of her mouth lifts in a small smile. "But I can't promise I won't just run away if she starts screaming."

"She won't scream. She'll want to control the rumors and if she loses her cool everyone will know it's you dumping her, not the other way around."

"Rumors?"

"Well..." I rub the toe of my shoe against the ground. "You know people are going to talk."

She leans her head against the locker and closes her eyes. "This is a terrible idea."

I lean close and whisper in her ear. "It's the only way out."

A snotty voice makes my spine stiffen. "What the hell are you two whispering about?"

Brianna.

I turn to face her and I can feel Mike shrinking against the locker. I nudge her foot with mine and smile at Brianna. "Just how great my party was. It's too bad you had to leave early."

Brianna's face turns from pink to a mottled red that clashes with her fuchsia sweater. She glares at me for one moment... two... three... then turns her attention to Mike. "I told you we're not friends with," she pauses to roll her eyes in my direction, "*her* anymore."

"Last time I checked, you aren't her mother." I don't know where this attitude is coming from. I must be channeling Sophia.

Mike pushes off the locker and crosses her arms over her chest.

"What are you doing?" There's a split-second hitch in Bri's bravado, a quaver in her voice that's almost imperceptible, then she straightens her back and it's gone.

Mike shifts so her shoulder's brushing mine. "I'm talking to Cally. Last time I checked, I can be friends with whoever I want."

Bri's jaw clenches.

This is it.

Her head's going to shoot off her neck.

I'm almost disappointed when it doesn't.

She steps toward us.

Don't step back. Don't step back. From the corner of my eye I notice heads turning our way.

Brianna points her finger at Mike. "We're not doing this right now."

"We're not doing it later, either."

Bri's lips part and she snaps them closed.

I want to whoop and shout I'm so proud of Mike but this isn't over yet.

Bri steps so close I can smell her mouthwash. She wags her finger between me and Mike. "I don't know what's going on here, but this isn't over." She spins around and walks away as the first bell rings.

I exhale. "That went well."

"You call that well?"

"She didn't scream or pull your hair."

She waves her hand at the kids around us. "Only because she had an audience. She isn't gonna let this go that easily."

A locker slams and we both jump. I force a smile. "I'll talk to you at lunch."

I just hope Brianna doesn't corner her in a dark alley before then.

twenty-three

"I'm a nervous freaking wreck. Every time I turn a corner I expect her to be waiting there, ready to attack." Mike is so amped that I didn't put up a fight when she asked if we can eat in the library. We grabbed a table at the end of the stacks in front of a window that overlooks the mountains and is far from the front door. I haven't seen Blake yet today and was hoping to see him at lunch, but Mike's sanity is more important.

"What do you think she'll do?"

"Rip out my heart?"

I snort, almost choking on my sandwich. "I wouldn't put it past her."

She smiles. "It could happen."

"I know it's gonna be awful when she unleashes, but what do you think she'll actually do?"

I find out on the way to English when a foot catches my ankle and I fall directly on my knee. I look behind me to see who it is and spot a blond ponytail whipping through the crowd of kids, but I can't say for sure that it was Brianna. I'd be surprised if she actually did her own dirty work—I'd expect her to send Kenzie or some freshman I don't know—but maybe she's so pissed she wants to see me go down—literally—in person.

I limp into English and for the first time since I started at Monarch, I don't hide that I'm looking for Blake. Our eyes meet and my cheeks flush as I think about our kiss on Saturday.

But he has a different reaction when he sees me: his eyes narrow and his jaw clenches. He's out of his seat and at my side before I have time to contemplate what it means.

"What happened? Why are you limping?"

My heart swells, but I can't tell him. Not until Brianna is done with whatever she has planned. "I tripped in the hallway. Landed on my knee."

"Oh shit." He slips his arm under mine and guides me to my desk. "Do you need to go to the nurse?"

I sit at my desk and run my fingers over my kneecap. It feels swollen but it's been so touchy this year that I won't be able to tell for an hour or so if it's actually serious. "Maybe after class."

He squats next to me and looks into my eyes, his hair falling across his forehead. "I'll help you if you want."

"All right class, take your seats." Ms. Simpson shuts the door and stands at the front of the room. She catches my eye and a soft smile plays over her mouth. "Please pass your papers forward, then open your books to..."

I turn around to look at Blake. He's already handing his paper to the person in front of him, but he catches my eye and gives me another smile.

After class, Blake is at my desk before I even try to stand. He slips his arm around my waist to help me up and his hand settles on the curve of my waist, turning my insides to mush.

"It doesn't hurt that bad anymore."

He tilts his head toward mine and whispers against my ear. "That's okay."

I can't fight the dopey smile that probably tells everyone in the hallway that this boy makes me ga-ga.

He keeps his arm around my waist but lowers it so I can walk normally. "Where's your next class?"

I blank for a moment, too busy scanning the hall for the Snow Bitches. "Um, just around the corner."

"Do you need help?"

As much as I'd love for him to scoop me into his arms, I shake my head. "No. But thanks."

"I'm this way." He points in the opposite direction. "I'll see you later." His hand slides out from around me and runs along my jawline. Everything inside me urges him to kiss me, and he does, but only on the cheek. I guess we're still a little new for PDA.

"Bye." My side is still warm from where he held me. I close my eyes, reliving the sensation of where his lips touched my cheek, and an elbow to the back sends me flying. I don't fall this time, but whoever pushed me is gone by the time I turn around. "Seriously?!" I shout at no one.

A group of freshman girls give me a funny look, but otherwise people ignore me. Just another day in high school.

***

The Attack of the Snow Bunnies is in full effect on Tuesday, and by Wednesday morning Mike is so anxious she's about to crawl out of her skin. "She hasn't said ANYTHING to me. Not a single bitchy thing. This is just weird."

I rub my arm. I've been elbowed, tripped, and straight-out pushed between every class. I haven't fallen again, but only because now I'm ready for it. "I think she's taking most of her anger out on me." A small part of me worries that this is my new reality, that I won't survive high school without Sophia and the guys, but I push it deep inside me and refuse to let it worm its way back up. This won't last.

It can't.

Tears well in her eyes. "I can't believe you're putting up with this."

My chest tightens just thinking about Bri, but it's not like I have a choice. "She can't do this forever. One of these times I'll see her coming and I swear I'll knock her on her bunnied-ass."

"I want to be there for that!"

But the morning is oddly quiet. Mike and I eat in the cafeteria, but as far away as we can get from her former friends. I catch Evan looking at us a couple times, but so far he hasn't approached me. I'm a little surprised he's caving to Brianna after everything he said, but I can't say I blame him. After seeing how she's treating me, maybe he's decided it's easier to be a follower.

But still.

I leave lunch a little early to meet Blake outside of English and breathe a sigh of relief when I see him leaning against the wall, one foot propped up, arms crossed over his chest. He smiles that adorable crooked smile when he sees me. I want to fall into his arms but there are too many people around, even for the end of lunch, plus we haven't really kissed since Saturday and I don't think Ms. Simpson would appreciate having to climb over us to get into her classroom. I settle for stopping inches in front of him.

He scans my face. "Everything okay?"

I haven't told him about the non-stop onslaught, but he has to have heard something by now. "Just a little tired."

"I wish it was already Friday."

Friday, when I can finally escape their harassment, but wait—he's smiling at me again and—*oh! He means our date!* I smile a moment too late. "Me too."

He cocks his head. "You sure?"

"Yes, more than you know." Okay, that might have been overkill, but I can't help it. He's so freaking hot that I just want to—*oops, now I'm touching his chest.* It's like my body has a mind of it's own and—*oh! He's leaning in. Finally!* His lips press against mine and I relax against him. His arms wrap around me and I'm reaching for his face when something hits me in the back of the head and my lip explodes in Blake's mouth.

Blake opens his eyes. "What the hell was that?"

I run my tongue over my lip. Blood. I am freaking bleeding.

That's it. I slam my books on the ground and whirl around. "Enough!" I shout. To my surprise, Brianna's standing there, hands on her hips. Her presence startles me and I lose my momentum. *Why didn't she run away? Why is this time different?*

Blake steps around me and glares at Brianna.

Her steely gaze falters for a beat, but she doesn't back down.

"What. The. Hell. Was. That?" Blake enunciates each word so sharply that Brianna blinks with each one. She glances over her shoulder like maybe she's regretting staying this time, but it's too late now.

She points at me. "Ask your girlfriend."

I shrug. "Brianna's got the hots for me and has reverted to elementary school where you assault the one you love." The look on her face—eyes wide, blush rapidly covering her face—almost makes the abuse worth it.

"I—what?! No!" She steps toward me but Blake blocks her approach. She points a perfectly manicured finger at me. "You know exactly what this is about."

"Yeah, I called you out for being a bitch and—shocking—you've responded by being an even bigger bitch." I'm about to accuse her of stealing Dad's notebook but I suddenly realize that all traffic in the hallway has stopped, pushing the three of us into the middle of an MMA cage. Any minute bets will be placed on who will win. Considering I'm already bleeding, my guess is the odds are in her favor, but they don't know that my body can take a hit and keep going.

Blake looks between us and settles on Bri, but points at me. "I don't know what crawled up your ass and made you worse than usual, but it's gone too far. She's bleeding."

I touch my lip. My finger comes away bloodier than I expected.

Brianna's face shifts from red to ghostly pale in a heartbeat. "She deserves it for—"

A shrill whistle makes everyone jump. "Get to class!" Ms. Simpson stands at the edge of the circle, arms crossed. Her gaze rakes over each student. "Now."

Brianna turns to flee but Ms. Simpson catches her arm. “Not so fast, Miss Vines.” She looks at me, then Blake. “All three of you to the principal’s office.”

The crowd scatters and Blake and I fall in step toward the office, Brianna trailing a dozen yards behind us.

“Are you going to tell me what’s going on?” he says low enough so Brianna can’t hear.

I press my sleeve against my lip, then yank it away. I’ve ruined my favorite sweater! “That bitch!”

“Cally.”

“It’s about Mike.”

“She wasn’t even there.”

“I know. I convinced Mike to break up with the Snow Bitches and they’re taking it out on me.”

He stops with his hand on my arm, then looks back at Brianna and keeps moving. “You’re taking this abuse for someone else?”

“Mike’s the one being abused. I know she’s not like them and I couldn’t sit by and do nothing.” The weight of the past week lightens from finally telling someone. I don’t regret going through this for Mike, but you can only be pushed and tripped for so long before you start to question if it’s worth it.

He squeezes my arm. “She’s lucky to have you as a friend.”

“Only if I survive.”

We enter the principal’s office but Ms. Simpson must not have called down yet because the secretary doesn’t know why we’re there. Brianna enters behind us and I clench my fists at my sides. Falling on her bunny-ass is minor compared to what I want to do to her now.

Blake must notice my reaction because he tugs me to the far end of the office. I glare at Brianna with my arms crossed until Ms. Simpson opens the door.

“We need to see Mr. Taft.”

The secretary ushers us past her desk into the epicenter of the school.

I met the principal my first week, but since then I've only seen him strolling the halls. Word is he likes to mingle with his students so he knows what's going on, but right now his usual relaxed smile is replaced with a scowl. His gaze lands on me and stays there. "Miss Clarke, why are you bleeding?"

I point at Brianna. "She pushed me." I leave out that it was technically Blake's teeth that broke the skin.

He turns to Brianna, but he doesn't just turn his head—his entire body shifts so all his focus is on her. "Is this true?"

Brianna shrugs.

"A verbal answer, please."

"I might have bumped into her when I was adjusting my book bag. The halls were really crowded." Her normally ice-cold expression melts into one of utter sincerity: wide eyes, full lips pulling into a frown, brow creased in concern.

But all I see is her noticeable lack of a book bag.

"Mr. Taft, you know I would never intentionally hurt anyone."

He clears his throat. "What I know is Cally is bleeding and Ms. Simpson felt that whatever happened was bad enough that she's missing class to be here. So let's try again."

Brianna seems to crumble under his stare. Her shoulders droop and the fake frown turns real. "Cally stole my best friend."

I choke on a laugh. *Best friend?*

Their eyes shift to me, waiting for a response. Blake's hand finds the small of my back and I draw courage from his touch. "Mike is not her best friend. She treats her like crap. Granted she hasn't made her bleed..."

Mr. Taft pulls a tissue from a box on his desk and hands it to me. "It sounds like we have some hurt feelings here. High school is a time for discovering who you are and," he pauses, "that often means making new friends. Brianna, I'm sorry if you feel like Cally stole your friend, but I suspect this won't have much effect on your social calendar."

I cover my mouth with the tissue to keep from laughing. He can't know how important that is to her, can he?

"But—"

Mr. Taft cuts her off. "Unfortunately for you, I don't tolerate fighting in my school."

"I told you, I tripped."

Ms. Simpson coughs, covering her mouth with her hand. Her eyes meet mine and I swear she's trying not to smile.

Mr. Taft lowers his head until his chin is almost touching his chest. His stare makes me squirm and he's not even looking at me. "You tripped, or you hit her with your bag?"

"I—" Any attitude left in Brianna dissolves into tears. I'm a little offended she's resorting to this. I figured she had more pride.

"The penalty for fighting is three days suspension, but—"

"What?! I can't be suspended! Do you know what this will do to—"

"BUT," he continues. "Because you seem to regret your error in judgment, I'll shorten it to one day."

The only thing Brianna regrets is getting caught.

If the tears were fake before, they're real now. "Mr. Taft, please don't suspend me. My parents will kill me."

Ms. Simpson touches her back. "Perhaps you should have thought of that before you started bullying Cally."

The word catches me off guard. Everything about Brianna screams bully, but I refuse to believe that's what this is. That would make me a victim. And I'm not a victim.

"I'm not a bully. I told you, I was upset because of Mike." She sniffs as she looks Ms. Simpson in the eye. "I really didn't mean to hurt her."

Maybe getting suspended will snap the attitude out of her. It's doubtful she'll change, but hopefully this thing with Mike will be over.

Mr. Taft sighs. "You're excused. Get a note for your class before you leave. A letter will be emailed to both your parents at the end of the day." He smiles, but it's a sad smile, like he's said these words more often than he'd prefer. "I like to give students a chance to tell their parents first."

Brianna leaves without another word. Mr. Taft looks at me. "How long has this been going on?"

"Just this week."

Blake stiffens. "Is she why you tripped on Monday?"

I nod.

"Do you need to see the nurse?" Ms Simpson asks.

I touch my lip. The bleeding has stopped but it hurts like hell. "I'd just like to get to class."

She looks at Mr. Taft. "I'll have the incident report to you by the end of the day."

"Thank you." We turn to leave but Mr. Taft stops me. "Cally."

I face him.

"Let me know if this continues. I don't tolerate bullying in my school."

"Okay." I hadn't really considered what Brianna was doing to be bullying, but when seen from an adult's perspective, I guess that's what it was. Being surrounded by guys, I never gave two thoughts about being bullied because they always protected me. Another fun thing I've learned at my new school.

Ms. Simpson leads us back to her classroom. "Cally, I'd like to talk to you about your essay."

"Is something wrong?"

"No, quite the opposite. I really enjoyed it. And I must say, I'm a little surprised that anyone who can do the maneuvers you can would put up with someone like Brianna."

"I was trying to help Mike. It seemed like as long as Bri's energy was focused on me, she ignored Mike."

Blake slides his fingers through mine.

She tucks her hair behind her ear. "So maybe what she said about considering Mike to be her best friend was true."

Blake snorts. "She sure has a funny way of treating her friends." The bitterness in his voice is heavier than I've ever heard it.

"That may be true, but maybe it's the only way she knows." She sighs. "But that's not what I wanted to talk to you about.

Can you stop by my class at the end of the day? I'd like to talk to you about your other topics."

I freeze.

Blake's hand is still on mine and my sudden stop jerks his arm. He raises an eyebrow at me.

Mom.

twenty-four

By the end of the day, the entire school has heard about the pseudo-fight and Brianna's suspension. "Her parents really are going to kill her," Mike says. I'm glad Bri got the punishment she deserves, but I'm too focused on talking to Ms. Simpson about my mom to worry about that now.

I knock on the open door to her classroom and she waves me in with a smile.

"Have a seat." She gestures to the seat directly in front of her desk but instead of sitting in her chair, she settles into the desk next to me. Her eyes are bright and she's clutching my paper like it's something far more valuable than a sophomore English essay. "I should start by telling you that I was on the ski team in high school."

"You?"

She gives me the side-eye, but her smile makes it clear she's teasing. "Yeah, me. I was in high school once, too."

I blush, feeling stupid. "Sorry. I guess I never really thought about teachers being kids."

"It's okay. I'm telling you this so you understand why your essay has me so worked up. Cally, I've never met a girl who can do the tricks you describe."

I'm about to rattle off my heroes—Hannah Kearney, Devin Logan—when she continues.

"I know there are professionals, but I've never met one in

person." She shifts in her seat. "I checked with Coach Michaels and he said you're not on the ski team."

Her excitement is contagious, but one mention of the ski team and my energy deflates. "I was on the team back home but I moved here too late to get on this team."

"Have you talked to him?"

I shake my head. "My dad checked before I started classes. I'm planning to enter the Dash at the end of the season. The top finishers from here and Nederland get a guaranteed spot. If it was based on tricks and stuff I'd say yeah, I've got it, but it's not."

"Have you been practicing?"

I shrug. "Not as much as I should. I'm running but the altitude here is killer."

She smiles. "If you don't win, will you still try out next year?"

I cock my head. Not trying out never entered my mind. "Definitely. But if I can get on the team this school year, I can practice with them over the summer."

She straightens my paper. "I'm glad to hear it."

I like Ms. Simpson. It's clear she has an agenda other than my writing prowess but she seems genuinely interested in me—she's not faking like some teachers do.

"The reason I want to talk to you about your other three essays is I want to make sure you branch beyond skiing for your topics. It's clear you have a passion—rightly so—but I want to hear about the other things in your life." She pauses. "Have you given thought to what else you'll write about?"

I knew this was coming, yet I can't stop the anxiety that creeps through my belly, up my throat, thickening my tongue and making it almost impossible to breathe. I nod.

Concern creases her face. She rests her hand on my arm. "What is it?"

I take a shaky breath. "Actually, I need help with my other topics."

Her brows furrow. "This sounds more serious than skiing."

And it all spills out of me. Mom. The accident. How I miss her every day and wish with all my heart that she was still here with me and Dad. How I can't ride on the left side of a car because—even though I never saw her after the accident—all I see is her battered body in the driver's seat. How I've always gravitated toward boys because that's what I know and suddenly I'm at war with the bitchiest girl in school when all I want is to be on the ski team and find friends who are normal.

I wipe my face with my sleeve and sniff loudly.

Ms. Simpson is quiet for a moment longer. "Wow," she says softly. "You're carrying a lot with you."

I sniff again. "The best day of my life was easy. It's the other three that terrify me. I've talked about Mom to lots of people, but I've never written about her. At least not when someone else is going to read it."

"I think it might be good for you to try. And I don't want you to write it with the fear that others will read it. Part of your grade is to read one of your essays to the class, so read the skiing one and the rest will stay between you and me."

I smile, but it's the most pitiful smile known to man. "So which essay should be about her? Worst day, most memorable, or event that changed my life?"

She doesn't answer right away. "Let's use the process of elimination. For which topic can you most easily think of another day?"

"I guess moving here for the event that changed my life. But that's the last one."

"What if I allow you to shuffle the order a bit? That will give you more time to think about the other two."

"Really?"

She rests her hand on my arm. "I'm here to help you become a better writer and hopefully gain some introspection. The order in which you write your essays won't change that." She winks. "Just don't tell the other students."

I slump in my seat, suddenly exhausted. She's so sympathetic that I'm tempted to tell her more about the bullying, to get her perspective on how to survive high school, but I hold back. This is about all I can handle in one day. “Thank you so much.”

“Just promise me one thing.”

“Sure.”

“Save me a seat at the Dash.”

***

My energy slowly returns on the drive to Eldora. Dad’s still quiet, but I can’t tell if his anger about the notebook has faded or if he’s bottled it up so tight that he’s going to explode.

“Dad?”

His eyes move my way, then back to the road. “Yeah, sweetie?”

“Are you ever going to forgive me?”

The car jerks. “What?”

“About the notebook.”

“Cally, what are you talking about?”

“It’s my fault it was stolen. And now I’m not even friends with those girls anymore. It’s like the only reason she talked to me in the first place was to get inside our house.”

“Do you really think that?”

“She’s a total bitch, so yes.”

He laughs softly. “I meant that it’s your fault.”

“I’m the one who let her in the house.”

“Yes, but you can’t control other people’s actions.”

“But the recipe...” I trail off. Because he hasn’t talked to me I still don’t know how this is going to affect the opening.

“Cally, I’m upset it was stolen, yes. But we’ve been working on that recipe for months. Everything’s in the system, safe and sound.”

This eases my anxiety a little, but not completely. “But what if Mischief releases the same beer?”

He shrugs. “We’ll have it first. I’ve met the owner and while I don’t know him well, I get the impression he thinks highly enough of himself that he doesn’t need to rip off a competitor to succeed.”

"But you don't know for sure."

"No, I don't."

"I'm still sorry."

"I know you are. Just do me a favor?"

"Anything."

"Stop hanging out with people who steal from us."

I laugh. "Deal."

Floodlights bathe Eldora, making it look like something out of a movie. A lump catches in my throat. I haven't been night skiing since our first week here, but in Vermont we went every week. Almost every day during the height of the season.

Dad parks in the lot and carries his laptop toward the lodge while I head for the lockers. Amber's waiting inside.

"Hey, you been here long?" I find a clear spot on the wooden bench to change my boots.

She shakes her head. "Just a couple minutes." She claps her hands together. "You ready for some real fun?"

I lift my head to raise my eyebrow at her.

"I'm taking you on the race course!"

I straighten. "Is it set up?"

"No, but I've seen it enough times to know the basic layout. You're still planning to enter the Dash, right?"

I stand and adjust my gear. "I wouldn't miss it for the world."

"Then hurry your skinny ass up and let's go!"

I throw my glove at her face but she catches it before it hits her.

"Come on!"

We take the main lift to the top of the mountain, then skate across the ridge to the slopes on the far end of the resort. We stop in front of a smaller lodge where people are sipping hot cocoa on the deck.

"The past couple years they've run it on Corona or West Ridge. Spectators always complain because they're the farthest from the main lodge, but you can't beat the view."

Colorado is breathtaking from ten thousand feet, but seeing it at night makes the rest of the world melt away. Stars blanket the sky as far as I can see. Darkness surrounds the resort, and even standing on top of the Rockies, I feel small, insignificant. And closer to Mom. Lights from nearby towns mark pockets of life; the largest and farthest away is Boulder.

My emotions are still all over the place from earlier and my body feels sluggish. "Where do you live?" I ask, stalling.

Amber points toward Boulder. "Just up the main road. You probably blinked on your way here and missed it." I don't respond and Amber nudges me. "Hey, you okay?"

I bounce on my knees. Maybe if I go through the motions my body will remember what it's supposed to do. "It's just been a long day."

This time her hand stays on my arm. "It's more than that. Is it about the party?"

The party seems like eons ago. So much has happened since then, but Mom is still at the front of my thoughts. I know I can trust Amber, but I don't want to get into all that for the second time today. "It's not a big deal. Oh, but Brianna got suspended today."

"Since when do they suspend people for being a bitch?"

I point at my lip. "When you push someone and make them bleed."

"Oh, shit." She peers at my mouth, frowning. "That can't feel good."

"Eh, I've had worse." I don't mention what I was doing when my lip split open, but I can't stop the blush that warms my cheeks.

"But other than your busted lip, you're okay?"

"Let's take this one a little slower."

She drops her hand and adjusts her goggles. A smirk dances on her lips. "I'm not making any promises." She drops over the edge and I follow close behind. We cut across the powder in an elegant game of follow the leader, Amber weaving around skiers like they're standing still, her wide arc blazing a trail that's easy for me to find, even under floodlights. My heart rate slows as our speed increases. I'm finally in the groove. My body reacts on its own—left foot lifting slightly off the ground when I cut right, then pressing hard when I shift to the left—as if the sound of fiberglass scraping over snow is all I needed to find my balance.

We crest a smaller hill and Amber crouches low to her board. "Oh, no you don't." I lower into a tuck and point my skis straight down the hill. Trees and skiers and light poles flash by in a blur—all I see is Amber up ahead. My heart flutters and I take a short breath as a sensation like runner's high sweeps over me. Here, when I'm flying down a mountain on the edge of losing control, is where I can almost feel Mom's arms around me.

The moment doesn't last long enough. I want to whisper to her about Blake and the stolen notebook and how my friends back home are moving on without me, but Amber rounds a bank of trees and the chairlift comes into view. I blink away tears and tuck tighter, intent on passing Amber before we reach the bottom.

She must sense my approach because she speeds up. She crosses the invisible finish line—the chairlift booth—a length ahead of me and we spray each other with snow as we stop. She laughs as we join the line for the lift. "Man, I wasn't sure what to expect from you. Usually you can do tricks or race, not both. But you..." she trails off, watching me.

I wipe the snow off my ski with my pole. My throat is still tight and it's hard to talk. I shouldn't bring this up when my emotions are all over the place, but I want to hold onto Mom as long as I can. "My mom taught me to ski as soon as I could walk. She was big time back in the day and I've always wanted to be like her."

We slide forward in line and the chair swings around, scooping us high into the night air.

"You've never mentioned her before. Are your parents still together?"

"She died when I was eight." It shouldn't still hurt to say those words, but fifty feet in the air—the place she loved most—it nearly breaks my heart all over again.

"Oh, wow. I'm sorry."

I shrug. The lump in my throat tightens.

Amber drags her hand back and forth across the safety rail. "Do you..." she takes a breath. "Do you want to take a break?"

I know that's the last thing she wants so I appreciate the offer. I smile, but my skin feels tight, like it's fighting being happy. "Actually, I feel her the most when I'm up here. In the air." I wave my hand at the dark trees lining the chairlift's path. "This is where she loved to be."

"That's awesome you still feel connected to her like that."

I hold back the protests that flood to my lips. It's not enough. It'll never be enough. It's been seven years and her death still feels raw, like a piece was ripped out of my heart. Everyone assured me it would get easier with time, but I sometimes worry I'll never move on.

Amber twists on the narrow seat to face me. "Hey, seriously. We can go hang in the lodge."

And then Dad will see me and wonder what's wrong. "No, I'll be okay. I don't talk about her much and this is the second time in a couple hours. I just feel a little off."

"I know the cure for that."

I raise an eyebrow, even though she can't actually see my eyes because of my goggles. "What's that?"

"A race."

"Oh, you're on." Nothing—not even getting all weepy-eyed over Mom—can turn off my competitiveness once a challenge has been made. I straighten, readying myself to dismount. Excitement worms through my body, shaking off my funk. I bounce on the seat.

Amber laughs. "That's all it takes to perk you up?"

"What can I say? I'm not very complicated."

"I like that about you."

I smile at her as the end of the lift nears. My skis hit snow and we round the tiny chairlift house in unison. Amber drops to her butt to hook into her board, then we're standing at the edge, our breath fogging in the air before us.

"Rules?" I ask.

She touches her gloved finger to her chin. "Don't wipe out?"

I bark out a laugh. "I don't plan to."

"Then let's go. On your mark, get set..." We ready ourselves to push off. "Go!"

I launch over the edge and feel a twinge of guilt at how quickly I pick up speed. Everyone knows skis are faster than boards—and Amber has to know that too—but that doesn't mean I'm gonna hold back.

I follow the same route as before. The people who were on this run the last time seem to have disappeared and it's like the mountain is here just for me. I stay in my tuck, picking up speed with each shift of my weight, everything else around me a blur. I crest a hill and catch air, soaring over the snow. I don't consider this a real jump—not compared to what I do on the terrain park—but the rush is the same. All adrenaline and the feeling like my heart's going to explode with happiness.

I can hear Amber's board behind me, but she's far enough back that I know I've got this. Even so, I keep my skis straight until I'm almost to the bottom, then stop in a spray of powder.

"You cheated!"

I flip up my goggles. "What? No, I—"

She throws snow at my face. "I'm kidding. You smoked my ass."

"Did you expect anything less?"

She nods at the lift. "Ready to go again?"

We run the course a dozen more times, until my legs are wobbling and I can barely stand. So of course we do one more. We're standing at the edge of the line for the chairlift and I lean forward, stretching the back of my legs. My knee's on the border between total exhaustion and holy hell, what are you doing to me. "Can we call it a night? My knee's ready to give out."

"Why didn't you say anything? Do you have problems with it?"

I shrug. "I do jumps. I have bad knees. Comes with the territory."

She rests her hand on my arm. "You should have told me." Her eyes focus on mine through our goggles. "Seriously. We're just having fun. I don't want you to risk an injury."

I smile. "Now you sound like my dad."

"He cares about you. I get that." She moves closer. "You've got snow all over your face." She brushes her glove over my cheek and before I realize what's happening she's leaning closer and her lips are touching mine and OMG what the hell is going on? Her lips are soft and way more gentle than any boys' but... but...

I pull back gently. Her eyes flutter open and she watches me with wary eyes. "Amber..." I don't know what to say, but the fact that I'm not smiling probably says enough.

She backs up. "I'm sorry. I thought... I guess I... I'm so sorry." She looks around, as if suddenly realizing there are other people around us. A few watch with curiosity, but for the most part no one's paying us any attention. Her gaze skitters over my face, to the ground, to her hands.

I hold up a hand between us. "It's not a big deal."

"I was sure—omigod, I'm such an idiot." She turns away, pushing off in the direction of the lodge.

"Amber, wait!" I hurry after her and yank on her jacket but she doesn't slow down. There's no easy escape when you're on the side of a mountain, plus she can only go so fast on her board, and I match her pace. "It was a mistake. It's not like you bombed a plane. Just forget it."

"I totally screwed things up."

When a friend you aren't interested in kisses you—nah, forget it. I don't have a rule for that!

Slope Rule #9: Make the best of a bad situation.

I can't hold back a laugh. "Maybe if you'd slipped me some tongue, but you didn't."

Her jaw drops. *Is she deciding she hates me?*

We move in silence, my comment growing more and more awkward as the minutes tick by. Finally, she sighs. "I feel really stupid."

"Don't.

"I'm terrible at this. I brought Bethany to your party to help me figure out if you were interested, but she spent most of the time talking to that guy Austin and didn't pay attention to you."

How could she think I was interested? Blake was there and as much as I tried to hide it, it was pretty obvious I'm into him. Oh—but she left right when he got there. And since we're not in the same school she wouldn't know. "I'm really sorry if I sent you mixed signals. This just shows how bad I am at relationships."

She risks a glance at me. "Why do you say that?"

I hesitate. Telling her about Blake when she's already upset is a total dick move.

She stops, and I pause next to her. "Cally, just tell me what's going on."

"There's this guy. The one who was at the door when you were leaving."

"Blake?"

"You know him?"

"Sure, he and Luke are always falling all over their asses on the terrain park."

I laugh. "That sounds about right."

"So you like him?"

"There's a little more to it than that, but..."

"Are you in love with him?"

Am I? It seems like a heart can't break as badly as mine did if I was just in like with someone. I sigh. "I don't know."

"But something's going on?" Her face is unreadable.

I don't want to hurt her more than I already have. It must've taken a lot of guts to kiss me—even more than kissing a guy—but she knows Blake better than any other girl I've met and maybe she can help me figure him out. So I tell her our long, drawn-out saga. I conclude with "We're going on our first real date this Friday, but I worry that whatever issues he hasn't told me about are going to get in the way."

She sinks to the ground. "Wow."

"Sorry to dump all that on you." I pop out of my skis and sit next to her.

She digs her fingers into the snow, flicking it into the air. "Blake's a cool guy but he's definitely got a hangup about money.

I've never understood it, but our schools are different. We don't have the 'rich bitches', as he calls them."

Is that what he thinks I am? A rich bitch?

"It sucks that he treated you the way he did. If it seems like he's opening up, I'd say go for it, but you tell me if he pulls that crap again and I'll take out his kneecaps."

I burst out laughing. The rush of endorphins feels good after having my emotions on full throttle all day. "Please don't hurt his kneecaps."

She rolls her eyes and smiles. "Maybe just an ankle."

My phone dings in my pocket. I check my texts. "It's my dad. I need to go."

We push ourselves to our feet and continue the trek back to the lodge. We stop outside the lockers, neither of us ready to go inside. Amber fidgets with the lift ticket on her pocket, once again refusing to meet my eyes. "Are we okay?"

"Yes. I swear."

"Will you be here Saturday?"

"As if my life depended on it. And hey, thank you for taking me through the runs tonight. I still need more practice, but I feel a lot better about the competition."

She snorts. "You could win that tomorrow on your wobbly legs."

"Ha, right. But I appreciate your confidence."

"So you're sure we're cool?"

"Seriously. Forget it." I lean forward and give her a quick hug. "I'll see you Saturday."

***

The next day is oddly calm. The halls are free of random arms and legs pushing and tripping me, and I go about my day like a normal student. "I could get used to this," I say to Mike at lunch. We're still sitting at the table on the other side of the cafeteria, but for the first time this week, I don't feel the need to keep an eye on the Bunnies. Of course, that could be because Brianna's home serving her suspension and it's only Kenzie today.

"I doubt it'll last. Bri puts on a good show for the teachers, but she'll consider this the ultimate humiliation." She lowers her voice like Darth Vader. "You will pay."

I snort, almost choking on my water. "Awesome. Can't wait."

"How was skiing last night?"

It's on the tip of my tongue to tell her about Amber, but I hesitate. I'm ninety-nine percent certain I can trust Mike—at this point I'm her only friend and alienating me would really make things suck for her—but some people get all weird about homosexuality. I'd peg Mike for the "you do you" crowd, but you never know. And while I don't tolerate homophobes, I'm a tiny bit afraid to lose *my* only friend.

"It was good. Amber showed me the race course so I ran that until I practically collapsed." I rub my thighs under the table. "I used to train a lot harder than I've been. I'm a little worried I won't be ready in a month."

"Cally, I've seen you ski. You have nothing to worry about."

I smile.

My good mood carries me to English, where Blake's waiting outside the classroom. "How's your lip?"

"See for yourself." I stick out my lower lip. There's a tiny cut from his tooth, but the swelling is mostly gone so it's not noticeable.

"I think I need a closer look."

My stomach flip-flops as he leans toward me. He doesn't kiss me, but his face is so close I can feel his breath. Everything in me tingles and my eyes flutter closed and—

"Didn't you two learn anything yesterday?" Ms. Simpson's standing in the doorway, arms crossed. A smile dances on her lips.

Heat flames my cheeks and I duck my head. "Sorry." I hustle past her into the classroom and don't look up until I'm in my seat. I look to see if Blake's as embarrassed as I am but he just gives me his lopsided smile.

I spend the rest of the class in a puddle on the floor.

The next day I bounce out of bed, dance through my shower, and practically float to my locker. Today's our date! I love seeing Blake at school, but being alone with him, away from everyone else... I shudder just thinking about it.

"You're in a good mood today." Mike raises an eyebrow at me.

"I'm going out with Blake tonight."

"Ooh, do tell. Where are you going?"

I pause. "I have no idea. He mentioned dinner and a movie but that's all I know."

She gives me a soft smile. "Sounds perfect to me."

I dump my stuff in my locker and we're heading down the hall when someone hits my arm and my books go flying.

Seriously?

I whirl on Brianna. "I guess you didn't spend your day at home thinking about how to stop being a bitch."

Brianna ignores me and glares at Mike. "So you're a dyke now?"

She startles. "What?"

Brianna nods in my direction but doesn't look at me.

I roll my eyes. "I'm not gay."

She scoffs. "That's not what I heard."

"I think your ponytail's pulling your brain out of your head."

She finally faces me. "I heard from a very reliable source that you were making out with that freak snowboard chick." She angles her head so she's looking down her nose, daring me to challenge her.

"We weren't making out."

Her eyes light up. "But you don't deny you kissed her!"

"I didn't kiss her."

"I have proof that you did." Everything seems to move in slow motion. Brianna reaches into her back pocket and pulls out her phone. Pulls up a photo. There's the base of the chairlift. There's me. And there's Amber, her lips on mine.

I straighten my shoulders. Amber's my friend and I'm not letting Brianna trash her reputation or mine. "Like I said, I didn't kiss her. She kissed me, but it was a misunderstanding." I smirk. "Don't tell me you've never made out with a girl. Just for fun? You know, just to see what it's like?"

Her face turns bright red and her mouth falls open. "I would never!" Mike chokes back a laugh and Brianna points a finger at her. "Don't even think about it."

Woah. Looks like I hit closer to the truth than I expected. "So I guess if anyone is turning Mike gay," I air quote that part, "it's you. Not me."

"I am not—I didn't—" She stops mid-sentence, gives each of us her deadliest glare, then turns on her heel and stalks away.

Mike and I exhale at the same time.

"Did you two really kiss?"

"For like two seconds in eighth grade. She heard about older girls making out at parties for attention and wanted to try it, but she never brought it up again." We pause at the corner that leads to her class. "Are things okay with you and Amber?"

"Yeah. She was super embarrassed but I'm not freaking out over it."

"That's cool of you."

"You're just saying that because I helped you escape the Bunny cult."

She laughs and gives me a quick hug. "Yes, yes I am."

The warning bell rings and we head our separate ways. The butterflies kick into full force as I enter English.

T minus six hours until the date.

twenty-five

Skinny jeans. Boots. Shirt and scarf that look good but don't look like I'm trying too hard.

Hair?

Down.

Perfect.

Were you this nervous for your first date with Jake?

Worse.

How is that possible?

I couldn't talk to you about it.

I stop in the middle of my room. *I'm a shitty friend.*

We already went over this. You were just a little self-absorbed.

Shitty friend.

Tomato tomahto.

I laugh.

Are you gonna tell him about Amber?

I think he has enough self-esteem issues without worrying that I'm switching teams.

Touché.

What are you guys doing tonight?

We're at a party.

I check the time. *Shitty friend forgot about time difference.*

The guys say hi.

Send me a pic! While I've talked to Sophia every day, I've barely heard from Hunter, Sam, or anyone else. It's like once I moved they forgot I ever existed and—

A picture comes through and I tap it to make it full-screen. Everyone's there, plus a couple girls I don't know squeezing themselves in on the ends. They're all smiling at something beyond the camera—it's like she caught them in the middle of something that was going on, rather than them stopping and posing for me. I should be happy they're happy—that's how a real friend would react—but instead a knot of jealousy works its way up my stomach to the back of my throat until tears burn my eyes.

Looks like fun! I text, thankful that she can't see my face.

Wish you were here!

xoxo.

I press my hands under my eyes, willing the redness that I know is there to go away. I'm supposed to be happy. I'm about to go on my first real date. I shouldn't be feeling sorry for myself because all my friends have forgotten about me.

I'm heading downstairs when my phone dings again. This time it's Mike.

Have fun tonight!

Thanks babe!

I settle at the kitchen counter until I hear an engine in the driveway. Nerves have me so worked up I almost can't move. I take a deep breath, smooth my jeans over my legs, and head for the front door. "Bye, Dad!" I yell down the hall.

He steps out of his office and points at me. "Be safe."

I'm reaching for the handle when the doorbell rings and my heart stutters.

This is finally happening.

I open the door and a blast of cool air chills me. Blake's standing on the front porch, hands shoved in his pockets, his lopsided smile waiting for me. His eyes lower for a beat before meeting mine. "Hey."

I step outside and pull the door closed behind me. "Hey."

His orange Jeep sits in the driveway, its chest all pumped out, ready for whatever we throw at it. The paint is faded and there's rust in a couple spots, but it's still the most amazing vehicle I've ever seen.

Blake slips his arm through mine and guides me to the passenger side. "Do you like Italian?"

My stomach growls. Per Sophia's advice I haven't eaten since lunch. "Carbs are my best friend."

He smiles. "Good." He opens the passenger door, helps me inside, then strides to the driver's side while I fasten my seatbelt. I'm thrown back to the second day I knew him, over Thanksgiving, and too many emotions get clogged in my chest. Even though I knew nothing would come of it, I fell hard and he broke my heart. Yet here I am, sitting in his car, on our way to dinner like it's the most normal thing in the world. Excitement over what might happen tangles with what already has and I blink back tears.

His hand slides over mine and he squeezes my fingers before he puts the Jeep in gear and we roll out of the driveway. A cloud blankets the moon, making the night sky darker than normal. He peers at the sky through the windshield. "Looks like it's going to snow."

Emotions be damned, I lean forward to take in the view. The cloud shifts and a canopy of stars stretch as far as I can see. "It's so beautiful." The clarity of the Colorado sky still catches me off-guard. Despite the occasional streetlight, darkness envelops us, cocooning us in our own tiny universe where nothing is impossible.

His hand reaches for mine, then he pulls my hand to his lips and presses a kiss to the tips of my fingers. I stifle a sigh, not wanting him to know how he's affecting me. I mean, I've been a puddle of mush since I met him but I wouldn't mind hanging onto a tiny shred of dignity.

Snowflakes dance across the windshield as we drive to the restaurant, making the night feel even more surreal. He parks in a lot across the street from an Italian restaurant lit with strings of tiny lights and we step into a snow globe. He tries to cover my head with his arm but I push him off.

"Come on." I break into a run across the street and we're laughing by the time we're under the awning. I stop to shake snow out of my hair and Blake slips his arm around my waist, pulling me against him. I look up as his eyes drift shut and his mouth closes in on mine.

His kiss is soft, and far too brief. His mouth moves to my ear and I hear him chuckle. "Everyone's watching us."

I twist around. The people seated at the tables along the window most definitely got a show. I press a kiss to his cheek. "Pause 'til later?"

I feel his smile against my cheek. "I'm holding you to that."

We go inside and follow the host to our table, then order an obscene amount of pasta from a waitress not much older than us. Once she leaves us alone I allow myself to look directly at Blake. Part of me fears that looking directly into his eyes will make me spontaneously combust, but we are on a date and it'd be weird for me to not make eye contact.

"How's Andrew?"

His face lights up. "He was supposed to be back at school today but begged his mom to let him have the full week off school."

"So he's okay?" Relief sweeps through me. I haven't been able to get the image of the unconscious boy out of my head. As a skier, thinking too much about what can happen if you land wrong can be more than just dangerous. It can be deadly.

"As okay as he was before." He laughs. "The first run this season he'd barely strapped on his board when he biffed a jump and broke his arm."

"Maybe someone should teach him how to land."

He holds up his hands. "I'm trying. Believe me."

By the time our food arrives, Blake's told me so many stories about the Half-Pipes that I feel like I know them better than Blake. And when he's not talking about his groupies, he's deflecting questions about himself. I keep trying to bring the conversation back to him, or get him to talk about his brother, but all he gives are one sentence answers before flashing that charming smile. I'm worried that he'll know all my secrets by the end of dinner and I'll barely know a thing about him.

When the check arrives, I pull a twenty from my wallet and set it on the table.

His brow furrows. "What are you doing?"

I tilt my head.

"I can afford to buy you dinner."

"I know—I just—"

"I have a job. I've got money."

"What?"

He pushes my money toward me and I slip it into my hand. I've got the sinking feeling that I've done something wrong but I don't understand what.

"I didn't mean to upset you."

"It's not your fault." He runs his hand through his hair. "It's me. I—"

"My dad never lets me leave without money and this is my first date so I guess I didn't think about whether you would pay for me." Sophia didn't tell me what to do when the check came and I sure as hell wasn't going to ask Dad. My cheeks are on fire and I'm sure he's about to leave me here when he laughs softly.

"Can we skip the movie?"

Panic grips me and I avoid his gaze as the magic from the past hour slips away. I screwed this up worse than I thought. Not only is he laughing at me, he doesn't want to spend any more time with me. "I—I guess." I blink rapidly, fighting back tears. *Save them for home.*

"Hey," he says softly. His hand grazes mine and I look up. He nods at the picture window overlooking the sidewalk. "I thought it'd be nice to walk around in that instead."

The snow is heavier than before. Any normal person would hibernate inside near a roaring fire, but I've never claimed to be normal. Snow is in my blood. "On one condition."

"Name it."

"You finally tell me the truth."

His smile fades.

"You owe it to me."

He drops his gaze to our hands and the panic bounces back. Maybe I've pushed him too far, but I'm done with tiptoeing around whatever it is that made him act like nothing happened between us.

"Blake?"

"Let's go."

Go home? Go for a walk? Where are we going?!

I follow him to the door. He pauses beneath the awning where we kissed earlier. "You're right."

At this point I'm so worked up I don't even remember what I said. "I am?"

"I owe you an explanation."

"Oh. Yeah."

He steps onto the sidewalk and it's like we've entered another world. He holds out a hand. "Walk with me?"

A girly squeal ricochets inside my head as I slip my hand into his. Snow covers the sidewalks and clumps in the trees that line the street, blurring their tiny lights, and the roads haven't been plowed since we've been inside. Soft light glows from the restaurant and bar windows along the street, but we're the only ones outside. "It's so beautiful."

"I love being outside before anyone else has touched the snow. It's like my own universe where anything can happen and..." he trails off.

I squeeze his hand. "I know what you mean." We cross the street to the pedestrian plaza, where the statues bury their faces beneath pillows of snow. I tug him under a tree and a flurry of snow shields us from the rest of the world. I look up at Blake. This moment is so perfect that I don't want to ruin it by bringing up the past, but I need answers.

I start easy. "Tell me about your job."

"That's not what you want to know."

"Sure I do."

He sighs. "My parents own a restaurant a couple blocks from here. I wait tables on weeknights and sometimes on the weekends if someone calls in. It's not exciting, but it pays for gas."

I caress my thumb over the back of his hand. "And this."

He smiles. "And this." He takes a deep breath and stares into my eyes, but several moments pass and he doesn't say anything. He leans his forehead against mine. His voice is soft. "I'm a dumbass."

"I was thinking idiot, but we can use your word."

He laughs. "I don't know where to start."

I pull back so I can see his eyes. "How about what you were thinking that first day when I called your name and you walked away?" In an instant, sadness pushes its way into my chest. I can still picture his face: confusion, then... nothing, because that's when Brianna staked her claim on me.

His smile fades and he closes his eyes, as if he's remembering. "I couldn't stop staring at you all through class. I knew you'd be here and that we might have a class together, but I wasn't prepared for you to BE here."

I swallow the impulse to shove him away from me and into the snow. I take a deep breath and let him continue.

"Luke wouldn't stop kicking me, like I was supposed to get up in the middle of class and be like, 'Hey, remember me?'" I smile. "I didn't know if you ever wanted to talk to me again. When you said my name, I couldn't believe it, but before I could say anything Brianna grabbed you and tried to kill me with her Medusa glare."

"Yeah, what's that about?" I know what Mike told me, but I'm curious what he thinks.

"Typical middle school bullshit. She's always been bossy and what-not, but we were in ski club together so I was sort of friends with them." He hesitates and looks over my shoulder, avoiding my eyes. "Then the summer after seventh grade, she decided I wasn't good enough to be her friend anymore."

"Just like that?"

He shrugs, and I know in my gut he's leaving something out.

I touch his cheek. "What happened?"

He takes a deep breath and meets my gaze. "Have you heard about my brother?"

"Just that—that he died." I try to hide my surprise. What does this have to do with Brianna?

He nods. "Brianna and I used to hang out a lot. At one point I thought she liked me, but nothing happened. You know how middle school is." I nod, even though up until Blake, high school has been like that for me too. "Since it was summer, I was in charge of watching Cody. We decided to bike to Eldorado Canyon to go hiking and Brianna wanted me to leave him home, but he was only nine and my parents made me take him everywhere with me.

"It was a perfect day—one of those you wish would never end. Bri packed a lunch so we hung out near a creek so Cody could play." My stomach twists at the picture he paints—he and Brianna all cozy under a tree, kind of like we are now—but I dread where this is going. "On the trail back to our bikes, Brianna kept slowing down. I thought maybe she'd twisted her ankle but when I stopped to see if she was okay—" he breaks eye contact. "She kissed me. And that's when we heard Cody scream."

My mouth falls open.

Blake blinks rapidly, as if he's fighting off the memory. "He'd been walking on this stone wall along the edge of the trail. One minute he was jumping from rock to rock, and the next he fell down the ravine."

"Oh my god."

"I jumped down after him. That's how I got this." He taps the chipped tooth that I previously thought was adorable. Now I see it as a painful reminder of what he went through. "He was still breathing when I got to him, but—" He stops again.

"You don't need to keep telling me this."

He squeezes my hand. "He died on the way to the hospital."

"Blake, I'm so sorry."

He bites his lip, his eyes searching mine. "When you told me about your mom, I knew I'd met someone who got it. Who understood what it's like to have someone you love ripped out of your life."

I nod, unable to find words. I remember being amazed that Blake appreciated the connection I have with Mom, but I never imagined this is why. "So what happened with Brianna?"

The softness leaves his eyes. "She was a wreck. We both were. But she handles grief differently than we do."

My breathing stills. "What did she do?"

He clenches his jaw and his grip on my hand tightens. "When we were waiting for my parents at the hospital, she said that if my family had money, Cody would have been with his nanny instead of us and this never would have happened."

I gasp. "She—she actually said that?"

"I didn't see her again until the start of eighth grade. That's when she came up with the Snow Bunnies and Moguls, and started calling me and Luke the Ski Bums. We've hated each other ever since."

"I knew she was a bitch, but this goes beyond anything—I just. I can't even believe it."

"You're the first person to stand up to her for as long as I can remember."

I run my fingers over the zipper of his coat. I feel more drawn to him than I did before, but that doesn't erase how he treated me. "Getting your heart broken does weird things to people. I guess I figured I didn't have anything else to lose."

His breath catches. "Hey." He lowers his head so he's looking me in the eyes. "I'm really sorry. I wish I could take back the past month—well, the past two months—but I don't know how."

My throat tightens and my voice comes out high-pitched. "You didn't talk to me. Not once."

His jaw clenches. "Can you forgive me?"

I break eye contact, focusing on the lights in the tree fuzzy with snow. Or maybe they're blurry because of the tears in my eyes. I blink several times to get myself under control. "I want to, but telling me you ignored me for a month because you thought I was friends with the Bunnies—I mean, I get it. She was beyond horrible to you. But it isn't enough. You really hurt me and I don't—I can't go through that again."

He touches my cheek, tilting my head so I'm looking at him again. "What else can I do?"

"Tell me what you were thinking. Did you want to talk to me? If I hadn't invited you to my party, would you have ignored me forever?"

He bites his lower lip, studying me. "Let's come back to the first one. Then yes, and no."

I mentally replay my questions. "Okay."

"As for what I was thinking, mostly just how stupid I am."

"You're not stupid."

"Okay, what a heartless bastard I was being."

The corner of my mouth turns up. "That's more accurate." He presses his hand to his heart like I wounded him and I shrug. "Your words." I rest my hand on his. "So there you were, being a heartless bastard and..." I raise my brows.

"I figured I'd screwed things up so bad that you'd never talk to me again. It was torture having you sit so close, where I could watch you and—" he stops, his cheeks reddening.

I smile. "Go on."

He turns his hand and slips his fingers through mine. "Cally, I told you before that I've never met anyone like you. I didn't think you'd ever forgive me. I guess I didn't try because I was afraid of what you'd say."

"And now?"

"I still can't believe you're here."

"Here in Colorado? Or here, like under this tree in a snowstorm with you?"

"Both."

"So now the big question." I take a breath as he watches me. "How are you going to make it up to me?"

Our eyes lock and everything around us comes to a stop. I realize he's going to kiss me a split second before his mouth touches mine, and I tilt my head up to meet him halfway. His arms slide around me, pulling me close, and I melt against him. The faint scent of garlic drifts between us and I mentally thank Sophia for suggesting I let him try my food so we both smell like it. Then his mouth parts and all thoughts of Sophia vanish. I move my arms around his neck and weave my fingers through his hair as his tongue touches mine. Electricity shoots from my toes straight through my body and I tighten my grip in his hair. He sighs softly against my mouth and my body reacts on its own, pressing against his chest. He spins me around and leans me against the tree, never breaking the kiss. A blanket of snow falls from the branches and we both jump.

"Gah!" Blake runs a hand over his hair, brushing out the snow.

I shake my head, sending snow down the back of my coat. I yelp and he cracks up.

"You'd think we'd be used to this."

I smooth out my hair. "You saying I need to wear a helmet on our next date?"

He smiles, and my stomach purrs when I realize what I said. He lifts his hand to wipe snow off my forehead, then slides it down until he's cupping my cheek and kisses me again. "Maybe we should find protection," he whispers against my lips.

"What?!" I push him away, mouth hanging open. "How do you get from kissing under a tree to—"

He points at the sky, a huge smile on his face.

"From the snow."

He nods.

"Omigod." *Quick! How can I shove my foot deeper into my mouth?* I reach for his jacket and pull him back to me. I tuck my head under his chin. "I'm sorry."

Laughter rumbles in his chest.

"Please say something."

"You're adorable when you're embarrassed."

I swat at his arm. "Not helping." I squint up at him. "And who uses that word when they're talking about the snow?"

"I'm broadening my vocabulary."

"Mm-hmm."

"So whaddaya say? Head back to the Jeep?"

"If you can find it out here."

He grabs my hand and tugs me into the blizzard.

By the time we reach the car, we're covered from head to toe and the magic of walking in our own personal snow globe has worn off. I'm shivering and wet and, despite yelling at him for suggesting such a thing earlier, I really want to get out of these clothes.

He starts the engine but doesn't put it into drive. His thumb picks at a piece of black tape wrapped around the shifter. "Do you want to get coffee or something? It's still early."

"Coffee sounds wonderful, but I'm soaked."

He frowns. "Do you want me to take you home?"

"I do, but I don't." Sitting in front of the fire sounds like the perfect way to end the night, but only if he comes with me. "Would you, uh, want to come over? You could borrow some of my dad's clothes while we..." I trail off as the image of us making out in front of the fire distracts me.

"While we what, Cally?" His teasing tone makes me blush even harder.

I smack his arm. "Oh, shut up. You were thinking it, too."

He chuckles and puts the car in drive. I send Dad a quick text to let him know we're on our way. He sends back a thumbs-up emoji, but I know it won't be that simple.

When Blake pulls into my driveway, I have to unstick myself from the seat. I hurry to the front door before my wet clothes freeze, and wait for him to join me.

He closes the door and brushes a kiss on my cheek. "You're sure your dad's okay with me coming over?"

"I can't promise he won't grill you a little." There was so much unsaid in that thumbs-up.

He runs a hand through his damp hair. "Can't wait."

I touch his hand. “I’ll protect you. Now let’s find you some clothes.” I lead him upstairs. “Wait here.” I step into Dad’s room and start opening drawers.

“Ahem.”

I jump.

Dad’s leaning on the doorframe, eyebrow raised.

I straighten. “Hey, Dad. You remember Blake?”

Blake stretches out his hand. “Sir.”

Dad shakes it and gives a little nod. “Do I want to know what you’re doing?”

“Looking for clothes for Blake to borrow. Where are your track pants?”

“Bottom drawer.”

“Bingo!” I hold up a pair of track pants and a hoodie—Dad’s go-to comfy outfit. “We got soaked in the snow so I invited Blake over and said he could wear something of yours while he’s here.”

“Sounds harmless enough.”

My eyes go wide and Blake shifts on his feet. “Dad!”

Dad smiles. “Meet me in the living room once you’ve changed. I have something... interesting... to tell you.”

He knows I have no patience for secrets. This is probably just a ploy to make sure we don’t linger with our clothes off—but it works. I show Blake to the bathroom and hand him the clothes. “See you in a minute.” I face Dad. “Do you really have something to tell me?”

“I do.” He tilts his head at the closed door. “And now I have a few questions of my own, but they can wait.”

I turn toward my room.

“Cally?” Dad’s voice is low. “I want to see you happy, but are you sure you want to go down this road again?”

I glance at the very non-soundproof door and nod. The little voice in my head warns that maybe Dad has a point, but I mentally tell her to shut her trap.

“Okay, I’ll see you downstairs.”

In my room, I peel off my clothes and toss them on the floor. Old Faithful calls longingly to me, her stretched-out sleeves reaching for my ankles, but I grab a fleece-lined hoodie that hugs my body instead. Just because I'm comfy doesn't mean I have to look sloppy. I slip into track pants like what I gave Blake, pull my hair into a ponytail, and rush out of the room.

Right into Blake.

He catches me before I fall, arms tight around me.

"I thought you'd be downstairs by now."

"And sit there by myself with your Dad?" He shakes his head. "Now I really need protection." He laughs, but the intensity in his eyes makes my breath catch. The quiet hallway feels oddly intimate. Maybe it's the fact that we were both undressed a minute ago, or that no one's watching us and this is the first time we've really been alone, but it feels like something shifts between us. He seems to read my mind because he doesn't hesitate covering my mouth with his. The urgency that started to build under the tree is back and our arms are wrapped around each other like we never want to let go.

A cupboard slams in the kitchen and I jump back. His eyes are glassy and he's staring at my lips. I clear my throat. "Ready?"

He shakes his head but smiles.

I toss his wet clothes in the dryer then lead him to the living room, where Dad's sitting on the couch.

He smiles.

Balanced on his leg is his missing notebook.

twenty-six

"You found it!" I rush to his side and grab the notebook. Dad's familiar scribbles peer back at me as I flip through the pages.

"More like it found me."

I hand it back to him and sit next to him on the couch. "What do you mean?" Blake's still standing in the doorway so I wave him over and he sits in the chair closest to me. His hair's sticking all over the place and his face is still flushed from our kiss—and it's grossing me out how unbelievably sexy he is in Dad's hoodie and track pants.

Dad sets the notebook on the table and stretches his arms out in front of him. "I had a visitor at the brewery today." He pauses long enough for my head to explode.

"The notebook fairy?"

"No..."

"Dad, you're killing me."

He glances at Blake. "This isn't a conversation for outside this house."

Blake shifts in the chair. "I can go."

I reach toward him. "No, you stay here. Dad, he's fine."

Dad levels his gaze at Blake. "She may have forgiven you, but you still have to earn back my trust."

Blake looks like he's ready to bolt. "Yes, sir."

"Dad, stop it."

He holds my gaze for ten excruciatingly long seconds, then nods. "Frank Vines from Mischief stopped by to chat."

Blake coughs. "Brianna's dad?"

My head whips between them.

"We had a pleasant conversation about business."

"I don't buy that," Blake says. "Nothing about that man is pleasant."

I tuck my leg underneath me. "Do you know him?"

"I haven't spoken to him since—in years, but I know he's a tyrant."

"Yeah, a tyrant with a soft spot for Switzerland." I watch Blake for a reaction but his face is a mask.

"Anyway," Dad continues. "He had the notebook and said he wanted to return it to me."

"Just like that?"

He leans back and pokes me in the side, making me jump. "Not everyone has the loving, understanding relationship that we do. He implied that his daughter gave it to him thinking he'd be thrilled. Business has been slow lately and while he insisted it isn't anything to worry about, it seems she had a different impression."

"So she stole it to help his business."

"He was careful not to say her name or that she actually took it, just that it was given to him."

"Are you calling the police?"

He shakes his head. "He swears he didn't read it." I open my mouth to protest and he holds up his hand. "I don't believe that either, but he knows that showing up in my brewery with it in his hands is enough ammo if I wanted to press charges. Same thing if he came out with one of our recipes. I trust that he's going to do the right thing."

"You trust him but you don't trust Blake?" Blake shoots me a dirty look and I mouth 'sorry.' I don't mean to keep making him uncomfortable, but that doesn't make sense.

"You're more important than the brewery."

I roll my eyes.

"I'm serious." He looks at Blake. "I apologize for putting you on the spot, but I watched what Cally went through when you two stopped talking, and frankly, that doesn't make me your biggest fan." He turns to me. "I can always come up with new recipes, but you're my only daughter and your mom would kill me if I screwed this up."

I melt against his side. I don't want to cry in front of Blake—again—but I get emotional when Dad gets all fatherly on me. He wraps his arm around me.

Blake stands. "I should go."

Dad releases me and rises. "No, no. You kids stay here and watch a movie." He moves around the coffee table and rests a hand on Blake's shoulder. Blake's a couple inches shorter than him but he stands tall, looking him in the eye. "I'm not saying I won't ever trust you. I see how happy you make Cally, and that means a lot to me. Just keep doing that and I'll come around." He shoots me his pointer finger. "I'll be in my office."

Blake watches him leave, then faces me. "Brianna stole your dad's beer book?"

I exhale loudly. "At the party. But before I tell you about that..." I move toward him until there's no space left between us and slip my arms around his neck. He lowers his lips to mine and everything inside me turns to mush. *What is it about a guy in a hoodie?* We're just getting into it when I hear the refrigerator open in the kitchen.

Which means Dad just walked by and saw us making out.

I jerk away from Blake and plop in the center of the couch.

He shifts from one foot to the other. "He's not gonna, like, kick my ass or anything is he?"

"No, but I probably shouldn't sit on your lap."

He grins. "Too bad."

Ten minutes into an action movie and I've wiggled my way against his side. His arm is around my shoulders, holding me close, and every so often he presses a kiss to the side of my head. When the movie ends, I stretch lazily against his side and realize with a start that this is the closest I've been pressed up against him without a thousand layers or my ski jacket between us.

He must be thinking the same thing because he scoops my legs across his lap so I'm facing him. His face is an inch from mine, but he pauses. "Is your dad gonna walk in here?"

I grab the remote and switch channels to another movie. "Only if he hears the credits."

His eyes close and he brushes his lips over mine. My fingers twist into his hair, pulling him closer, and he deepens the kiss. *This! This is what I've been waiting for!* Just me and Blake and a kiss so good it's making my toes curl. I lean back, tugging him with me, but he stops with a hand on the back of the couch. We're both breathing heavily, our lips almost touching. "Your dad," he whispers.

I glance at the doorway but don't hear anything. The desire to be a good daughter battles with my need for Blake. I close the gap and kiss him again, but he pulls away. "I don't want to make him hate me even more."

"He doesn't hate you."

He smiles. "He will if he comes in here and I'm on top of you."

Heat flares in my belly at the thought, then sinks lower, warming me in an even better way.

"I should probably go home soon."

I flop back onto the couch, my legs still sprawled over his. "Stupid curfews."

He runs a hand from my ankle to my hip, settling at the curve of my waist.

"You can't do that if you're leaving."

His eyes darken and he leans over me, his eyelids heavy. "Maybe one last kiss."

My arms are around his neck before he can change his mind. The intensity between us makes me want things I shouldn't be considering when Dad could walk by any second, but the risk of getting caught makes me kiss Blake that much harder.

When we finally break apart, my mind is fuzzy. All I see is him.

He leans back and I disentangle myself. We stare at each other for another minute before I stand. "I'll get your clothes."

Once he's changed—and I've fantasized about what he looks like behind the closed door—I lead him to the front door to send him off into the blizzard.

He stops me from opening it. "Do you need a ride tomorrow?"

Right, skiing. With everything that's happened I forgot that I don't have a ride. "Actually, that'd be great."

"Is ten okay?"

I press a kiss against his cheek. "Perfect."

He exhales against my neck and I shiver. "Good night."

"See you tomorrow." I close the door and swoon like the lovesick lead in a rom-com. All I need now is to race up the stairs, flop onto my bed, and clutch my hands to my chest and the part will be mine.

I'm no less swoony the next morning. I slept like a rock—probably all that frolicking in the snow—and wake to a text from Sophia asking about the date.

It was heaven.

Did he finally explain?

Yeah, and then some.

I don't want you to get hurt again...

Me neither, but he's so hot.

LOL.

But seriously. I get it now.

Too much for texting?

Yeah. I'll call you later. He's picking me up to go skiing soon.

This is getting serious.

Is it? I don't know if I'd call this serious—not yet—it just feels right.

Maybe.

Be careful.

Gah, between you and Dad...

We love you.

xoxo

Now that I'm thinking of him, I have an intense urge to talk to him. I settle for texting.

Good morning.

That's a nice way to wake up.

And now I'm imagining him in bed with a lot less clothes and much messier hair and I kind of wish I hadn't let him leave when I did.

We still on for ten? I ask.

Unless you're ready sooner.

The sooner the better. Does that sound desperate? He knows how much I love skiing so hopefully he's thinking that.

I miss you too.

Even though he can't see me, I blush.

Be there in half an hour.

I start to reply my standard sign-off with Sophia—*xoxo*—then quickly erase it. No need to scare him off now that we're finally—I don't know—together? Back together?

I crawl out of bed and trip over my laptop. Ugh, I still have to write my life-changing event paper. Moving to Colorado is definitely the number two event that changed my life, and not just for the obvious reasons. I've never lacked a backbone or followed along with my friends just because they said to, but all the drama with Brianna's shown me that I'd rather stand up for myself and have no friends than be bullied around. If we'd stayed in Vermont I might not have ever learned that about myself. Convincing Mike to ditch Brianna is just a bonus.

Dad's at his usual spot in the kitchen, an empty bowl of cereal and full cup of coffee in front of him. And his notebook by his side where it belongs. "Wasn't sure if you needed a ride."

I pour myself a cup and grab a banana from the counter. "Blake's picking me up in a little bit."

He raises an eyebrow. "Does this mean you've forgiven him?"

"I haven't completely let him off the hook. I made him explain all the crappy things he's done and there was a lot more going on than I realized." I tell him the highlights of our date—leaving out the kissing, even if he did see us—and how Blake explained why he acted the way he did, including what happened with his brother.

"Wow, that's a lot to deal with at his age."

I cock my head. I don't mean to compare me losing Mom to Blake losing his brother, but I didn't expect that reaction from Dad.

"It was awful when your mom died, but we've never dealt with the kind of guilt that Blake carries with him."

I pick at the banana peel. "I guess I didn't think about it that way."

He smiles. "Don't be too hard on him."

I top off my coffee and kiss his cheek. "I better go get ready."

An hour later, we're cruising down the highway in Blake's Jeep, my skis and his board strapped to the roof and our boots and helmets in the backseat. When we arrive at Eldora, I reach for the gear in back while Blake stands on the running board to get our equipment. His shirt lifts in the front, revealing a patch of his belly, and I can practically feel the drool running down my face.

He pokes his head inside to smile at me and I flush. The shit-eating grin hasn't left my face since he picked me up. He hops down and for the first time in forever, I'm actually nervous to ski. It's stupid because he's seen what I can do and thinks I'm amazeballs, but I can't help feeling like I need to impress him. I guess hanging out with guys all the time has rubbed off on me. They're always showing off to impress a potential mate.

Blake slides his hands over my waist and nuzzles his nose against my cheek, and my insides turn to mush. "Ready?"

I shake my head.

He pulls back to look at me. "I thought you were in a hurry to get here."

I duck my head so I'm not looking in his eyes. "I was... but then you went and did that and..." My face is so hot I'm sure I'm melting the snow in the parking lot. I look up at him through my lashes, expecting to find a teasing smile, but his face is serious. I rise on my toes and he meets me halfway, kissing me like he did last night outside my bedroom.

We break away, both of us breathing heavily. He presses a gentle kiss to my lips. "If we keep doing this we're never going to get out of the parking lot."

That wouldn't be so bad. Except I need the practice. I pick up my gear and we head for the lodge. In another ten minutes we're on the chairlift to the terrain park.

He rests his hand on mine. "I didn't know if we'd ever do this again."

'This' could be so many things. "Me too."

"Have you been practicing for the Dash?"

"Amber led me through the race course on Wednesday but I want to be more familiar with it."

"Want to hit that first?"

"I thought you weren't entering?"

He shrugs. "I'm not, but that doesn't mean I can't race you."

Lightness fills me. That, and adrenaline. "Oh, it's on."

Skis by nature go faster than snowboards, but Blake is stronger and more agile than Amber and he doesn't waste time cutting from side to side. From the second we drop off the top lip of Corona, he's crouched low, barreling straight down the mountain. His aggressiveness shouldn't surprise me, but I've never seen him on a straight-away so I didn't know how intense he is.

I especially like that he isn't going easy on me.

Everything's a blur except the trail ahead. I shift my weight from left to right, letting my edges do the work, while the rest of my body remains in a tuck. I whip past him midway down the run, but let up enough so that we hit the final drop side by side. We both catch air, and for a moment the entire world stops. We're flying feet apart from each other, our bodies locked in position, trees and other skiers frozen in time. My heart yearns to look at him but I stay focused on the bottom of the run.

The chairlift.

The finish line.

My knees bend as I land and I don't let up until I reach the line of people waiting for the chairlift. Blake slams to a stop seconds after me, his spray barely missing a couple kids from our school.

A huge smile lights up his face. “Not bad. Go again?”

I beat him three more times before he calls mercy and we make our way to the terrain park. We pause at the top, assessing the boarders already there. He shifts so our arms are touching but his attention stays on the tricks. “I knew you were good, but you’re good.”

“Thanks?”

He smiles. “Almost makes up for the fact that you don’t board.”

“What?!” I smack his arm and he pretends to lose his balance.

“I’m just saying.”

“Yeah, well say this.” I push off, but instead of the big jumps like I normally do, I cut for the series of boxes and rails. They aren’t my favorite, mainly because they’re so hard on your gear and you have to wax more often, but I can hang. I go easy on the first rail—a simple one-eighty mount, then one-eighty dismount. The box is next so I twist to start in reverse, then let my skis carry me off. I stay backwards leading up to the next rail, spin to land on the rail going forward, then take a deep breath and pull off a full three-sixty dismount. I come to a stop at the bottom and watch for Blake.

He hops forward to gain momentum and takes the first rail with a one-eighty mount and dismount. He copies my motions on the box too, and by the third rail, I’m bouncing in my boots. *Follow the leader!*

He slows before reaching me and grabs my waist as he comes to a stop. He brushes a kiss across my lips and my eyes flutter closed. His face is as cold as mine but somehow his lips are still soft. I lean into him, kissing him back, when a snowball bursts against his helmet.

We both jump. Luke is tossing another snowball in his hand, smiling.

Blake shakes snow off his head. “I thought you were getting your beauty sleep.”

He shrugs. "Ian convinced me I'm already beautiful."

"Well, let's go!" Blake squeezes my arm. "I go first this time."

Ian catches up to us when we're in line for the lift, cutting through people until he's next to Luke.

At the top, Blake eyes Luke. "No flips?"

He holds out his hands like he could go either way, and Blake nods. "Follow me!"

We take turns being the leader and all the stress from school and the party and even Blake melts away. I'm in my element flipping and twisting and hanging with the guys, and it's like I'm finally home.

Until we get to the top of the lift and the Snow Bunnies are there.

twenty-seven

I'm glad Mike's not with them, but I feel bad that she's not skiing today. Evan and the guys are in line for the big jump and the Half Pipes are right behind them. They wave at Blake and he gives them a thumbs up.

I stop while he straps on his board and glare at Brianna. I don't know if she knows her dad returned the notebook, but it proves she stole from me—from Dad—and I'm done being civil with her. "Did you miss a turn at the last green?"

She rolls her eyes. "You think you own this run?"

"No, but I've seen you ski."

Kenzie's eyes narrow. "Where do you get off acting like you're all that?"

"Didn't seem to bother you before."

She huffs, and I try not to smile. If these two want to make fools of themselves, who am I to stop them?

Evan pushes off first, and Austin and Reece follow close behind. They hit the jumps right after each other—boom, boom, boom—and land perfectly at the bottom.

"Ready, Kenz?" Brianna pushes Kenzie to go, and Kenzie hesitates.

As much as I want to be a bitch, I know what can happen when you don't know what you're doing on a jump. "It's harder than it looks." My voice is flat. I really don't want to help them. "Just keep your skis straight and don't miss the landing or you might break your neck."

Andrew laughs. "Yeah, I'm proof of that."

Brianna's eyes go wide, and Andrew is my new best friend.

"Bet my helmet doesn't seem so dumb now, huh?"

She narrows her eyes at me and her mask of composure resets. "You people are ridiculous." She uses her poles to get going and slides to the top of the jump, Kenzie at her side. With a quick glance at Kenzie, Bri straightens her skis so they're pointing downhill and she starts moving.

"This oughta be good," Blake murmurs.

Her skis wobble as she approaches the first jump—the first time I've seen a crack in her composure, at least on the slopes—and a high-pitched squeal echoes off the mountain when her skis leave the ground. Arms flailing, she somehow lands on both feet and immediately snowplows. By the time she reaches the second jump she's going so slow that she coasts over the top, her skis never leaving the snow. All of us at the top exhale when she does the same on the third jump.

She comes to a graceful stop at the bottom and Austin pulls her into a bear hug.

"Well, that was anticlimactic." I flick snow off the tip of my ski, sending it high above our heads.

Ian laughs. "Show's not over yet."

Kenzie's still standing at the top of the jump. By now there's a line of boarders behind her and their taunts carry to where we're standing.

"Go already!"

"Get out of the way if you're not jumping!"

Luke cups his hands around his mouth and shouts, "Go back to the bunny hill!"

She turns her head our way, mouth clenched in a firm line.

"Not so nice when it's directed at you, is it?" Blake's voice is low, but the disgust is unmistakable.

Kenzie inches forward until ever-so-slowly her skis begin to move.

Blake shakes his head. “If she doesn’t pick up speed she’s not gonna clear the jump.”

And that’s exactly what happens. Kenzie’s going so slow that she doesn’t have enough momentum to crest the jump and she starts to slide backwards.

He snorts and I nudge him. “You should do commentary.”

“Screw this. I’m hitting the rails.” Luke hops, slapping his board against the snow, then takes off down the hill. The Half Pipes follow him, leaving me alone with Blake.

Kenzie tries to skate up the hill but her skis keep slipping. By now a small crowd has gathered above her, their shouts getting obscene.

I shift my weight. “Should we help her?”

Blake looks at me. “You’re joking, right?”

“I guess.” Kenzie and Brianna have gone out of their way to make my life miserable, but she’s out of her element here. I remember how my stomach cramped the first time I pushed off the top of a scary mountain. I still get a twinge of nerves at the top, but I know I have the skills to get me safely down the hill. Kenzie doesn’t have that.

What she does have is a cheering section because she’s given up trying to go uphill and cuts to the side, freeing up the run. Boarders fly by her—a couple even flip her off—before she points her skis toward the bottom and glides to Brianna’s side, head high and form perfect like nothing happened.

Brianna gives her a quick hug at the bottom, then they get in line for the same lift.

“They’re coming back for more?”

I shrug. “Let’s wait until they’re on the lift so we won’t keep running into them.” We get in line for the jumps, but my adrenaline has faded. The Snow Bunnies are the only thing that make me not want to ski.

“You okay?”

I nod. “Just a lot of standing around.”

“Mind if I go first?”

I’ve never seen him do his thing from the top—er… from the top of the jumps. And now I’m thinking of really inappropriate things. I blush and Blake raises an eyebrow at me. "Go for it." I flush even more and he leans his head toward mine.

"I'm dying to know what you're thinking."

"Not a chance in hell."

He winks. "Maybe later?"

I smile. Later, when the Bunnies are gone and it's just us and... "Mmm, maybe."

He pecks my cheek, then hops forward. "See you at the bottom." Then he gives me another wink that sends my heart into convulsions. His first jump is a smooth three-sixty. He lands easily and crouches to gain speed for the second. As soon as he leaves the ground, he grabs his board behind him and arches his back. It looks like an easy move but it takes a lot of control to keep yourself steady.

And a lot of muscles.

Muscles.

Like probably a six-pack.

I bite my lip and give up trying not to blush.

The third jump is all big air. Body tucked, arms steady, soaring far beyond where most people land. He sticks the landing and turns around to wait for me.

My thoughts are so rattled from imaging him without clothes that I play the jumps safe and copy him—three-sixty, ollie, and big air—although his air was way bigger. I come to a smooth stop next to him and my hand reaches for his belly. I can't feel muscles through his heavy jacket, but I can imagine.

His brows furrow. "You okay?"

I run my hand over his torso. "Better than okay. Let's go."

We head back up and my stomach sinks. The Bunnies are still at the top. "Why would they come back up if they're too scared to do anything?"

"I've never claimed to understand what they do." He glances at me and rests a hand on my thigh. "Hey, just ignore them. They don't own this place."

"I know, it's just..." I hate the squicky feeling I get when I'm around them, like I'm waiting for the other shoe to drop. "Being suspended clearly didn't make Brianna change her ways and I trust Kenzie about as far as I can throw her."

He squeezes my leg. "Do you have plans for winter break?"

Oh, right. That's next weekend. When we first moved I'd hoped I could go back to Vermont, but I never made plans and now it's too late. "What did you have in mind?" I realize he didn't actually ask me out, but I never claimed to be bashful.

He smiles. "More of this? Maybe go to that movie?"

I lean so my shoulder's pressed against his. "I'd love to."

We fall silent until we reach the top. The Bunnies are still there, watching the jumpers.

"Ignore them," Blake whispers.

They're in the middle of the lip so I hang back while Blake fastens his boots, then follow him to the jump. This time I'm leading. I crouch to gain momentum and hit the first jump at top speed. Spread eagle. Not super difficult but I'm dying to see how Blake handles that on a board. I barely notice my landing and am prepping for the next jump when a flash of neon orange alongside the jump catches my eye. I ignore it and launch a three-sixty. I'm going inverted for number three so I want to keep my speed up and—*what the hell?*

The spot of orange drifts into my landing zone.

"Watch it!" I shout, but it's too late. I twist to avoid hitting her and land sideways, but instead of my skis popping off, I end up sitting on my skis, shooting sideways on the hill toward the tree line and the chairlift. A chorus of "Ohhhhs" sound above me but I'm too pissed to care. I roll to my side to stop and am back on my feet in a flash, but a bolt of pain rips through my knee and I fall back into the snow. I look up in time to see Kenzie glide away, her black ponytail swinging.

"I can't believe she did that! What is wrong with you?" I shout after her, but she's already gone.

A spray of powder above me makes me jump.

Blake.

He's at my side in a heartbeat. "What happened? I didn't see you land, just that you didn't make the third jump." He gives me a visual once-over, making me forget my anger for a second, and pauses on my knee.

I'm gripping it without realizing.

"Is it bad?"

"I don't think so. I landed at a weird angle to avoid crashing into that stupid B. I should have just—"

He shakes his head. "Then you'd be just like them. And you're not."

I thrill at his words. I feel like I've been battling this impression he made of me when we first met—however right or wrong it was—and to hear him say that means he's finally seeing me for who I am. Just Cally. Not some stuck-up rich girl who cares about stupid crap like money and clothes and—

The whine of a snowmobile stops my thoughts.

"No. Uh-uh. No way."

Blake stands to look down the hill. "They're coming this way."

I push myself off the ground and am standing almost completely normally by the time they reach us. "I'm fine. Really."

A patrol woman jumps off the back. "We have instructions to check more people after that boy hurt his neck last week."

"Frigging Andrew," Blake whispers.

She glances at him, then focuses on me. "Chairlift operator says you took a hard fall off the jump. Considering you're still here I'm guessing he wasn't making it up."

I shift from foot to foot. There's a twinge in my knee, but it's nothing a little rest and some ice won't fix. "It looked worse than it was. I swear."

She looks at the patrol guy still on the snowmobile. "Whaddaya think?"

He shrugs. "She seems okay."

I breathe a sigh of relief. "Thank you."

She climbs back onto the snowmobile and they drive off.

When the whine of the engine fades, Blake leans his head close to mine. "I was really hoping to see those bunny pants again."

"That's too bad." I smile. "Today it's hearts and rainbows."

He raises an eyebrow. "Really?"

I give him a half-smile. "Maybe."

His eyes darken. If I had more experience with boys I'd guess that now I've got him thinking of me the way I can't stop thinking of him, but I'm not sure. The moment passes and he rubs my arm. "You okay to get to the lodge?"

I bend my knee, but rather than pain, I just feel exhaustion. "Yeah. But no more jumps for me."

I follow him to the lodge. He secures our gear on a rack and we head inside. Half the mountain seems to be in here. I eye the line snaking along the far wall, then take his helmet. "You get hot chocolate, I'll find a table."

He stuffs his gloves and goggles in the helmet and kisses my cheek, causing my pulse to skitter. I'll take a sweaty boy with hair sticking all over the place over a neatly groomed one any day.

I meander through the lodge in search of a table when I spot Evan and the guys. I turn around but he calls my name and waves me over.

Their feet are propped on two empty chairs.

"Is there room for two more at the inn?"

Evan nods at the chairs and Austin gives him a sideways glance. Brianna and Kenzie are nowhere to be seen, but I'm sure these are for them.

"I'm not taking their seats."

Evan shrugs. "They're still skiing."

"More like hiding after making me fall." The words are out before I catch myself.

Evan sits straighter and gives me a once over. "What'd they do now?"

I wave his feet off one of the chairs and sit. "I'm sure Kenzie will claim it was an accident, but she cut in front of me when I was landing a three-sixty."

Now it's Austin's turn to look concerned. "On purpose?"

I roll my eyes. "When do they do anything on accident?"

"That's not cool."

"Yeah, no kidding." I look across the room to check on Blake's progress and spot him halfway to the cashier, talking to two girls in line behind him. A stab of jealousy makes me grip the table, but I force myself to relax and stop being a hypocrite. While he's in line talking to girls, I'm over here talking to boys. I turn back to Evan and he gives me a small smile, making me wonder for the hundredth time why he's friends with the Snow Bunnies. If what Mike said was true about why they broke up, then he's not into all that superficial crap, and while I get that he's friends with Austin and Reece, that sounds like a miserable way to go through life. "I really don't want to cause a problem when they get here. I've had enough drama this week."

Evan leans toward me and lowers his voice. "Brianna doesn't tell me who I'm friends with."

I appreciate the sentiment but that's not going to stop Bri from throwing a fit when she comes inside. "So why—never mind."

"What?"

"I was going to ask why you hang out with them, but—" I nod at the guys. "I get it."

He glances at Austin to make sure he's not listening. "Some day Austin will realize what a raging bitch she is and put an end to whatever it is they have going on, but until then..." He shrugs.

Kind of like Mike. I smile, happy that she seems to really be free of them.

"Am I interrupting something?" Blake's standing at my side, a cup of hot chocolate in each hand and a bag of chips dangling from his fingers.

I jump back, noticing how close Evan and I were and how it must look. I nod at the other chair. "I found seats."

The guys shuffle so Blake can sit next to me and he sets the drinks on the table. He locks eyes with mine as he sits, seeming uncertain.

I lean so my cheek is pressed against his and whisper in his ear. "We've commandeered the Bitches' chairs."

I feel his smile. "Nice."

The guys fall into an easy conversation and before long I'm laughing and joking like I've known them forever. Reece is in the middle of a completely disgusting joke about a pig and a bottle of baby oil when he suddenly falls silent, his gaze locked over my shoulder toward the entrance. I don't need to turn around to know who's there.

"The eagle has landed," Evan whispers. "Repeat. The eagle has landed."

Blake snorts. "You mean the vultures."

Austin gives him a dirty look but doesn't contradict him.

I remain still, dreading what's about to happen. I refuse to turn around. Blake slips his hand into mine and smiles like there's no one else in the room. The distraction lasts all of five seconds.

"This looks cozy." Brianna's fake-sweet voice makes the hair on the back on my neck stand up.

I twist in my chair and smile up at her. "Sorry, this table's full." *Go big or go home, right?*

Her calm demeanor vanishes and her lips curl into a snarl. "I thought we got rid of you."

I pat my knee. "Nice try, but I'm still here."

Kenzie stiffens beside her. I won't give her enough credit to think she feels guilty for what she did, but it's nice to see she has a reaction other than total bitch.

Brianna nudges Kenzie's arm. "Maybe next time."

Blake yanks his hand from mine and is on his feet, toe-to-toe with Brianna. "When are you gonna realize this isn't a game? She could have really been hurt."

She lifts a shoulder and rolls her eyes at me. "Maybe your girlfriend shouldn't go where she's not welcome."

I start to rise but Evan pulls me back by my shoulders.

The gesture doesn't escape Brianna. "It's not enough to have a Ski Bum trailing after you? You're still stringing him along, too?"

I look between Blake and Evan. "What? No, I—"

She sneers. "Don't play innocent. I invented that game."

Austin cocks his head and there's a flash of concern on

Brianna's face, like maybe she said more than she intended, but she shakes it off.

Blake moves a step closer to me, as if his body can shield me from her venom.

She crosses her arms. "Oh, so now you're her bodyguard or something?"

"Enough, Brianna."

"Since when do you care about anyone but yourself?"

"You've treated me like shit for years and I've never said anything. As of today, I'm done."

The Brivolution is real!

But she's not backing down that easily. "You'll never be anything but a Ski Bum."

Blake laughs, but it's filled with disgust. "That name didn't stick the first hundred times you tried calling me that. Give it up."

I snort. "Ski Bum? Seriously?"

Blake turns his head toward me. "I guess it was supposed to keep me and Luke in our place. You know, as far away from the Snow Bitches as possible." He turns back to Brianna, whose face has turned a garish shade of red that clashes with her bright pink jacket. She should really reconsider her wardrobe choices if her face keeps doing that.

"Snow *Bunnies*," Brianna corrects. Her eyes have taken on a glassy sheen and I don't think she's blinked in at least a minute.

Blake matches her glare. "My mistake."

It's so quiet at our table that noise from the surrounding tables suddenly seems much louder. Bits of conversations from other groups drift over to us, but no one seems aware of the Blake vs. Brianna showdown.

Austin finally stands and tugs at Brianna's arm, but she shakes him off without looking at him. She points at me and Blake. "You two are not welcome here."

I cross my arms. "Funny, no one complained when I was invited to sit here."

Her eyes flick to Evan, then back to me. "There's no explaining some people's taste."

I glance at Austin. "I could say the same thing."

She takes a step closer. For a second I think she's going to launch herself at me but she just stands there with her finger frozen in midair.

I'm tempted to grab it like I sometimes do to Dad when he's giving his Behave warning. That would snap her out of her power trip.

"I'm complaining now."

I exhale loudly. I could keep going back and forth with her, or I could go someplace more private with Blake. Plus I can't guarantee I won't kick Kenzie in the kneecap if she decides to add her two cents. I rest my hand on Evan's shoulder and he looks up at me. "Thanks for saving us seats, but we're gonna take off."

Blake quirks his eyebrow at me.

Evan smiles at me like Brianna isn't fuming two feet away. "See ya, Cally." He nods at Blake. "Blake."

Brianna huffs. "Don't act like this was your idea."

I wave at the other guys. "See you at school." I loop my arm through Blake's and lead him through the maze of tables to the exit.

He chuckles when we step outside. "I can't believe you caved."

"Well, I figured I could trade insults with Brianna for the next hour," I slide my arms around his neck and focus on his lips. "Or I could spend time with my Ski Bum bodyguard." I barely notice his lopsided smile before his lips brush mine. "Does she really still call you that?"

"She tries. But nicknames are only fun when the person hates it and since I don't ever react, she's the only one who cares."

"That's a good strategy."

"I don't waste my energy on people I don't like." He pulls me closer and nuzzles my neck. "I have lots of energy for you."

I know he doesn't mean the innuendo that pops into my head, but he's turned me into a lovesick horndog who can only think about all the inappropriate things we could do in an hour. "What did you have in mind?"

twenty-eight

She's still giving you crap?

Like it's her life's mission.

Winter break is this weekend. Want me to come kick her ass?

OMG that would rock. But really just to see you. I can handle Brianna.

You sure? I wouldn't mind meeting Blake too.

Do it. Having Sophia come to visit would be amazing. Not that I need help with the Snow Bunnies, but not seeing her every day makes me feel like there's a piece of me missing. A long weekend together might be enough to get me through the rest of the semester, when Dad's promised I can go back for a longer visit.

:(I wish I could. Summer is too far away.

My phone dings with a text from Blake. I swipe to the other screen.

You write your paper yet?

I glance at my laptop on the bed next to me. I know I'm writing about moving to Colorado but I've been stuck on where to start. *Sort of. You?*

Almost done.

Show off.

What can I say, I like to write.

For real?

English is my favorite class.

I tilt my head in surprise. I assumed Blake wasn't into school since he was late my first couple days, but I guess that wasn't fair. I totally judged him instead of getting to know him first. I silently tuck that away with everything else I'm learning about him.

Actually...

??

I kinda want to be a teacher some day.

You would be an amazing teacher. And you already have groupies.

;)

Sophia dings. *Go write your paper.*

You have a camera on me?

I know you...

sigh.

xoxo.

I swipe back to Blake. *Help me, oh wise one.*

What's the problem?

I don't know where to start.

Write down what's in your head, then fix it later.

Tell me more.

LOL.

I'm serious.

Do you know what you're writing about?

Moving here.

That's your worst day??

No! Simpson's letting me do them out of order.

His text bubble bounces, indicating he's typing, and my mind wanders to my paper. I need to go deeper than just 'moving changed my life.'

What if you compare what you expected with what it's really been like? I know you were freaked out to move—

It occurs to me that he knows that from when we were texting right after Thanksgiving.

—and Bri's been a bitch, but there's been good stuff too, right?

My pulse quickens. *Are you suggesting I write about you?*

No! I meant... the text bubble bounces, then stops, then bounces again. *New school, new friends. There has to be something worth writing about.*

Thanks. This helps.

:)

See you tomorrow.

Sleep tight.

It's not an xoxo but it's got me thinking of his bed and that's not going to get my paper written. Two hours later, I turn off my computer, still wrapping my head around the idea that while I may not have wanted to move here, now I couldn't imagine ever leaving.

***

The happy glow lasts until I spot the Bitches at their usual table in the cafeteria. *Let it go, let it go,* I sing in my head as I carry my tray to where Mike's already waiting.

But I can't. I thought speaking up on Saturday would have some kind of effect, but they're still laughing down their noses at everyone beneath them, oblivious to the torment they wreak on the little people. And frankly, I'm pissed they've killed my good mood.

I drop my tray next to Mike's. "Be right back."

"What are you—"

I shake my head. "I've had enough." I spin on my heel and march over to Bitch Headquarters. Evan catches my eye when he sees me coming but doesn't warn the girls, whose backs are to me. I stop near Kenzie's shoulder and cross my arms. "You owe me an apology."

Kenzie and Bri's heads swivel toward me in unison.

"Excuse me?" Kenzie says as Bri's mouth falls open.

My pulse pounds in my ears but it's too late to back down now. "You heard me."

Kenzie turns so she's facing me. "And what, exactly, do you think I did that requires an apology?"

"I'd say you should apologize for that pathetic attempt at a jump, but I'm being selfish. An apology for making me crash will do."

She turns to Brianna. "Do you believe this crap?"

A low voice behind me makes me jump. "What's going on?" Blake touches my waist and meets my determined gaze with curiosity.

Brianna pushes her chair back and stands. "You think you can just waltz in here and be one of us." She sneers at Blake. "You don't even have good taste in men."

I lean toward Blake and whisper, "I dunno. I think you taste pretty good."

He laughs, which only infuriates Brianna more.

"Why would you choose him over Evan? You're hopeless."

I glare at Kenzie, who's only too happy to have Brianna battling for her, then scowl at Brianna. "Maybe I'm interested in more than just a bank account. But that's something you'll never understand." I step closer and take a breath. I won't be able to take back my next words. Once they're out there, especially in the middle of the cafeteria, there's no going back. "I know you stole my dad's recipe book."

Kenzie gasps.

Brianna's composure breaks, just for a second. "I don't know what you're talking about."

"It makes sense. As soon as you found out my dad owns a brewery, you never left my side, even when it was obvious—and I can't stress this enough—that we have nothing in common. And the party." I shake my head, feeling stupid for playing into her hands. "That was just a way to get inside my house."

Brianna crosses her arms. "Why would I need to steal anything? In case you haven't noticed, money's his problem, not mine." She points at Blake, who bristles beside me.

Anger and frustration and disbelief war inside me. I'm vaguely aware of people staring at us so I take a deep breath, refusing to take the bait she's dangling in front of me, and dangle a bit of my own. "Except that's not true. Mischief isn't doing very well. In fact, your dad's close to filing for bankruptcy. You thought stealing the book would help his business."

Several people gasp and Kenzie stares at Brianna, eyes wide.

Brianna dismisses me with a wave of her hand. "You're going to listen to this... this... nobody?" She whirls around, facing the crowd that's gathered, then turns back to me. "I should have kicked your ass when I had the chance."

I look down at myself, then back at her. "I don't seem to be running away."

She moves toward me, fists clenched at her sides.

"Careful, Bri." I lower my voice. "Don't want to get suspended again. What will your minions think?"

A flicker of fear darkens her eyes.

"But that's not who you're worried about, is it?" I pause, making a guess. "This is all for your dad. To make him proud of you." When she doesn't disagree, I keep going. "Manipulating people isn't the way to earn their respect—that just pisses them off. I'd rather be friends with people who genuinely like me, not people who are so afraid to speak up that they do whatever I say."

"You're just jealous."

"I'm not the one everyone hates." I slip my hand into Blake's and lead him to our table, where Mike's jaw is practically detached. I sit next to her and tuck my shaking hands beneath my legs.

"I can't believe you did that."

"Somebody had to."

"Yeah, but holy shit."

Blake rubs my back. "You alright?"

"The adrenaline is fleeing my body."

Mike laughs. "Food. Stat."

Blake pushes my tray of now-cold food closer to me. "Eat."

I reach for my sandwich, then glare across the room. "Hey, I never got my apology!"

But I get something better: another date with Blake. Winter break is four days long which means more days to ski and more days to hang out without commentary from the Super Bitches.

twenty-nine

Winter break starts off the same as last weekend—Blake driving me to Eldora—except today Mike's crammed in the backseat of the Jeep. She keeps the chit-chat light, and if it weren't for the fact that Blake's hand keeps drifting toward mine, I'd almost forget he's here.

Ha, who am I kidding? I flush every time he touches me.

Fresh powder fell overnight and drifts of snow still cover the edge of the road. It's no match for Blake's Jeep, but it takes longer to get there than normal. When we finally arrive, Blake parks in the lot and hops out to get our skis off the roof, and Mike nudges me. "So things are going well?"

I force the smile from my face and glance at Blake. "Is it that obvious?"

"Uh, yeah. He's got the same dopey expression as you."

I rest my head on the seat. "This is bad."

"It doesn't sound bad."

I peek at him through the window to make sure he's not listening. "It's good, but it's bad. He crushed me so hard before and part of me's scared he's going to do it again."

"If he does—and from the way he looks at you I don't think he will—but if he does, I promise I'll be the first in line to kick his ass."

"You'd do that for me?"

"After what you went through with Brianna? I owe you way more than a little ass kicking."

"Whose ass are we kicking?"

We both jump at Blake's voice.

"Uh, no one," I say.

His eyes grow serious and his chest puffs out in that way guys do. "Is it Brianna?"

"No!" Mike and I exclaim.

I reach for his arm. "Nothing else has happened. But I promise to tell you if it does."

"Okay." He deflates and nods at our gear. "Ready?"

Mike catches my eye, then presses her hand to her chest and flutters her eyelashes.

I burst out laughing. "Shut it."

We're on the slopes in ten minutes. I promise to meet Blake on the terrain park after a few runs with Mike. Normally I'd do my own thing with Amber and catch up with Mike later, but Amber's visiting family over the break. "Are you sure I can't get you to try a few jumps? It's really not hard and you're a good skier."

We're on the chairlift that leads to the easier runs. "Maybe. I admit these runs get a little boring." She bites her lip. "What are you thinking?"

"Either the moguls or a black. You choose."

"Is there a third choice?"

"You won't run into Brianna and Kenzie there."

She sighs. "You win."

"I swear I'll go easy on you."

When we get to the top, instead of going straight down the blue, we cut across the ridge to the more challenging runs. "This one's a black, but it's like a baby black. The scariest part is the top."

Mike peers over the edge. From here it looks like a straight vertical drop, and it doesn't help that we're the only people up here.

"If I go first, will you follow?"

She nods, lip firmly clamped between her teeth.

I glide the tip of my skis to the edge, take a final look at Mike, then let gravity do the rest. I keep my knees bent and body relaxed. Instinct and reflex carry me through the steepest part and I come to a gentle stop at the first semi-level spot.

Mike's still hovering at the top. Her poles are planted on either side of her and she seems frozen in place. I clear my throat to shout her name but before I can, she inches over the crest. Her shriek carries all the way to me. Her form isn't as graceful as when she's trailing behind the Bunnies, but she doesn't fall—and best of all—she doesn't snowplow. When she reaches my side she flips up her goggles, a smile plastered to her face.

"I think I pissed my pants but holy crap that was amazing!"

I laugh. "I wasn't sure if you were going to do it."

She looks over her shoulder at the top. "I wasn't either."

"You ready to keep going?"

"How many more drops are there like that?"

"One more near the bottom. It kind of sneaks up on you so I'll stop right before it."

"I feel stupid that you know this place better than I do. Are there any runs you haven't taken?"

I shake my head and smile.

She laughs. "Lead the way."

We fall into a rhythm, gliding back and forth over the freshly-groomed powder. A few kids race by us and I bite back the urge to pick up the pace. I've already pushed Mike out of her comfort zone—getting her on a hill she's not familiar with will have to be enough for today.

"You look like you're plotting something," she shouts.

I burst out laughing. "Maybe, but it's all good."

"There better not be a giant jump at the end of this run."

"I promise. Just the one drop—"

A thundering crack echoes all around us and I lose my edge. It sounds like a gunshot but it's too big, too all encompassing. I come to a hard stop as birds swoop from the trees around us, their squawks piercing the eerie silence that follows.

Mike stops next to me, eyes wide.

"What was that?"

"We need to go." Her voice is strangely quiet. I don't think she's blinked since we stopped.

"Mike, what was that?"

Another boom echoes through the trees, followed by a low rumbling that shakes the ground beneath us. Snow falls from the branches, filling the air with a fine powder.

"I can't believe—Cally, we have to go now!" She pushes off and crouches low to her skis.

I scramble to follow. "Is this—is it an avalanche?" The ground continues to shake and I quickly catch up to Mike. Determination barely covers the terror on her face as she stares straight ahead. "Is it really an avalanche?" I shout.

She glances at me out of the corner of her eye, never leaving her tuck. "I've never seen one, but—" she takes a quick breath "—they teach us about them in school. Big boom. Freaked out animals." Another breath. "Ground shaking like an earthquake."

My heart gallops in my chest. All I know of avalanches is what I've seen in movies or read online. The idea of the mountain turning against me fills me with a fear I haven't felt since Mom died.

I crouch lower, pulling away from Mike. Maybe if I go faster she'll keep up.

But she doesn't.

I check over my shoulder. Terror has completely taken over. Her mouth is open in an ugly grimace and her upper body is locked in the same crouch she started in.

I slow so we're side by side. "You need to loosen up. You're going to hurt yourself."

Her knees bend as we follow a curve in the trail, but otherwise nothing on her moves.

"Mike!"

She risks a look at me. Tears slip beneath her goggles, wetting her face. "We can't stop!"

This is a real avalanche. The kind from the news. The kind that sweeps people away, never to be heard from again.

I shake that thought away. "I know, but you can't stay that tense. Do what I do." I push my arms straight above my head, careful not to decapitate her with my pole.

Her arms lift as high as her shoulders, then they snap back into place.

"Now this!" I straighten my back, keeping my eyes focused ahead. The big drop is close but I'm not sure if it's after this bend or the next. I know I can stop on a dime but I'm not sure how fast Mike can slow down. A crash while we're trying to outrun an avalanche could be deadly.

She unlocks her shoulders and gets a little more upright.

"Good! That drop is coming up so I'm gonna slow—"

Another boom shakes the ground beneath us. Mike's edge catches, jerking her sideways. I duck as she flips forward but her ski tip catches mine and my legs buckle beneath me. I land hard on my side but am on my feet in a heartbeat. My skis popped off and are a few feet below me, but Mike's are a good twenty yards away.

Up the hill.

And Mike's lying facedown in the snow, legs splayed.

I rush to her side and press my hand to her shoulder. "Are you hurt?" *Please don't let anything be broken.*

She groans and rolls to her side. Snow's packed around her goggles but there isn't any blood. "My skis." She gropes for her feet. "They're not here."

I run up the slope as fast as my boots will let me. I slip twice, landing hard on my bad knee. "They popped off," I shout back to her. "Can you get up?"

I don't hear her answer but it doesn't matter. Her skis are ten yards away.

Five.

The ground rumbles, knocking me to my feet.

I scramble for her skis. I grab one in each hand and throw myself down the hill toward Mike.

She's sitting up, tears burning rivulets in the snow still sticking to her face. "Save y-yourself."

"This isn't a war movie and I'm not leaving you. Come on." I maneuver her boot into the bindings, wedge the bottom of the ski against my leg, and press until it snaps into place. Then I do the same with the other foot.

She stifles a cry against my arm. "I don't think I can do this."

I get to my feet and pull her upright. "You have to." She wobbles, nearly falling over, and I catch her in my arms. I bring my face close to hers. "You can do this. We just have the last drop and we'll be at the bottom. But we have to get off this mountain."

She nods, tears running into her mouth.

I release her arms and take a flying jump to my skis. I'm snapping the second boot into place when Mike slides past me. "I'm right behind you. Just don't stop."

She's going painfully slow. Most of her weight is on one leg and she's using her poles to keep her balance.

"You're doing great. That next hill is the top of the drop."

She wobbles, but catches herself with a pole. "I don't think I can do this."

"I'm right next to you."

She stops.

I look up the mountain, expecting a wall of snow. It looks the same as it did when we were farther up, but that could change in an instant. "I have an idea. Here, take my poles." I shove a pole into each of her hands, then shuffle behind her. "Put your legs closer together."

She twists around. "What are you doing?"

"I'm getting you out of here." I put my skis outside of hers so she's tucked between my legs in a snowplow, the same way Mom taught me to ski. I slip my arms under hers and lock my grip to support her, then push off. *Help me, Mom.* Mike's high-pitched moan gets louder as we reach the lip, but I don't stop. Momentum carries us over the edge and it's like her body forgets what to do. I nearly fall as she crumples into me. "Mike! You have to help me!"

"I'm t-trying!"

Her ponytail whips me in the face. The base of the chairlift winks up ahead, and the whine of a snowmobile steels my resolve. "We're almost there."

She clenches her arms against her side, pinning mine.

"Stay loose, Mike."

The pressure lessens but her body is locked in position.

Our skis bump as I steer us. She lets out another squeal but her body doesn't fight mine. "Almost there," I whisper, reassuring myself as much as her. As if on cue, a snowmobile carrying two Ski Patrol rounds the bend and I exhale.

Mike waves her arms, dropping all the poles.

They turn our way but I can't relax yet. If Mike falls again her injury could get worse. I force my legs into a wider snowplow, slowing our descent. The snowmobile whinnies to a stop a few feet away and I finally release my grip. Mike collapses to the ground.

The guy on the back jumps off. "You girls need to get off the mountain. We got reports of an avalanche."

A shudder passes through me.

Mike fumbles with her bindings. "I hurt my leg. I can't ski."

He jumps into action, removing her skis and scooping her into his arms. I've never seen them move someone before checking their neck. He sets her on the back of the snowmobile, where he'd been sitting. "You're gonna have to hang on. There isn't time to get a sled." He looks at me. "Are you hurt?"

I shake my head. "Just her."

"Can you carry her skis?"

"Yeah."

He runs up the hill behind me and grabs our poles. "You okay to follow us?"

The panicked look on his face scares me more than the rumbles and booms.

I grab Mike's gear and nod. "Where's the avalanche?"

He catches the driver's eye, then looks back at me. "Let's go."

Why won't he answer?

My stomach drops.

What if it's the terrain park?

thirty

I skate behind the snowmobile as fast as I can carrying skis and two extra poles. By the time I reach the lodge my legs are burning and sweat runs down my back. But I barely notice any of that. All I can think of is the terrain park. Every one I know—all my friends—are there. If something happened to them... A cry catches in my throat as I try to push away thoughts of Blake. He can't be hurt.

He can't.

I lean Mike's equipment against a rack and head for the terrain park. They've already got her inside the med station and while I should probably make sure she's okay, I need to see the park for myself.

I'm pushing against the stream of people rushing toward the parking lot when a loudspeaker crackles to life. Hundreds of eyes lift to the speaker mounted on a nearby pole.

"All runs are closed effective immediately. Please make your way to the base of the mountain. The lodge and medical station will remain open. Repeat: all runs are closed immediately. Please make your way..." The voice drones on and people hurry toward the lodge, their faces an identical mask of panic. I search the crowd for Blake. Groups of friends cluster together, all pointing at the top of the mountain.

Two of the Half Pipes run by.

"Joey!" I shout.

He stops and turns.

"Have you seen Blake?"

He glances toward the park, then back at me and shakes his head, eyes wide. "No. Is he here?"

I nod, and his eyes grow wider. "Stay with your friends. I'll have him text you when I find him." Because I will find him. I have to.

Joey gives me a wobbly smile and catches up with his friends.

I reach the chairlift and am stopped by Ski Patrol. "Sorry," she says. "All lifts are closed. You need to make your way to the parking lot."

"But my friends. Was anyone hurt here?"

Her eyes soften and her jaw clenches. "Not here."

Fear grips my chest. "But people are hurt?"

She blinks rapidly and I realize she's trying to keep her emotions in check. "It's too soon to tell." She touches my arm. "If your friends were on the terrain park, we've already cleared them off. Go check in the lodge or the parking lot." Her voice is sympathetic but firm.

"Okay. Thanks."

I turn to leave as a snowmobile screeches to a stop next to us. "All clear here."

Exhaustion grabs hold of my legs but I have to keep looking. *What if he didn't come straight here?*

Stop it. He's probably in the lodge.

I make my way to the med station, numb to the shouts and cries around me. It's like someone took our snow globe and with one violent shake, disrupted everything. *Why haven't I seen anyone I know?* I try to text Blake but it won't go through. Probably because everyone on the mountain is jamming the signal. Tears blur my vision. I flip up my goggles and wipe my arm across my face.

Inside the med station, Mike's lying on her back on a padded table, her elbows propping her up so she can see what the medic is doing to her leg. She greets me with a weak smile. "My hero!"

I hurry to her side. "You'd be fine if I hadn't made you take that run. I'm so sorry."

"Yeah, it's totally your fault there was an avalanche at the exact moment I got a burst of courage."

The medic finishes wrapping a bandage around her knee. "This'll have to do for now. We need to clear you out for when—" He stops, his face pale.

For when they bring in victims from the avalanche.

Mike nods, understanding.

"Go to the hospital today. I don't think it's broken but you might have torn a ligament."

She gently swings her legs over the side of the table and I help her to her feet.

"Be safe, girls."

We both murmur our thanks and head outside. "Can you walk okay?"

"I'll manage." She takes in the chaos at the base of the mountain. "Thank you for not—" she takes a breath. "For not leaving me."

"That's what friends do."

She shakes her head. "When I fell, all I kept thinking is that Brianna would have left me there."

I start to object, but she's probably right. Brianna only does what's in her own best interest. "Then it's a good thing you weren't with her." I loop my arm through hers, swallowing back the panic that's still bubbling in my chest. "Let's go find Blake."

She looks at me, eyes wide. "You haven't found him?"

I bite my lip. "I haven't seen anyone we know."

"Well, quit screwing around with me. Go find them." She shoves me away from her and I stumble.

"Are you sure?"

"Get my poles and I'll be right behind you."

I retrieve them from the rack, make sure she's steady, then weave through the crowd as fast as I can.

I'm on the patio outside the lodge when a shout stops me.

"Cally!"

I whip around. Evan and Austin are huddled around the fire pit with Brianna and Kenzie and some other kids from school. I'm relieved to see they're okay—even the girls—but one very important person isn't with them. "Have you seen Blake?"

The guys look at each other, then turn to me and shake their heads.

Brianna rolls her eyes.

I resist the urge to pile drive her into the fire pit. "I need to find him."

Evan steps toward me. "Have you seen Mike?" His ever-present smile wavers and concern creases his brow.

"She was with me. Ski Patrol had to carry her off Muleshoe."

His face goes ashen. "Were you near the avalanche?"

I go still. The Ski Patrol who helped Mike were probably on their way to search for people when we waved them down. "Omigod."

He grabs my shoulders. "Is Mike okay? Where is she?"

"I'm right here." Mike's soft voice stills him.

He lets go of me and turns around.

Mike's standing on one leg, using the poles for balance. She starts to smile, then stops, like she's unsure what to do.

But Evan doesn't seem to have that concern. He reaches her in two strides and pulls her into his arms. I can't hear what he's saying but based on the way he's burying his face in her neck, I'm thinking it's good. Her poles clatter to the ground as she wraps her arms around him.

"What a soap opera." Brianna's mocking tone makes the hair stand on the back of my neck. I meet her glare and open my mouth to tear her a new one when her eyes flick over my shoulder.

I turn around.

Blake's running from the parking lot toward the front of the lodge, away from where we're standing.

"Blake!"

He stops mid-stride and looks around, following the sound of my voice.

I shout again and his eyes lock on mine. In an instant he's running toward me. I jump down the steps from the patio, my boots skittering on the brick, and my legs decide at that moment that they've had enough for today. They shoot out from under me and I land hard on my hip.

Blake's at my side in seconds. Instead of hauling me to my feet, he's on his knees, folding me into his arms. "I didn't know where you were. You said you'd been practicing the course and when I heard where it hit and I couldn't find you..." He tightens his embrace.

I bury my face in his chest. The adrenaline from the past twenty minutes drains out of me, leaving me shaking in his arms.

"God, get a room." Brianna's voice sets my teeth on edge.

I turn to glare at her and for the first time notice someone else who's missing: Reece. I tug Blake's arm. "Help me up." He pulls me to my feet and I look closer at the group around the fire pit. In my panic to find Blake, I didn't notice how still everyone is. "Something's wrong," I whisper to Blake.

"You mean besides the avalanche?"

"Reece isn't with them. He's usually joined at the hip with Austin." I pull him toward the group. "Hey, where's Reece?"

Brianna crosses her arms and pointedly turns her head away from me, but I ignore her and lock eyes with Austin.

His face is whiter than normal and his jaw's clenched so tight the muscle ticks. "We haven't heard from him."

Blake stiffens next to me. "Was he practicing?"

Austin nods. "We both were. I wanted a break so he stayed for one more run. Said he might hit the back trails before coming in."

I cover my mouth with my hand and look in the direction of the Corona Bowl. From here it looks peaceful, just a fine mist of powder in the air, but who knows what's actually happening up there. What the people who were there—a lump catches in my throat. *Are people trapped? Could they already be dead? How long can you survive being buried alive?*

My legs buckle. Blake catches my arm before I hit the ground and pulls me to his side.

"Have you texted your dad?"

I shake my head. "I couldn't get a signal."

"He's probably freaking out."

I nod and dig my phone out of my inside pocket. *I'm okay. Will call on way home.* It finally goes through.

There's an unread text from Sophia. *OMG AVALANCHE ARE YOU OK WHERE ARE YOU?*

I smile weakly. I don't know how she already heard. *I'm ok. Was skiing when it hit. I'm safe.*

Are you sure?

Some friends might not be.

:((((

yeah.

Call me later.

xoxo

I look up at Blake. "Did you text your parents?"

"Yeah. My mom's ready to come here and get me herself but I promised I'd be home soon."

I startle. That's the first time he's ever mentioned his mom. I knew his parents are still together, but he's only ever talked about his dad and work. Even when he told me about Cody he didn't mention his parents. "Should we go soon?"

He glances at Mike, who's still wrapped in Evan's arms. "You wanna check if she's still riding with us?"

I can't help but smile. I'd hoped that once she ditched the Bitches Evan would change his mind, but I didn't know if it'd actually happen. I guess extreme situations really do show you what's important.

We walk over to them and I clear my throat. Mike looks up, tears still running down her face, and the lump in my throat gets worse. I can only handle so many emotions in one day.

"We're gonna get going. Are you still coming with us?"

She nods. "They're waiting for Reece."

We fall silent. No one mentions that it could be a really long wait.

Evan runs his hand over her arm. "Where's your stuff? I'll bring it to the car."

"I'll grab it. It's still where Ski Patrol brought her in."

Blake follows me to the med station. We have to fight our way through groups of people clustered together, all waiting for news from the mountain. I find our skis leaning against the building just as the loudspeaker fires up again.

"Please make your way to the lodge or the parking lot. All runs are closed. Please make your way..."

People around us start talking all at once.

"I heard people are trapped."

"Do they know if anyone died?"

"They've already got the dogs up there."

"It's too soon to know."

A shiver travels down my spine. I grip Blake's arm. "Let's get out of here."

We haul our gear to his Jeep, where Mike and Evan are already waiting. I give Evan a hug while Blake straps everything to the roof. "He's gonna be okay."

He shakes his head against me. When he steps back, his eyes shine with unshed tears. Mike leans into his arms and I climb into the front seat to give them a moment alone, and the past half hour catches up to me. The trembling starts in my hands, then works its way up my arms and shoulders until my entire body's shaking. I rest my face in my hands and rock back and forth. *I'm okay. I'm okay. I'm okay.*

The driver door opens. "You okay?" Blake's voice is low and full of concern, but I can't help but smile. At least the chanting was all in my head.

"I'm ready to go home."

He tilts his seat forward so Mike can climb in the back, then gets in the car. We wave at Evan through the open window.

"Text as soon as you hear anything," Mike says.

He nods once, his lips tight.

Blake joins the line of cars snaking toward the exit and I twist around in my seat. "Should we bring you to the hospital? The medic guy said you need to get your leg checked out."

"My mom's gonna take me as soon as I get home. I want to change first so I'm not stuck in my Pokemon long underwear."

Blake snorts and I can't help but laugh. "Believe me, I get it."

The ride home is quiet. The longer we don't hear from anyone still at Eldora, the worse it gets. No one wants to say out loud what we're all thinking: we might never see Reece again.

thirty-one

That night, news footage shows a candle-light vigil at the lodge and the search team still on the mountain, long after the sun has set. "Crews will continue to search until everyone is accounted for. At last count, there are twelve people missing. Officials say—"

"Twelve? Omigod." I clap my hand over my mouth and Dad squeezes me closer to his side. We're on the couch, our half-eaten pizza growing cold on the coffee table.

"—may cancel the Eldora Dash, the annual race scheduled for the end of the month. But right now the focus is on locating the missing skiers."

"Did she say?"

Dad presses a kiss to my head. "Don't worry about that now."

"But—" A ski competition is silly compared to what's happening. I know that. But I want this so bad and I've worked so hard.

We watch the news until they switch to a more uplifting story, then Dad puts on a movie and I fall into a restless sleep on the couch. I dream that I'm with Reece, buried under ten feet of snow, then that I'm the one trying to dig him out and no matter how deep I go, I can't get to him. When Dad finally sends me to my room I'm an exhausted, sweaty mess.

A text from Blake came while I was sleeping. *Still nothing. :((*

Still on for tomorrow?

Yeah, noon at the brewery.

Night.

I start to write xoxo, then delete it. "Ahh, screw it." *xoxo.* I press send before I can change my mind. Time stops until my phone finally dings.

<3

I hug my phone to my chest, glad that no one can see my goofy smile. It feels wrong to be happy when Reece is buried on the side of the mountain, fighting for his life, but I chalk it up to appreciating things more in the face of tragedy. Or something like that.

I stay up later than I mean to, not wanting to go to bed until there's been news. The unknown is almost worse than knowing. My brain won't stop running through everything that could be happening, and the longer I don't hear anything, the more I come to terms with the idea that Reece might be dead.

The next morning, I drag myself out of bed early to head to the brewery with Dad, and there's still no news about Reece. We set our bagels and coffee on a table near the bar, and I make a mental checklist of what needs to be done while we eat. He claims he needs my feminine touch for the opening.

I nod at a stack of boxes pushed up against the bar. "Glasses?"

"They came in yesterday."

I wipe my hands on my jeans and rip the tape off a box. The looping, whimsical Calliope Brewery logo is etched on one side. "Dad, they're gorgeous."

He smiles, and his eyes glaze over to a faraway place. "I've always liked that logo."

The story is it was inspired by my large, loopy handwriting from when I was a child—prettied up, of course—and Mom insisted that if they were naming the brewery after me, it may as well have my mark. "She'd be proud of you."

He looks at his hands, the smile lingering. "I was going to say the same thing to you."

We sit in silence, both lost in our memories of Mom, when the door opens.

Dad turns, wiping his eyes. "We're not—oh."

Blake's standing in the half open door.

I glance at the clock over the bar. It's not even nine. "I thought we were meeting at noon?"

He shrugs and steps inside, sealing the cold air outside. "You said you were getting things set up so I thought, I don't know, maybe I could help?"

The uncertainty on his face makes him even more adorable.

I look at Dad, who frowns. "Sorry, you need to be twenty-one to come in here." Blake pauses, and Dad laughs. "Come on in. Who am I to turn down free labor?"

Blake relaxes and slips out of his coat. "Where do I start?"

Dad puts us to work filling the shelves behind the bar with the tear-inducing glasses while he does something in the office.

"Thank you for coming."

Blake turns a glass so the logo is facing out, then slides another next to it. "I had ulterior motives."

I raise an eyebrow.

"Well, I wanted to see you, but I've been curious about this place, too. And," he looks over his shoulder toward the office, "I figure it doesn't hurt to let your dad see what a swell guy I am."

I snort. "Swell?"

He pushes his hair out of his face. "You know, clean-cut, straight-laced. All that stuff."

I take in his hair that's tousled so perfectly I want to run my fingers through it and laugh again. "I don't think that's how I'd describe you."

"Oh yeah? How would you describe me?" He rests his forearm on the edge of the top shelf and I want to tuck myself into the space beneath his arm.

"Let's just say clean-cut and straight-laced isn't it."

He reaches for a strand of my hair and twists it around his finger. "Now I'm really curious."

Sexy. Funny. Mischievous. "Well, you're not so bad to look at, and you're pretty funny most of the time. And I guess you're fun to be with."

He moves closer. "You guess?"

I look up at him through my lashes. "From what I've seen so far."

His lids grow heavy and he trails his finger along my cheekbone, sending shivers down my back. I'm closing my eyes to kiss him when a drawer shuts in the back room. I jump away just as Dad emerges from his office.

"Those glasses look great! Blake, how are you at moving tables? Cally doesn't seem to think the way I've arranged them has the right flow."

Blake crosses his arms and puffs out his chest. "Just tell me where you want me."

I press my hands to my cheeks. Dad doesn't seem to realize what he almost interrupted but I still feel like we were caught with our tongues down each other's throats. Blake smiles so his dimple shows and I swat his arm. "You're not helping," I whisper.

Blake leads me out from behind the bar and stands with his hands on his hips, surveying the room. "What are you thinking?"

Tables. He means the tables. I weave through the tables to the front door, then turn and face them. "You want to create a path that sucks people to the bar."

Dad smirks. "I thought my excellent beer would do that."

"Well, yeah, but you want people to feel welcomed, like the brewery's giving them a hug from the minute they walk in." They both raise their brows and I wave a hand at them. "Come on, you know what I mean. Haven't you been to a place where, from the moment you step inside, you feel comfortable? Like you want to settle in and never leave?"

They nod half-heartedly.

"This space here," I wave at the large opening near the front door, "this is too open. People come out because they want to be a part of the action, so put them in the middle of it as soon as they step inside." I touch my finger to my lip. "Although if you do that, then you don't have a place for people to stand while they're waiting for a table."

"What about here?" Blake points at two tables wedged against a wooden support pole. "This is prime leaning space." I tilt my head at Blake, and he shrugs. "We had the same problem at the restaurant until we rearranged the tables."

Dad rubs a hand over his jaw. "That makes sense. I've been to places where you have nowhere to wait."

I nod. "You feel like you're in the way and by the time you get to your table, you're in a bad mood. Or at least I am."

Dad rests his hand on the beam. "I wonder if it's too late to add a ledge for glasses." He grabs a notebook off the table with our bagels. "Remind me to increase your allowance." He scribbles a note and nods. "What else you got?"

I walk them through the rest of the brewery, channeling my inner HGTV and pointing out details that will make Calliope stand out. "The artwork seems a little high. Maybe lower it so it's eye level?" I glance at Dad and he's still writing, so I take that as approval. "The bookcase with games should be closer to the area with couches, and you need hooks under the bar and on the ends of the booths."

Blake tilts his head. "Hooks?"

"For purses and coats. I will never forget these ladies who sat near us last winter going crazy because the tables had hooks and they didn't have to rest their purse on the table or the floor."

Dad nods. "Got it."

I turn in a circle. "And I think that's it."

Dad gives me a hug. "It sounds like I need to make another trip to the hardware store. Can you two handle the other things while I'm gone?"

My stomach flips. More time alone with Blake. "Sure, Dad."

He grabs his keys off the table and points a finger at me as he walks out the door.

"Yeah, yeah." I face the bookcase. "Let's start with the games. It makes sense to have them by the couches, right?" I look up at Blake just as his head dips toward mine. His arms slip around me and I melt against his body as his lips move over mine, sending my nerve endings on fire. I reach for his hair, tangling my fingers behind his head and pulling him closer. He tightens his grip and takes a step forward, moving us toward the couches. I pause when the back of my legs hit leather. "The store isn't far away."

His normally bright eyes are dark, and his lips are swollen from our kiss. We're both breathing heavily and I want to fall back onto the couch and lose myself in him, but Dad won't be long. I press another kiss to his mouth then slide away from him.

He clears his throat and runs a hand through his hair. "Bookcase. Right."

I smile at him and we burst out laughing.

We've got the boxes of games rearranged and are in the middle of a fierce game of Jenga when Dad returns. "Don't worry, Blake's about to lose, then we'll get back to work." I slide a piece from near the bottom and place it at the top. The tower wobbles, but doesn't fall, and I smirk at Blake.

I expect a teasing comment from Dad, but he's watching us from the doorway, his face pale.

My stomach twists. "What?"

"You haven't heard the news?"

The avalanche. I've been so preoccupied with Blake and setting up that I didn't think to check. I shake my head. "Did they find everyone?"

Dad nods.

Blake's voice cracks. "Are they alive?"

"They rescued nine people, but three people died."

I lean back and the Jenga pieces scatter. "Omigod."

"Who?"

Dad clears his throat. "A married couple and," he pauses, watching me. "And a boy from your school. They've already released the names of the victims."

Blake stiffens next to me. "Was it Reece?"

Dad nods and a wave of nausea sweeps through me. Reece can't be dead. He's so full of life and energy and— "Are they sure?"

"I'm sorry, sweetie."

We sit in silence, each lost in our thoughts, the only sounds the furnace kicking on and the tick of the clock over the bar. This doesn't feel real. Kids my age aren't supposed to die, especially not on the side of a mountain. Driving, sure. But the mountain is my safe place and now I don't know what to think.

I rest my head in my hands, my eyes burning for a boy I barely knew. But while I might not have known Reece very well, I know what this will do to his family. And so does Blake. I lean closer so our shoulders touch. "You okay?"

He shakes his head. When he speaks, his voice is thick. "Everything about Cody is playing in a loop in my head. When he fell, being at the hospital, the funeral—" He stops abruptly and I rest my hand on his. Sometimes words can't make things better.

After a while Dad moves to my side and rests a hand on my shoulder. "You know I'm here if you need me. Both of you."

I nod, and look at Blake. His face is pale and his eyes shine with unshed tears. I squeeze his hand as my phone dings with a text.

It's Mike. *Have you heard?*

Yeah. I can't believe it.

Everyone's going to school.

Now?

Yeah. It's some sort of vigil.

"Everyone's at the school."

Blake faces me, his expression unreadable.

Dad clears his throat. "You should go be with your friends. I can finish up here."

"Are you sure?"

"Be home in time for dinner."

I nod, feeling numb. I slip into my coat on autopilot and Dad pulls me into a hug.

"Are you gonna be okay?"

I tuck my face against his shirt. "I don't know. I feel helpless."

"I'm here if you want to talk."

"Thanks Dad." I step away and Blake holds out a hand to Dad.

"Thanks for letting me help today, sir."

"You're thanking me for letting you work?" Dad smiles at me. "Okay, maybe I'm starting to like him."

I try to roll my eyes but give up mid-roll. My heart's not in it.

Dad gives me another hug at the door and whispers, "At the very least, I can see why you like him. He seems like a good kid."

Blake's parked in front, but I hesitate in front of his Jeep, not ready to leave just yet. "Can we walk a little?"

We wander through downtown hand in hand, not talking, but taking comfort in each other's presence. I stop near a sculpture of a frog.

"Reece is the first person I've known who's died since my mom. I don't know what I'm supposed to do."

Blake pushes a pile of snow with his toe. "I don't think we're supposed to know."

It's not an answer, but knowing he feels as helpless as I do makes me feel less alone and I'm grateful that we have each other. He doesn't mention his brother again but he has to be thinking about him.

When I'm so cold I can't feel my face, we head back to his Jeep and drive to school. With death so strongly on my mind, I can't help but think of Mom and the way she died. Blake's motions are effortless—step on the clutch while he shifts, turn the wheel with one hand—like he doesn't have to think about how to make the vehicle move. I don't know if I'll ever be able to do that.

He turns into the school parking lot. Dozens of cars are parked near the main entrance. I spot Mike—on crutches—and head her way.

I give her a hug. "Is it broken?"

"Torn ligament. I might need surgery but they won't know for sure until the swelling goes down."

"I'm so sorry. I shouldn't have made you go on that run."

She adjusts her grip on the crutches. "It's not your fault. I was doing fine until the mountain exploded."

I smile. "Yeah, you were."

A girl carrying a cardboard box stops next to us and hands us each a candle. Mike's gaze falls to the ground. "I can't believe he's gone."

"Did you know him well?"

"He and Evan are pretty tight so he was pretty much always there." She bites the corner of her lip and closes her eyes. "I can't even imagine what he's going through."

Blake puts his arm around my shoulder. "Is he here?"

"Yeah, but I haven't seen him."

People continue to arrive, filling in the sidewalks and grass in front of the school, but the candles aren't lit until Evan makes his way through the crowd. He looks exhausted as he climbs onto the low wall along the main sidewalk and looks out over the crowd. He starts to talk, then closes his eyes. Pressing his hand to his throat, he tries again. His voice is hoarse but he holds his candle out for everyone to see. "Reece was my best friend. Anyone who knew him... loved him." His voice cracks. "It won't—it won't be the same without him. He just made everything... better." He lowers his head and the people closest to him touch his arms in an attempt to console him. When he lifts his head again, tears stream down his face. "I can't believe I'll never see him again." He jumps off the wall and is engulfed in a group hug.

Tears burn my eyes and I lean into Blake's body. He tightens his grip.

Mike's eyes haven't left Evan. I expect to see tears when she turns around, but she's scowling. "I can't believe those bitches are acting like they care."

I crane my neck to see who she's talking about, but I know who she means before I see them. Of course the Bunnies are front and center. Forget that Evan's made it clear he doesn't like them—they've got their arms wrapped around him as if their world is collapsing, too.

Blake shuffles toward Mike, keeping me tucked against his side, and I wrap an arm around her. She tucks her head into my shoulder and her body shakes.

Other people stand on the wall and share their memories of Reece, and soon everyone around us is sniffling. Even Blake. I touch his cheek and his eyes meet mine. I search for the right words but nothing is right. Kids our age shouldn't die.

A hand grazes my arm that's holding Mike.

Evan.

His normally bright eyes are red and swollen, and he looks like he'll never smile again. I gently push Mike toward him and they hold each other, sobs wracking their bodies. I nudge Blake away and rest my head on his chest, lost in thoughts of death and loss and how just when you think you have life figured out, something happens that rips it all to shreds.

thirty-two

The week passes in a daze. The majority of the student body wears black in honor of Reece and the halls are eerily quiet, like someone pressed pause on life. I write my most memorable event paper—hello, avalanche—and I'm already dreading the final essay. I try not to think of the awful day Mom died, but knowing it's due next week when Reece hasn't even been buried is making it hard to breathe. Fortunately the teachers are being super understanding about the comatose students and are going especially easy on us.

The only thing that snaps me out of my stupor is a rumor that they might cancel the Dash. "How long does it normally take to clean up after an avalanche?"

Mike shrugs. We're in the cafeteria, picking at our lunch. "Considering people died, probably longer than normal."

I look down at the table and Blake rubs my shoulder. "We know. You really want to be on the ski team. But winning the Dash isn't the only way. There's still tryouts."

I sigh. For the first time since I found out about the competition, my excitement weakens. As much as I want to be on the team, it no longer feels like the most important thing in the world. "I know. It's just that I've gotten myself so amped up for this thing."

Mike smirks. "Yeah, we know."

I throw a fry at her, but Blake snatches it off her tray and pops it in his mouth. "No wasting fries."

It's not until Thursday, the day of Reece's funeral, that a decision is made. The loudspeaker clicks on during English and all eyes lock on the speaker above Ms. Simpson's desk.

"Good afternoon. We know many of you have been waiting to hear about the Eldora Dash. Officials have decided that because Corona wasn't affected—" Everyone in the classroom takes a breath, "—the race will continue as planned. Good luck to those of you competing." The speaker clicks and there's a beat of silence before the speculation on which run was affected begins.

"I heard the chairlift got taken out on West Ridge."

"Thank god they're not moving it to Pacer Glades. That's a double black."

"Like an easier course will make a difference for you."

I twist in my chair and lock eyes with Blake. He smiles, sending a flurry of butterflies loose in my stomach.

The Dash is on.

The school allowed anyone to go to Reece's funeral, regardless of whether or not they were actually friends with him, and even though I'll miss his quick smile and perverted comments, I can't bring myself to go.

I haven't been to a funeral since Mom died and I can't imagine being back in that dusty pew, the air thick with sickeningly-sweet floral arrangements that make it almost impossible to breathe, pretending not to be overwhelmed by the crushing realization that she's gone. I'm sure it would be different since it's Reece, but I don't want to chance it.

So many kids took advantage of the opportunity to miss class that the teachers in my last couple periods don't even bother giving a lesson, so I'm caught up on homework before the end of the day. The only thing I still haven't started is my final essay. You'd think it would be easy with death constantly on my mind, but I'm like a deer frozen in the headlights of an oncoming car: every time I start to write, I freeze.

***

Friday night Blake and I are snuggled on my couch watching a ski-movie marathon: Better Off Dead, Ski School, and a little known gem called Aspen Extreme. I've also got Jonny Moseley's greatest hits running on my phone.

"This is how you get amped up?" he asks for the hundredth time.

I nod, entranced with Jonny's aerials.

He leans closer, resting his head on my shoulder. "Should I be concerned?"

I turn my head and our noses bump. His blue eyes are focused on mine and all thoughts scatter. "Hmm?"

The corner of his mouth lifts. "You're gonna do great."

I blink, clearing away the haze that envelops my brain whenever he's this close. "And I can't convince you to enter?"

He closes his eyes and presses his forehead against the side of my head. "I told you..."

"That it's not your thing. I know." I don't want to push him if he really isn't into it, but he's so good. I pick at the blanket covering our laps. "I wish you could see you the way I do. It's like your board is a part of you and your movements are as natural as breathing."

"Funny, that's how I'd describe you." He kisses my cheek. "I know you want me to do this, but I can't commit to practice with my work schedule."

Oh yeah. Spoiled, selfish me keeps forgetting that one detail. I snuggle against his side and his hand finds mine, tucking it against his chest. I eventually fall asleep that way and don't wake up until the movie ends and he's sliding out from beneath me.

I walk him to the door and he kisses my nose. "Good luck tomorrow."

Panic stiffens me. "You'll be there, right?"

He runs his hands over my arms. "Yes. I wouldn't miss it. But in case I don't see you..." he brushes his lips over mine and I lean into his embrace. Every now and then I still can't believe that he's here—that I'm here—that after our brief thing over Thanksgiving we've ended up together. His heart pounds against my chest and I pull him closer. If it weren't for Dad clearing his throat in the hallway I might never let him leave.

We jump apart and Blake dips his head. "Sorry, sir."

"See you tomorrow, Blake." Dad's voice is stern but he's fighting a smirk.

I kiss Blake on the cheek and shove him out the door. "Bye." I turn and face Dad, heat flaming my cheeks. "Sorry."

"Kissing by the door I can handle. Just let me believe that's all you're doing."

My mouth drops. "It is!" Well, sort of. Just kissing anyway. And maybe a little groping. But nothing else. For now.

"You should get to bed. Big day tomorrow."

"Understatement of the year." I head toward the stairs and he pulls me into a hug.

"You'll be great."

I manage to sleep despite my nerves. This anxiety is unfamiliar but I haven't competed in so long it's like my body forgot its routine. In the morning, Dad's got oatmeal with a cut-up banana waiting for me, and we're on the road while the sun's still rising.

The parking lot is already full when we arrive. Dad stops in front of the lodge. "Go check in while I park." I make my way to the registration table and take a deep breath. "Cally Clarke."

The girl hands me my bib and points to the main door. "You're in heat five. They'll let you up during the fourth. They're alternating skiers and boarders every two heats so you'll be after boarders."

"Thanks." I move away from the table and look around for a familiar face. Evan and Austin are across the room with—ugh, cringe—Brianna and Kenzie hanging on their arms. Mike's supposed to be here and I really hope she doesn't see that. I'm debating whether or not to break up whatever's going on when I'm hugged from behind by someone too short to be Blake. I spin around.

Amber's dressed in head-to-toe navy and beaming. She's literally bouncing on the balls of her feet. "You ready?"

I laugh. "Not as ready as you. How much caffeine have you had?"

"Just a large coffee. Plus one at home. And another when I got here."

"Please tell me you've eaten? I don't wanna be around when you hurl."

She ticks off her fingers. "The standard: banana, oatmeal, and a spoonful of peanut butter. Plus pasta last night."

"Ha, that's better than me."

She glances at my bib. "Which heat are you?"

"Five."

She jumps up and down. "I'm four! We'll be up there at the same time!"

I'm beginning to wonder if Amber's on more than just a caffeine high, but everyone around us is fully amped. I seem to be the only one still waking up.

We move away from the registration table, and farther away from the Bunnies, and she grows serious. "So were you here when it happened?"

I nod. "I convinced Mike to run Muleshoe with me—her first time on a black—and that's when it hit." I fill her in on my personal avalanche story, still a little amazed I was able to get Mike off the mountain in one piece.

"That was quick thinking to ride her down like that."

"It's how my mom taught me to ski. I figure if it works on a newbie, it can work on someone who's injured." Even now, my legs tremble thinking about how close we were to real danger. "But she never would have been hurt if I hadn't made her go up there."

She pushes open the door and we look out over the crowd. "Stop. You didn't make her—"

The squeal of the loudspeaker cuts her off. "Racers in heat one, make your way to the top. The first heat will begin in thirty minutes."

I sigh. "Ugh, we have to wait forever."

"Let's get closer so we can watch them finish."

"Hang on, I need to find my dad first." And hopefully Blake. I was hoping to see him before the race but it's getting more crowded by the minute and it might be impossible to find anyone. I unzip my phone and send him a text. *You here?*

He replies right away. *Not yet. Sorry. I'll see you at the bottom.*

My heart sinks, but I try not to let it show. *Okay.*

I'm really sorry. Good luck. You don't need it.

That makes me feel a little better, but I still wish he was here.

"What's wrong?"

"Oh, nothing. Blake isn't here."

She smirks. "That's probably better anyway. You need to stay focused on the race."

My eyes widen, but I smile. "What's that supposed to mean?"

"I've seen how googly-eyed you are when you talk about him. I can't imagine what it's like when you're together."

"We're two normal teenagers who happen to be dating."

"Attached at the face, got it."

I burst out laughing and swat her arm. "Guilty."

She nods at my phone. "Ditch your stuff so we can go."

I find Dad waiting by the lockers. I hold up my bib. "Heat five."

He frowns. "Long wait."

"Amber's in four, so it won't be so bad." I open a locker and dump in everything but what I need for the race. "We're gonna head up so we can watch the earlier heats."

He smiles. "I'll be the one down here screaming my heart out."

I give him a quick hug.

"Knock 'em dead."

"Thanks, Dad."

I hit the bathroom to adjust the knee brace Dad convinced me to wear, then find Amber and we head for the base of the run. I come to an abrupt stop when we round the bend and see the crowd. The energy in the lobby is nothing compared to what's pulsating around the mountain. A sea of people crowd the barrier holding homemade signs and waving American flags like it's the freaking Olympics. Skiers and boarders mingle beyond the perimeter, the bibs on their chests marking them as the stars of the day, and little kids swarm them, asking for signatures on their helmets.

It feels like home.

I take a deep breath. "I've missed this."

Amber gives me a soft smile. "Let's get closer."

It's not long before competitors fill the chairlifts. I'm anxious to go up, but we have to wait or there won't be enough room at the top of the mountain.

"We're too far away to see much but the big air on the last bump."

And do we ever. The first racer soars into sight, sending the crowd into a screaming frenzy. He lands smoothly and stays in a tuck until he crosses the finish line.

I smile.

Amber nudges me. "That's beatable."

"Sucks going first."

The rest of the heat ends much the same way—big air, soft landing—but the second heat is a mess. The first three skiers lose their edge on the landing and barely make it across the finish line. The crowd groans with each fall. A couple of skiers who already finished high-five each other but I know better than to be glad they're out—there's still a lot of people left and bad luck can strike anyone.

Slope Rule #10: Save the cockiness until the race is over.

The snowboarders bring a new level of excitement, if only because there's some variation to their movements. They still rely on their edges to gain momentum, but one off-balanced move and they're eating half the mountain with their face.

When the third heat starts, Amber and I push our way toward the chairlifts. Technically I'm not supposed to go up yet but I figure there's gotta be enough room for me for moral support.

Once on the chairlift, the silliness from earlier is gone and we don't speak. It's time to get in race mode. They check our numbers at the top—the guy scowls at me but I smile and he lets me pass—and corral us to the heated tent to wait. The race is different up here. The cheers from the crowd are a distant roar, drowned out by last minute pep talks and skiers singing to themselves, earbuds in.

I stand when the fourth heat starts, stretching my legs and running through the course in my mind. I need to stay focused and concentrate on what's directly in front of me.

And maybe pretend I'm racing Blake.

I shake him from my head. Amber's right. Seeing him before the race would've just been a distraction. But still, it would have been nice to—

"I'm next." Amber's standing over me and I straighten.

I give her a quick hug, then smack her on the ass. "You got this!"

She straps into her board and the attendants part so she can get in place. The starting bell ticks down—beep, beep, beep—then a shotgun sounds and she pushes through the gate. I lose sight of her immediately but shout her name anyway, then move closer to the start.

After this heat, I'm up.

Seconds tick by, then a low murmur echoes up the mountain. Static comes over the walkie-talkies. "Racer down. Hold the start."

My chest clenches. I don't need to ask if it's Amber, even though my brain insists that it can't be her. She can't have fallen.

No one moves in the tent, and they certainly don't speculate about how bad the fall was. That's the last thing you want in your head right before racing. No, you stay focused on the course and pretend you don't know it happened.

Except it's Amber.

She could be hurt, or it could be she caught an edge and biffed it. Either way she's gonna be pissed.

I touch my knee brace to reassure myself that I'll be okay. Every second that ticks by without them giving the all clear is another dozen scenarios in my mind.

Finally a voice comes through the walkie. "All clear."

The starting bell beeps and in seconds the next boarder is off.

A man with a clipboard shouts over the chatter in the tent. “Heat five starts in three minutes.”

The attendant at the gate points at me. “You’re up.”

thirty-three

I glide into place and bounce my knees. I close my eyes for a moment, imagining myself pushing out of the gate, dropping off the edge, and flying. I don't wear earbuds like some people, but a jumble of songs skitter through my mind, keeping my adrenaline pumped. I roll my shoulders, then bend at the waist, stretching the back of my legs one last time. Deep breath in and out before looking to the sky. "Wish me luck, Mom."

"Racer is finished. Get ready."

The beeps begin then the shotgun sounds and I'm exploding through the gate, just like I imagined. Instincts take over as I crouch into a tuck, gaining speed as I hurtle down the mountain. The gates are spaced looser than my last race—way back in November—and I lean into each turn, cutting so close that the plastic supports slap my legs. My edges skitter across a patch of ice, and I tighten my stance, refusing to let the mountain beat me. I slice through a wide turn and cut across tracks where someone went off the course.

The tracks end at the plastic barrier.

Don't look.

Don't think about it.

Keep going.

I push harder, willing my body into a rhythm I used to be able to do on auto-pilot. Shift, cut. Shift, cut. The air is silent up here—nothing but me, the powder, and my skis—and I feel like

I'm the only person on the mountain. My breathing slows, the cold air barely registering on the edge of my consciousness. All I see is the next gate.

The course curves with the terrain. The next turn has air and I take a deep breath. This isn't the time for tricks—this is all about speed. I crest the hill and soar over the ground and it's like everything pauses. My chest expands. I can feel Mom. She's here, pushing me to go faster, to be better, to win this thing.

And there's the crowd screaming at the bottom.

I take a steadying breath.

Don't lose it now.

I bend my knees for the landing, then bend them further for a tuck. Go. Now. Don't hold back. Time seems to stand still and scream by all at once and the finish line's a blur. I stop in a spray of powder that dusts the spectators closest to the barrier.

People are jumping and screaming and waving their signs. I turn back to see the leaderboard and the crowd falls silent.

I'm at the top!

I pump my fist in the air and the screaming starts back up. People I don't know reach for me over the barrier and I hold out my arm, soaking it all in.

"Cally!"

I turn at Dad's voice. He's shoved between a couple kids from school, waving his arms like a crazy person. I skate to him and he pulls me into a hug.

"You looked like you were flying when you came over that hill!"

I look back as the next skier soars into view, the mom-love glow already fading. "I was." I pop off my skis and hop the fence. "Did you see what happened with Amber?"

"She fell on the last jump. They had to bring the sled to her."

"I hope it's not serious. Although I don't put it past her to keep riding even in a cast." I want to check on her but I don't want to miss anyone from school. I feel naked without my phone. "Let me know if you see her."

When the seventh heat starts, the loudspeaker booms. "Please join us in a moment of silence for those who lost their lives here last week." Like a switch, signs drop and people fall silent, all eyes on the mountain. Some lower their heads in prayer. Dad loops his arm through mine and pulls me tighter to his side. The silence drags on, and finally the voice returns. "Thank you."

People continue their conversations, but the energy-level has dropped. It's not until the first boarder crests the hill that everyone cheers.

"I'd hate to be the first one after that announcement."

His name and time flash on the leaderboard: Evan. He's not last but he's nowhere near first. "Man, I can't believe they did that right before his turn. Reece was his best friend."

Evan pulls off his helmet when he reaches the bottom and scans the crowd, tears in his eyes. For the first time I notice he's wearing a black arm band.

I push to the barrier. "Evan!"

He looks up at my voice and heads toward me. Tears aren't just in his eyes—they're running down his face. "I almost couldn't go."

I wrap my arms around his shoulder and stand on tip-toe to hug him. "You did great."

He pulls back to smile at me. "I did awful, but it felt like he was there with me. Does that sound weird?"

I glance up the hill at the final jump, where I felt Mom all around me, then run my finger over the arm band. "Not at all."

"Mike's supposed to be on the other side. You coming?"

I look up at Dad.

"Lead the way."

We follow Evan until we spot Mike tucked against the barrier. He sees her first and he's already hugging her by the time we make our way through the crowd. We get a couple stink-eyes for shoving to the front, but they cut me some slack when they see my race bib. I get a couple high-fives when they notice the number.

"Hey, nice job!"

"You were awesome!"

"Sign my helmet?"

Seriously? A marker is pushed into my hand and I scrawl my boring-old signature on a bright green helmet.

The kid beams up at me. "Thanks!"

Mike turns to me. "I'm so proud of you!"

"I haven't won yet. There's still two more heats of skiers."

She smiles. "Technicality."

"Hey, have you seen Amber?"

Mike shakes her head.

"I might head over to the med tent to check on her. I don't know if she's got anyone else here for her and since we don't have our phones, I hate to think of her trapped in there by herself."

Dad scans the crowd. "She's probably here someplace."

"At least wait until the next heat," Evan says. "Help us cheer on the Monarchs!" He pumps a fist in the air and I raise an eyebrow. That's a lot of school spirit, even for Evan.

"Okaaaaay."

Evan and Mike exchange smiles and I roll my eyes.

Another boarder soars into view, and my pulse accelerates. For as much as I love racing, I love being here at the bottom, where the first time you see the racer is when they literally come flying at you. I imagine what's going through their head and what they're doing to stay balanced, a non-stop synchrony that, if all goes well, ends with them cruising past the finish line.

The name for the next racer flashes onto the screen and I freeze.

Blake McMillan.

"What?"

Evan nudges me. "Surprise."

"You guys knew?"

"Just this morning. He had a hell of a time not running into you."

"So he was here the whole time?"

This time Mike nudges me. "Here he comes."

I like to think that I can be impartial and rate skiers and boarders on their skill and not what I think of them personally, but when Blake appears in mid-air, arms barely off his body, something inside me bursts. He soars higher and farther than all the other boarders and lands with a grace that makes it looks like he's still in the air.

"He's perfect."

I don't realize I said it out loud until Mike snorts.

But any response I might have is lost because everyone around us explodes into cheers. Jumping, screaming, arm-waving cheers. Blake pulls off his helmet and the higher-pitched screams get louder, but he doesn't look at the crowd. He's watching the leaderboard.

His time appears and his name bumps the top boarder to number two.

"Blake!" I scream, but he can't hear me. I can barely hear myself. I lean over the barrier and wave my arms until he finally spots me. For a moment it's like everything freezes and we're the only people here, then he's running toward me and drops his board and hugs me like he never wants to let go. "I'm so proud of you."

His lips move against my ear. "Thanks for convincing me."

Evan barrels through the crowd and reaches over me to slap Blake on the shoulder. "Great run, man!"

Blake grabs his hand in a weird guy-handshake and I'm relieved that they finally seem okay together. He smiles at me. "And you too."

I glance at the leaderboard. "It's not over yet."

"It's over." Blake and Evan say at the same time.

"In that case, help me find Amber."

Blake hands me his board before hopping the barrier, then we follow Mike and Evan through the crowd, our gear clutched vertically against our bodies to keep from decapitating spectators. Smiling faces blur together into a sea of excitement, and hands slap my shoulders as I pass. We're almost to an opening when someone grips my elbow.

"Cally!"

I tug Blake's jacket to stop him as I turn. "Ms. Simpson!"

I almost don't recognize her in her ski jacket and hat, but there's no mistaking the pride on her face. "Cally, that was amazing! Reading about what you can do was nothing compared to seeing it in person."

I'm not sure if that says more about my skills on the slopes or lack of skills on paper.

"If Coach Michaels doesn't put you on that team..." she shakes her head. "Let's just say he'll get an earful from me if you don't make it."

"Thanks. I'm really glad you were able to be here."

"I wouldn't miss it for the world."

"Cally, come on!" Evan shouts from beyond the crowd.

"Go catch up with your friends. I'll see you on Monday."

Blake grabs my hand and leads me to the clearing. Evan and Mike stand near a tent at the edge of the groomed snow.

"Is she in there?"

Mike nods.

I hand Blake my skis and push through the plastic door. Pop-up cots form two rows, one on each side of the tent, but only three are occupied. Amber's in the cot farthest from the door, her red curls hiding her face, her leg elevated in an air cast. I'm at her side in two seconds and on my knees, clutching at her arm before she sees me.

She jumps. "Jesus, Cally, you scared the crap out of me." The smile that's usually so quick to offset her sarcasm doesn't touch her lips.

"Amber, I'm so sorry." I glance at her leg. "Is it bad?"

Her eyes squeeze shut. "Broken in three places."

I rock back until I'm sitting on the floor. "You're kidding."

"I wish. I'm done for the season."

My mouth falls open, but I don't know what to say.

She smirks. "I really showed that wall who's boss."

I risk a smile back. "Those were your skid marks?"

She shifts on her side to face me, but freezes, jaw clenched. Several deep breaths later she refocuses on me. "How'd you do?"

I lift a shoulder.

"Cally."

"Last I checked, I'm in first."

She pushes up on her elbows, her eyes bright, the grimace gone. "I knew you'd crush it!"

"It's not final yet."

"Whatever." She leans back and closes her eyes. "Now I can die happy, knowing you won."

I smack her arm. "Stop it."

She juts her chin at the door. "Go watch the rest of the race. You don't want to be in here when you win."

I frown. "I don't want to leave you alone."

"Just promise not to forget about me in here."

"I promise." I give her arm a final squeeze.

I emerge from the tent to find everyone staring at the leaderboard. Dad's here, too. He smiles at me. "It's down to the last two skiers."

I stand between Dad and Blake, slipping my arm through Blake's.

"You've got this," he whispers.

"So do you," I whisper back.

I barely breathe during the final two races. Only when the final competitor crosses the finish line and my name stays firmly at the top do I allow myself to smile. Mike and Evan jump in the air, hugging and screaming. Dad and Blake reach for me at the same time, enveloping me in an awkward hug that feels strangely like home.

"Hey," Evan says, grinning from ear to ear. "You know what would make this even better?"

Let's see. I won the Dash, got the guy, and put together a pretty kick-ass group of friends. What else do I need? "I have no idea."

"How about a puppy?"

"Holy whiplash, Batman." I touch his black armband, my thoughts all over the place. The race. Amber. Reece. And now puppies.

"Dolly had them last night. Not what I thought I'd be doing the night before a race, let me tell you."

"Puppies?" I flutter my lashes at Dad, who laughs.

"Don't give me that look."

"But a puppy!"

He closes his eyes and shakes his head, but it's more a look of defeat than denial.

"Is that a yes?"

epilogue

LATE JUNE

"Cally, you can do this." Blake's leaning against the driver's side of the Jeep, his hand on the open door. I'm five feet away, eyeing the seat like it's the electric chair. "Come on, take another step."

Driver's training starts in a couple weeks and despite threats from Mike—who got her license last month—to stop bringing me places, I've yet to actually sit behind the wheel. At this point I won't get my license until long after my birthday, which is next week, but I'm okay with that. Blake's upholding his promise to get me over my fear, but it's not going as easily as he expected. Even his unceasing charm is no match for my irrational phobia.

Speaking of charming, after Calliope's opening in March—which was a huge hit, to the point that Dad had to hire extra staff after the first two weeks—Dad and I started looking at houses. The McMansion in Harmony Hills was nice, but it never felt like home. Dad didn't seem freaked out that it was taking forever to find something I consider normal, but we finally did. It's not purple, but it oozes character and it's in a neighborhood filled with normal families who grill out and drop by with lettuce from their gardens.

I touch a folded piece of paper in my pocket and take a breath. I've been carrying my fourth essay since Ms. Simpson returned it with a giant A scrawled across the top and a note that I should use it as a reminder of what I can overcome. Instead of focusing on the details of Mom's accident, I wrote about how it's affected me and my family, even after all these years. In a moment of impulsiveness, I shared my fear of being on the left side of a car and she's since become my personal cheerleader, insisting I talk to Dad about it, which I did. The thing is, I already knew my fear was irrational, but my brain and my body won't listen to logic.

Which brings us here, in the empty school parking lot. Just me, Blake, and his kick-ass Jeep which my brain seems to think is out to get me.

"Maybe if you get in first." He moves around to the passenger side and I shake my head. "No, the driver's side."

He stops, hands on the hood. "You've seen me drive a million times."

"Just get in."

He obliges, and I take a step closer to the Jeep. As if understanding what I'm thinking, he drops a leg out the door to make room for me. I grab the door and rest the other hand on the roof. Deep breath.

He runs a hand along my side and I shiver. Even after all this time, he still makes me googley whenever he's around. "You got this, Cally."

I lift my leg and rest my foot on the running board, and he kisses my cheek. I graze my hand over the steering wheel but quickly jerk it back like I've been scalded. *This shouldn't be this hard. Just climb in.* This time I avoid the steering wheel and use my legs to push up and into the seat. Blake's arms wrap around me, holding me close against his chest.

My breathing is ragged. I squish my eyes closed and focus on his arms. If it weren't for the steering wheel pressing into my legs I could pretend we're on the couch watching a movie.

"Okay so far?"

I nod, smacking the back of my head into his chin. "Sorry!" I twist around as best I can in the tight space and touch his face.

My gaze drops from his eyes to his lips and his breath hitches. I press my lips to his, pushing away thoughts of cars and driving and irrational fears, and he pulls me closer.

My leg starts to cramp from the awkward position. I break the kiss, but don't pull away. "Can't I just have a chauffeur for the rest of my life? This whole driving thing is overrated."

He laughs against my cheek. "Yeah, driving, independence... totally overrated."

"I mean, I get the allure, but people pay big money to not have to drive. I'm not being completely irrational."

"Not completely."

"But you're gonna make me do this."

He pushes my shoulders back so he can look me in the eye. "I won't make you do anything you don't want to. But I know you can do this. I mean, have you seen the crazy stunts you do on skis? This should be easy."

I drop my gaze. "Should be."

He lifts my hand and brushes his lips over my knuckles. "Turn around."

I do, and ignore my heart as it tries to claw its way out of my chest.

He slips his hands beneath mine so my palms are on the back of his hands, then places his hands on the steering wheel. We sit like that for several minutes and even though I know what's coming next, I feel like I'm watching a horror movie, waiting for the bad guy to spring out of the closet with a chainsaw.

But Blake's movements are slow, patient. He removes one hand from beneath mine, finger by finger, so now I've got one hand on the wheel and the other still on his.

I take another breath, then he does the same thing with the other hand. He keeps his fingers pressed lightly against my wrists—not holding me there, but reassuring me that I'm not in this alone. I lean my head against his shoulder, close my eyes, and wrap my fingers around the wheel. The grooves on the backside cradle my fingers the same way ski poles do. My eyes flutter open and I look more closely at the wheel. "I never noticed that before."

"What?"

"How the steering wheel is molded to fit your hand." I run my fingers over the bumps that cover the wheel.

"If you think that's cool, you're in for quite a treat." He reaches around me and before I can stop him, turns the key. The engine rumbles to life, a sound I've heard a bazillion times but this time is different. Terrifying. And a little thrilling. This time I'm in charge—literally in the driver's seat—and this beast will do whatever I tell it.

He turns the key again and the engine quiets. "Baby steps."

I drop my hand to rest on his thigh. "Thank you."

He squeezes his arms around me, then smacks my leg. "That's it for day one."

I hop out of the car and roll my shoulders, staring at the dashboard. Maybe I *can* do this.

"Let's go. We're gonna be late for practice."

Remember the Eldora Dash? Yeah, we both won our divisions. Blake didn't think he could be on the team and have a job, but his dad was so excited that he not only won, but made the team, that he let him cut back his hours. Evan was able to earn a spot at spring tryouts—yeah, stupid me never thought about the fact that there would still be tryouts for the team at the end of the season—and I've slowly cobbled together a new group of friends. Evan and Mike are still going strong, the Snow Bitches have melted into oblivion—well, not completely, but I ignore them so to me they've ceased to exist—and best of all, Sophia is coming to visit for my birthday.

I climb into the passenger seat, smile at Blake, and remember the most important Slope Rule: None of this means anything if you're not having fun.

to you, the reader

I've said it before and I'll say it again: you are why I do this. I've always loved telling stories and being able to entertain people with my imagination, so thank you for spending time with me.

Want more of Blake?

If you write a review on Goodreads and the bookseller website where you bought this, email the link to MelanieHooyenga@gmail.com and as a thank you, I'll send you bonus scenes from Blake's perspective.

One final note.

Boulder, Eldora, and Monarch High School are real places, and while I did my best to research them (thank you internet!) any factual errors are entirely mine. As for the bullying at Monarch, the students have an active anti-bullying campaign and would NEVER tolerate someone like Brianna. To the students and faculty at Monarch, thank you for letting my imaginary friends roam your halls.

acknowledgments

Writing a novel is a solitary endeavor, but it's never written alone. So many people helped me along the way:

My early readers, whose insight and red pens shaped this book: Stephani Martinell Eaton, Brigid Gallagher, Lynne Cox, Nadine Nettmann Semerau, Sara Spock Carlson, Nancy Matuszak, Tammy Ruch, and Judy Hooyenga. (Yes, that last one is my mom but there's no better proofreader.)

My numerous friends who've continued to support me, the crew at the Bookman (the best local bookstore in the world), and everyone else who innocently asks what's new and gets an earful about my writing.

The online writing community, who have graciously accepted me as one of their own and answered my questions with patience and professionalism.

My Facetious Friends, Sara and Nadine, thank you for being you. Navigating the writing, editing, and publication journey has been so much easier with you by my side. I'm so grateful to have you both in my lives and in my phone 24/7.

And finally, my husband Jeremy. Your unceasing encouragement gets me through the hard parts and makes the good ones even better. Thank you for always being up for a competition—regardless of the event—and for acting out the tree scene in Chapter 7.

Turn the page for a peek at the next book in the Rules Series, THE TRAIL RULES.

one

"Mike, you've got this!" Evan's waiting at the bottom of the trail. I can't actually see him, but I know he's there because I watched him ease his mountain bike down the path barely wide enough to fit his body like he was strolling down the sidewalk in front of his house. I adjust my grip on the handlebars. My arms are too stiff—he's told me that a hundred times—but you try to relax when you're facing a twenty degree incline with nothing but a plastic helmet and a few scraps of spandex to break your fall. With one final squeeze to test my brakes, I take a deep breath and let gravity carry me down the trail.

A girlish shriek pierces the air. I'd be embarrassed except I am a girl—Mike is short for Mikayla—and I'm more worried about staying on my bike and not decapitating myself on a tree branch than anything as silly as my pride.

My front tire winds its way down the path and I focus on staying upright. On staying on the path, where the trees are sort of cleared away. A rock catches my back tire and my center of gravity shifts, but I'm moving fast enough that it doesn't topple me over.

Deep breath. You've got this.

The dirt on the next turn is churned up—Evan keeps telling me it's called loam or something, but whatever—and I tighten my grip. The ground hardens as the path straightens, but the danger isn't over yet. A root snakes into the clearing up ahead and if my wheel isn't perfectly straight I'll be up close and personal with that cypress in two seconds. I squeeze the brakes as the root nears and yank up on the handlebars like Evan taught me. The front wheel clears the ground and a smile breaks over my face.

"Yes!" Evan shouts from the bottom of the trail. "You show that root who's boss!"

A giggle escapes me but I don't look up. Wiping out at the bottom is not an option. I guide the bike through the final turn and come to a shuddering stop next to Evan. My arms and legs are rubbery and I collapse against the handlebars.

"That was your best run yet." Evan's voice is close to my ear. I turn my head and startle for the millionth time at how bright his green eyes are and how beautifully they contrast with his dark skin. A smear of dirt on his cheek only makes him look better. He's half a head taller than me and I fit perfectly into the space beneath his arm—when I'm not wearing a helmet.

I push a loose piece of hair out of my eyes and look up at Evan. "I don't know how I let you talk me into this."

"Because you can't resist me." His lips curl into a smile that lights up his eyes, but rather than kissing me like I deserve after tackling that hill, he tucks my hair under the strap of my helmet. "Ready to go again? We can fit in a couple more sessions before it gets too dark."

I glance up the trail and scowl at the cypress that almost jacked my run. Part of me wants to be done and relax on the tailgate of Evan's SUV while the sun sets before we head to Austin's party, but another part—a newer part that I'm still learning to appreciate—wants to get this right. "One more."

"Two." It's neither question nor command. More like a challenge. Like he can sense the old Mike battling with this new girl who stands up for herself and doesn't take crap from anyone.

Well, I'm still working on that part.

"One and a half?" I flutter my eyelashes at him and he closes his eyes in an attempt to resist my charms, a smile playing on his lips.

It doesn't work.

His eyes open and lock onto mine. "One it is."

I stand on tip-toes to press a quick kiss against his full lips, then fling my leg over my bike and give him a nod.

He leads me along an easier route that winds uphill to the top of the trail I just barreled through. It's marked as a green—they're labeled the same way as ski slopes—and I can't imagine what blues or blacks look like. I'd love to try going back up the way we just came but Evan doesn't think I'm ready.

My thighs burn as I force the pedals down, down, down. We're in granny gear and going so slow I could walk faster, but as Evan likes to point out, that's cheating. Everything about mountain biking is challenging. Going up is brutal because it takes all your leg power to keep moving. Going down is a lesson in willpower overcoming the sheer terror that you'll lose your grip and smack into a tree, or you won't turn fast enough and smack into a tree, or you'll hit an obstacle like a tree root or rock and—you guessed it—smack into a tree. I'm also afraid of breaking my arm falling on a rock, but right now the trees are my biggest concern.

We stop in a small clearing that's semi-level and Evan faces an opening in the trees to take in the view. The parking lot looks tiny down below, and miles beyond that sits Boulder and the smaller town of Louisville, where we live. It's crazy to think my whole world is right in front of us. The drama and everyday problems that seem so big and threaten to overwhelm me can disappear in a blink. I close my eyes and they're gone. Open them, and they're still far enough away that I can push them aside—for now. But in two more days my biggest problem will be back: it's the first day of junior year and I'll have to face Brianna for the first time in months.

Evan faces me. "Ready?"

"Last one, right?"

He touches my arm. "Yeah. We should probably head back if we're gonna make the party."

No sunset lounging for us. It's Austin's end-of-the-summer bash and I've never missed one. A twinge of sadness catches in my throat. Our group has changed so much since last year—the Snow Bunnies and Moguls are disbanded and Reece, Evan's best friend, is dead. I'm not sure what to expect tonight.

Evan peers at me from beneath his helmet. "You okay? We can take this one slow if you're tired."

I run my hands over my thighs. They're aching, but it's a pain I've learned to appreciate. I smile. "I don't think it's possible to go slower than I already do."

He fiddles with his gears and laughs. "Mike-speed coming up." He mounts his bike and pushes off, moving as slowly as we were during the climb.

I take a deep breath to steady myself, then plunge into the trees behind him.

about the author

While not a fan of matching Day-Glo outfits, Melanie's been skiing since she was five and always points her tips up while exiting the chairlift. She lives in the land of lake effect snow—also known as west Michigan—with her husband Jeremy and Miniature Schnauzer Gus, and is always looking for ways to enjoy the outdoors.

This novel, her fourth, inspired her to purchase her first helmet.

Connect with Melanie online:
www.melaniehoo.com
MelanieHooyenga@gmail.com
Facebook/MelanieHooyenga
Twitter & Instagram: @melaniehoo
(she tried SnapChat and just doesn't get it)

Or if you prefer pen and paper:
Melanie Hooyenga
PO Box 554
Grand Haven, MI 49417